SOL CYCLE

Visit us at www.boldstrokesbooks.com

By the Author

No Experience Required

In the Cards

Can't Leave Love

Sol Cycle

SOL CYCLE

by
Kimberly Cooper Griffin

2022

SOL CYCLE

ISBN 13: 978-1-63679-137-1

This Trade Paperback Original Is Published By
Bold Strokes Books, Inc.
P.O. Box 249
Valley Falls, NY 12185

First Edition: June 2022

CREDITS
EDITOR: BARBARA ANN WRIGHT
PRODUCTION DESIGN: SUSAN RAMUNDO
COVER DESIGN BY INKSPIRAL DESIGN

Acknowledgments

Thanks to Rad, Sandy, and everyone at Bold Strokes for not only providing a platform that allows me to write the stories I write, but also for the support they provide to their writers.

Barbara Wright, I can't tell you how much your edits transform what I've actually written into what I think I've written. I'm thinking about getting a tattoo of your oft repeated comment, "But what are they feeeeeeling?"

Enormous gratitude goes out to my writing partners, Avery, Cindy, Finn, Jaycie, Janeen, Millie, and Ona, for the time we write, the advice you give, and the encouragement that keeps the stories flowing.

Finally, every writer should have a Michelle Dunkley in their life. You are so much more than a wonderful beta reader, you keep reminding me why I write.

Dedication

Summer, my favorite cycling partner…
actually, my favorite everything.

PROLOGUE

One Year Ago

Fat flakes of snow began to fall in the crisp air, and Angelique Kennedy watched them land like tiny snowballs, quickly collapse, and turn to water. Something about it seemed like a metaphor for how her relationships typically ended. She thought about what was going on in her house while she sat a few blocks away in the park giving Portia the space she'd requested to gather her things. The time to try to work things out had passed. She watched the park around her without seeing it, acknowledged the falling temperature without feeling it, and thought her thoughts without connecting with them.

The problem was, she hadn't dressed for the weather, having left the house without a coat when Portia tried to start yet another argument, recycling the same old grievances. *You're always working. Even when you're not working, you're thinking about work.*

She'd been told the same thing before, pretty much verbatim, by the women she'd dated, and she understood why they got so upset. She'd tried to learn, tried to find women who were more like her, women with career-focused minds who would accept the way she was, foibles and all. She'd thought she'd found some at times. However, they'd all grown sick of her dedication to her job. She'd tried to give them a head's up, usually during first dates but always by the second. She'd wanted them to know what they were getting into by dating her. Her mistake had been that she hadn't been direct enough. She was aware of that now.

They might not think she cared, but she did. She cared a lot. She wanted the relationships to last. She wanted to find a person who understood her. She always stuck with the relationships, optimistically hoping it would finally happen. But inevitably, they left her, proving once again that lovers would come and go, but she could always count on the one rock-solid thing in her life: the career she'd worked so hard to build.

Despite her warnings and hopes, she should have known it would only be a matter of time before Portia left, too. It had still come as a surprise, though. They'd lasted almost two years, longer than most. Ang had tried to do this one differently. She'd told Portia straight-up why her previous relationships had failed. She'd warned her before they'd started dating and again when Portia had moved in. Portia had simply said they were more alike than she thought, and she found ambitious women attractive. Ang had believed her.

Ultimately, it was the cat that had set the breakup machine in motion, though.

Portia had brought Jet, the little black fluffball, home to keep her company when Ang worked late or had to be out of town. Ang liked the kitten, a snuggler and a rascal. The thing was, the cat's dander didn't like Ang. She'd never had a cat, so she didn't know. But at the recommendation of her allergist, she'd started shots in an effort to make life with Jet enjoyable and to show Portia how invested in their relationship she was. She'd wanted Portia to be happy, for *them* to be happy.

She'd tried, she really had. But the shots required a weekly commitment, and as the weeks went on, more often than not, she'd ended up missing her appointments. She couldn't always get out of the last-minute meetings, plan trips around her appointments, or leave mid-situation when things blew up at the office. Adaptability to the ever-changing and brutally demanding technology retail industry played a major part in her success, and weekly shots had eroded the management team's perception of her adaptability. Unfortunately, on the verge of obtaining her dream promotion, she had to choose between remaining adaptable or successfully completing the shots. Choosing the job she'd worked so hard for had meant the cat couldn't sleep in their bed because she had to restart the shots from the beginning…again. It was the last straw for Portia.

Ang had debated whether she should be there when Portia packed and left or not. She didn't want Portia to leave without knowing that she loved her. And she did, just not in a forever way. She'd miss her. She'd miss Jet. But if Portia wasn't happy, Ang couldn't fix it without making herself unhappy. Her mother had always told her love wasn't the way the romance books portrayed it. People didn't complete each other. They needed to be fully formed before they came together. There was no magic moment when it happened. A lasting love came from balance, from time and familiarity. Ang had always thought that her mother's view was bleak and colored by her own failed marriage to Ang's father, who'd left before Ang had created memories of him. But her mother had a point. Her second marriage had begun as a marriage of convenience, but now her mother and stepfather obviously loved one another. A love honed over time. Was that what she had to look forward to?

As if in answer, the snow started to come down heavier in Wash Park, sticking to most surfaces, save for the bike path. Ang pushed her braids into her slouchy knit cap. At least she'd had the presence of mind to wear it when she'd left the house. She didn't have the time to fit in a special trip to her hairstylist to fix the frizz if she got her hair wet.

A big dog with long red hair and a white underbelly ran by her, dragging its leash, apparently escaped from its companion and chasing a bicyclist who had just flown by.

"Alfur! Get back here. You're chasing the wrong bike," a woman's voice called. The dog immediately retraced his steps. He and the woman met almost directly in front of Ang's bench. "Not everyone in a yellow hat is Swifty." She ruffled his neck and picked up the leash.

"He's a very good dog," Ang said, glad to be distracted from her thoughts. "And gorgeous."

The woman had dressed properly for cycling in this weather, from the tight biking leggings to her sporty all-weather goggles. She pulled down her balaclava and presented Ang with a beautiful smile. "Thanks, even though I had nothing to do with it. He's aware of it, too."

As if to prove it, Alfur approached Ang and sat before her, tail wagging. She paused the job of putting her braids under her cap to bury her fingers in his soft warm fur. "Alfur. What an unusual name. What kind of dog is he?"

They were having the universal conversation of Denver residents. It was customary for people to ask for people's dogs' names before they asked for each other's.

"Mostly Icelandic sheep dog, I think. Alfur is a common name for horses in Iceland, and he's so big, so..." She let the sentence dangle.

"He certainly is. If I hadn't met him, I'd have a heart attack if a monster like him charged me."

The woman, still astride her bike, dropped her head and shook it as if embarrassed, and when she looked up again, her pale cheeks were pink. "I know. I stopped to put on lip balm and dropped both it and the leash when I took off my glove. A cyclist in a yellow knit cap happened to roll by right then, and...well, one of Alfur's best human friends sometimes takes him on bike runs like I'm doing now, and he always wears a yellow cap, so..."

"He thought he needed to follow the bike. I get it."

They were quiet for a couple beats while the woman wrapped the leash securely around her hand and adjusted her pedals, presumably to bike away. Ang wished she'd take off the goggles and reveal the rest of her face.

She stopped herself in her thinking tracks. She had no room in her life to flirt with beautiful women in the park when her current girlfriend wasn't even out the door. Or maybe she did. But it didn't matter. Weariness fell over her because of the cycle she'd found herself in, ruining all her relationships because she couldn't find balance in her life. She had to figure out why she kept dating women who wanted more than she could give. It sucked the soul right out of her, leaving little left to try again. Maybe it was time for her to heed her mother's advice and stop looking for something that didn't exist. She sensed armor encasing her bruised heart at the resolution.

The cyclist gazed down the path. "Well, I better let him finish his run. Typical Colorado weather. Seventy degrees just two days ago, and we're poised for a blizzard today."

Ang stood. "Blizzard? Really? I better get home before it hits."

The woman lifted the goggles, and her clear blue eyes almost pierced Ang's newly resolved heart. "Maybe we'll run into each other in the park again." She lowered the goggles, pulled up the balaclava, and pedaled off.

Ang watched until they were out of sight around a bend and then finished putting her braids under her hat. She pulled her fingers into the sleeves of her light running jacket and took a deep breath, girding herself for more of Portia's resentment.

Pushing her hands into her pockets, she started to walk, dreading the fight, or worse, the silence if Portia was gone.

She already missed Jet.

Maybe she'd get one of those hairless cats.

She didn't want to think about it so she pulled up the memory of anything but icy blue eyes, which helped keep her warm during her walk back home.

Krista Ólafsdóttir forced herself not to glance back. She told herself she needed to keep her eyes on the bike path because of the heavy snow coming down, when, in fact, if she looked back, she might just turn around and ask the beautiful woman on the bench for her name and number.

Her heart still beat a little faster than normal. She couldn't remember the last time a woman had given her the jitters. She'd practically lost her ability to speak a coherent sentence. And all the rambling? If she hadn't been holding Alfur's leash and the handlebars, she'd have slapped her forehead. What a dork! And completely unlike her.

Krista had passed the woman while walking along the perimeter during her first lap around the park, and she'd caught Krista's eye, even at a distance. Walking with a confident stride, her chin up, as if she had a reason to be there. Her long braids, flowing down her back from under a black knit cap, had softened her appearance, and although she'd dressed casually in warm-ups, she'd made it appear crisp and put together. Altogether, she'd possessed an attractive, mysterious vibe. Normally drawn to women with a more casual appearance, Krista had been filled with rippling waves of anticipation at first glance.

She'd come to the park to make a single loop with Alfur before the forecasted snow was dumped all over them for the next few days but had begun a second lap in the hope of spying the woman again. Her pulse ramped up when she caught sight of her sitting on a bench. The woman's sophisticated countenance drew her gaze. Still several feet away, she slowed her bike and stopped. Something about the woman held her in thrall, distracting her with the simple yet seductive activity of pushing her hair under her cap. It caused a response inside her that she couldn't explain, as if static under her skin gave her a sense of being extra alive, and magnets were pulling them together. She'd become so distracted that she'd dropped both her lip balm and Alfur's leash.

Divine synchronicity caused Alfur to mistake a biker for Swifty. It gave her an excuse to get closer to the woman, whom she found even more beautiful up close. She regretted not having asked her name, but the striking amber color of her eyes, complimented by thick lashes and glowing dark skin, blew Krista's thoughts into the wind. The stormy weather complemented the woman's beauty, accentuating her chiseled jaw, her high cheekbones, her perfect brows. Her perfect mouth, despite all her imposing features, held the hint of a gentle smile, a contrast that enveloped Krista in a web of reverence.

What had they talked about? She couldn't remember. Her memory consisted of those eyes and that mouth.

It was just as well she hadn't asked her name. The woman deserved someone special. Someone who could keep and nurture a relationship, not just have a good time and move on, as Krista had been doing all her adult life, something she'd been thinking about for a while, something she wished she could change. She didn't want to stand in front of another crying woman, wishing she could say that she'd try, knowing that she wouldn't even if she could. There was something broken inside her, something that made it impossible for her to let go and fall in love.

She'd tried. She really had. There had been a time when she'd gone into each new relationship with the hope that it would be different, that it would last. But almost from the beginning, every time, she could see that it wouldn't. There was always something missing. That something special that would catch her heart, something she'd recognize from the first moment. But she never found it, and it was just a matter of time before her lover would realize that Krista was just biding her time. Soon after, things would fall apart, and they would leave. It happened every time.

She wanted that special something, though. She wanted to fall in love, wanted to give her heart. She just hadn't found the right person, and she was beginning to believe she never would.

Maybe someone like the woman on the bench. But she'd never come close to anything like that.

Done wasting time, she decided right then and there to put dating aside for a few months, if not longer, to figure out why she couldn't stick with a relationship. She had enough in her life to keep her content...for now.

Chapter One

"Y ou *are* going to love me."
Ang stared into Cleopatra's unblinking, lake-blue eyes, speculating about what wonders roamed the head of the hairless Sphynx cat. Their stare-off continued across the corner of the kitchen island until Cleo blinked once, lifted a paw from the barstool cushion, and began licking it, dismissing her as usual.

Almost a year together and the only time Cleo acknowledged her presence came when she wanted a treat or a human warming pad for her hairless body. Theirs was an amicable relationship until Ang had started spending more time at home. Now that she was there all day, the just-barely-tolerating-you attitude of the cat had seriously started to get to her. It didn't look like Ang's expectations of becoming cuddly best friends would ever be a reality, and it made her sad. All the cutesy pet posts on her social media had given her unrealistic expectations.

She sighed and gave the cat's ears a good rub. At least Cleo allowed that. She didn't hiss and slink away anymore. They were making *some* progress.

Ang's toe hit the plastic bin she'd set on the floor before petting Cleo, and the clatter of glass reminded her she needed to get her shit together. She pulled her gaze from the empty wine bottles in the bottom of the bin and surveyed the room. She'd put her housekeeping service on hiatus when she'd quit her job. She had time now. She could do it herself. Best laid plans and all that. Now the house was a mess, and she had a hangover. The stupid cardboard box sitting on her counter caught her eye, but she didn't want to deal with it today. She could do something about the thirsty rubber plant, though. So she did. But her satisfaction didn't last long.

Her head ached, and the scrambled eggs she'd made for breakfast were now in the garbage can, uneaten. The fading scent of cooking was masked by freshly brewed coffee. She hoped the caffeine would expedite the delivery of the pain relief pills she'd popped moments before.

Cleo jumped from the barstool onto the counter, sniffed the plant, and hopped onto the cardboard box to sit with imperial disregard of the no-cats-on-the-counter rule. Flouting the rule completely, Cleo curled into a ball and shut her eyes.

"Oh no. This is not gonna go down like that. You may be named after a queen, but you aren't the boss of this house, cat."

Ang shooed Cleo, and the cat made her escape across the counter between the last two bottles of wine Kat and Geri had brought over the night before, hitting one as she leapt to the floor. As if frozen, Ang watched the bottle noisily roll across the counter, over the edge, hit the wooden barstool, and continue its descent. A foot from the granite floor, Ang had the presence of mind to kick the recycle bin under it, and the bottle landed with a mighty crash of broken glass. Somehow, the unopened bottle remained intact and only shattered one of the empties in the bin.

The whole incident exacerbated the throb in her head, and she lowered it to the cold surface of the counter. Wine hangovers were the worst. Poisoning herself with too much alcohol was just another failure to add to her list of many failures in the last week.

"What's all this noise?"

Ang looked up, surprised at the sight of Kat leaning against the archway to the kitchen wearing one of Ang's old T-shirts that barely covered her lady assets and showcased her long dark legs. Their romance ship had sailed years ago, but it was the one and only relationship she'd successfully transitioned from lovers to friends.

Cleo, the traitor, began to wind a figure eight through Kat's legs. Kat picked her up and gave her kisses. "Of all the naked women in my life, you're my favorite, Queen Cleo."

"Since when did my weird cat make higher standing than your plethora of rotating naked women?" Ang asked, carefully extracting the unopened bottle from the bin and trying not to reveal the extent of her hangover. Kat always ribbed her about being a lightweight.

"Check her out. She gets me." Kat kissed Cleo's nose, and the traitor let her.

Ang's frown eased at the sight of Cleo pressing her head against Kat's. She couldn't help it. Two of the most implacable females in her life were showing their softness to each other. "You stayed over?"

"I wasn't sure if you'd need a little extra support this morning."

Ang snorted. "I have a little bit of a headache, but I didn't drink enough last night to warrant this kind of concern."

Kat chuckled. "I guess Geri wins the bet, then."

"What bet?"

"The one we made last night about your reaction when you saw your hair in the morning."

"What are you talking about?" A sense of dread swept through Ang as she lifted her hand to her head.

Kat dropped her chin and gave her the look. The look that said she'd figure it out in a minute.

Ang patted the side of her head. The feel of the familiar silk bandana she normally slept in reassured her until she explored along the back where the bulk of her braids usually gathered, and it all came back to her.

She rushed to the bathroom in the short hallway between the kitchen and the garage, nearly tripping over a bag of garbage she'd set on the floor. Kat's laughter chased her across the cold floor tiles. She didn't turn on the light as she peered at herself in the mirror. The high small window in the bathroom didn't provide much light, but she was afraid of what she'd see.

Memories from the night before started to trickle in. She closed her eyes. With her head angled down, she leaned her hips against the cold granite countertop surrounding the sink and slowly untied the bandana. The usual fall of braids against her back did not happen.

Holding the silk in her fist, she opened her eyes and stared into the empty sink, afraid of what she'd see.

The slap of Kat's feet against the floor forced her to peek. "Oh my God," she whispered.

Kat stood in the doorway, and Ang glanced at her in in the reflection before returning her gaze to her own visage. Kat flipped on the light and lifted a large freezer bag full of black braids. "Searching for these?"

Ang took a deep breath and slowly released it, running a hand over her newly shorn hair, her tight curls now hugging her scalp and revealing the graceful shape of her head. The woman staring back at her looked familiar but different. She'd always associated close-cropped hair with models and actresses who could pull it off, but the cold stare she expected, the one that always seemed to accompany the hair statement, wasn't there. Just her large searching eyes, which, despite being bloodshot and slightly panicked, still appeared warm and inviting. She relaxed her shoulders. Her eyes remained soft. Still feminine. Not so anxious. Confident. Better. Aside from the redness, Ang liked what she saw, someone who might not be so afraid to let go once in a while.

She turned to Kat. "Thank goodness you went to hairdresser school before becoming a chef. I don't know whether to kill you or thank you, though."

Kat dropped her chin and sashayed away. "Thank the tequila."

She was right. Tequila made her do things she never thought she would.

CHAPTER TWO

Krista slouched over the keyboard in the dim back room of her bicycle shop, distractedly pulling on the hoop in her bottom lip. The familiar din of customers talking to her sales crew on the floor and the ubiquitous odors of rubber tires and chain oil barely registered as she tried to make sense of the accounting software she'd recently installed. She must have done something wrong when she'd imported the numbers because nothing made sense. She wished she'd gone to business school instead of majoring in health medicine.

She sighed, shut down the computer, and pushed the rolling chair away from the desk. Spinning around a few times, she stood and faced the doorway leading onto the sales floor. Her team could probably use help, but she had to clear her head. She pulled her bike from the rack and rolled it to the front, pausing at the maintenance counter.

"I'm going cross-eyed, Swifty. I'm gonna take a quick ride to clear the jumble of numbers out of my bean."

Krista's top mechanic tied an intake form to the bike next to him. "I told you I'd take care of it, boss."

"You're too good to me. I have to figure it out on my own."

Swifty frowned and shook his head. "You're as bad as your uncle. Always gotta experience things for yourself rather than let people help you out."

Krista laughed. "It's in our Icelandic blood to be the helpers and not the helpees, and the main reason I told Raggy he couldn't keep coming in after he retired. All of his help"—she did air quotes—"harshed my vibe."

He chuckled. "Well, when you give up on it, call me. I'm a wizard at spreadsheets."

"I'm aware of your talents, but I'm trying to get us more automated. This new program will do both inventory and our accounting so neither of us have to do it. We just zap it with the scanners and bang. It's all magically tabulated and reported."

"If it's easy, why are you having such a hard time with it?"

Krista wondered the same thing. It was supposed to be as easy as uploading their old inventory spreadsheets and doing some sort of mapping thing. The person who'd sold her the software had only asked for inventory and sales sheets, which she and Swifty always meticulously kept. Before them, her uncle had done the same. In less than a few hours, the salesman had migrated all the data into the new system and had showed her how to make updates and run reports. And then he'd left, giving her a card with a support center email she could contact if she had any questions. Before she'd caught the errors. She'd emailed their support desk, but they couldn't tell her what to do to fix it, leaving it up to her to go through and manually reconcile all the data. One of her least favorite things in the world

"Who knows? The technician-sales guy who set it up probably screwed something up. Someone divided when they were supposed to multiply, or we forgot to hold our tongues right when we pushed the go button. I'll figure it out. If I can't, I'll hit you up."

Swifty's brow relaxed. At least as much as it ever did these days. Worry made him appear years older. The familiar deep creases on his face were a result of fifty-five years in the sun, biking and hiking in the Colorado Rocky Mountains. But the worry came from his husband Dirk's battle with lymphoma and the related chemo. Swifty had a lot to deal with, thus her reasons why she didn't want to worry him with the books. He had enough problems without having to untangle an input mistake she'd probably made herself.

"Okay. Go take your ride. I'll have an iced coffee waiting for you when you get back."

Krista pulled some cash from her pocket and held out a twenty, but he waved it away.

"My punch card is full. I get a freebie this time."

Krista pushed the bill back into her pocket. "Sweet. A couple of loops around the park in this spring sunshine and a free coffee are exactly what I need to forget about all the math-y software stuff."

CHAPTER THREE

Ang lifted her bike from the hooks hanging from the wooden beams in the garage, careful not to let it fall onto her BMW. Compared to the other bike hanging next to it, the street bike was several pounds lighter and in much better shape than the well-used mountain bike she'd owned for almost twenty years. She'd only ridden the street bike a couple of times since she'd bought it three years earlier in the hope of commuting the five miles to work and getting some long rides in on the weekends. But the rides to work had never happened. There'd never been enough time, and the logistics of juggling work, wardrobe, and laptop while riding were more difficult than expected. Besides, she enjoyed sipping coffee during her morning commute. On the weekends, she was either too tired or getting caught up on work she hadn't been able to get to during the week. The bike only gathered dust.

She glanced at the team poster she'd hung on the wall behind the bikes. Her days captaining the cycling team at the University of Denver had been some of the best days of her life. How had her priorities gotten so out of whack? It made her sad she'd given up the thing she loved the most in the world to pursue a soul-eating career. And for what? A nice car and a big house she lived in alone in the good part of town. She peered down. The heart rate monitor on her wrist showed her pulse in the nineties. She closed her eyes and did the deep breathing thing Geri had reminded her to do when she found herself getting worked up. She let her mind go blank, and when she opened her eyes again, a sort of calmness had fallen. Not serene like she wanted, but at least her chest wasn't as tight.

The bike tires were a little low, so she concentrated on fluffing them up and wiping the bike down with a rag. She then rolled it out of the garage, grateful for the sunglasses she'd remembered before leaving the house. Sunshine warmed her bare arms and her shoulders beneath the tight fabric of her favorite jersey. Her head still ached, but the throb had reduced to a dull roar. She hoped this ride would sweat the rest of it away and help her forget the mess she'd let her life get into.

She adjusted the chin strap on her helmet, tightening it a little more than usual to adjust for her missing braids. She still couldn't believe she'd allowed Kat to cut her hair last night. She'd always wanted to try short hair, but she'd been told by work friends that the braids made her more approachable. She also knew being an out lesbian further intimidated people. So she'd worn the longer hair to soften her appearance in the hope that she wouldn't give them reasons to think of anything other than the work she did.

Well, no use rehashing all that she'd done to make other people more comfortable now that it didn't matter. Anger about the events that had gone down at work that week flared briefly. She stabbed at the cypher code to shut her garage door and concentrated on deep breaths.

The back wheel emitted a slight squeak as she pushed the bike farther into the alley behind her house, helping bring her mind to the present. Out in the sun, the bike's paint appeared a little dingier, with dust caked to the grease in the chain and gears. It definitely required a tune-up. Ang straddled the bike and pushed off. Even in need of a little TLC, the bike moved smoothly. After a few clunky shifts, the gears moved well, and she took off toward Washington Park.

Being the middle of the week, there were only a couple of neighbors out walking their dogs. She waved as she passed. Early spring sunshine prickled her skin, and the smell of freshly mowed grass helped improve her mood. Before she knew it, she'd arrived at the park, turned onto the bike path, and began to circle the inside perimeter. Glimpses of sunshine reflecting off the water of the lakes filled her with peace.

Without her braids, the wind moved freely through the vents of her helmet, and she liked the sense of lightness the new style gave her. Maybe it was the one good thing that had come out of her crappy week. She imagined Neil's reaction if she'd gone to work with the new haircut. Knowing him, he'd probably like it. She even considered sending him a text with a picture to get his opinion, but things were still too fresh, and she needed distance. Maybe in a week or so. She could do with a little of his support. Sometimes, he was too supportive, as if it was more of an act than an authentic emotion, but she didn't care. He'd always been kind. He'd never gotten in her way. They made a good team.

Until a week ago.

But it wasn't his fault. The blame fell squarely on Robert's shoulders, her boss, the lying piece of—

She stopped those thoughts, slowed, and took a few more deep breaths. Nope. Those kinds of thoughts were useless, and they threatened to make her headache worse. She coasted down a slight incline and picked up the pace when her emotions leveled out again. She even smiled at a little girl peddling furiously on her tiny bike with training wheels. A cyclist wearing a tie-dyed jersey passed her, and the woman's well-formed calves gave her more incentive to get out on her bike more often. She remembered when her calves had been almost as sexy. Ang sped up and drafted the woman for a few minutes, admiring the view before the pace tired her, and she slowed. Yep, she had to get out more often. Or stop drinking like a college freshman.

On her third lap around the park, she changed gears, and a heinous noise erupted from the bike. She tentatively kept pedaling, and the noise diminished, but it continued to click, and adjusting the gear paddles didn't help much. She pulled off the bike path into the grass to check it out, thankfully remembering to click from the pedals before she attempted to dismount. Once off, she rolled the bike forward and back, trying to tell where the noise came from.

Everything appeared fine, so she flipped the bike upside down to get a better view, resting it on the handlebars and seat.

"Are you doing okay there?"

The woman in the tie-dyed jersey pulled up, smoothly clicking from one of her pedals as she rolled to a stop. Ang found it hard to keep her gaze away from the woman's well-defined legs. Sunglasses and a helmet covered most of her face, but her bright smile caused Ang to smile back. Sunlight glinted off a small hoop in the woman's lip, somehow making the smile more charming. Ang wasn't usually attracted to women who installed hardware in their faces, but the sporty cycler vibe appealed to her. The hoop suited her.

Ang cranked the pedal to rotate the back tire. "I think my chain is just a little off. It's making a grinding sound when I change gears."

The woman leaned forward, elbows on the handlebars of her bike. With the dark lenses, Ang couldn't tell if the woman watched her or the bike. Behind her own sunglasses, she swept her eyes over the woman's body. Something familiar teased at her, but she couldn't place it.

"It looks like you might know a little about bikes," the woman said, gesturing.

Ang snorted. "At one time, maybe, but not now."

"Can I take a gander?"

Ang waved a hand. "Gander away."

The woman jumped off her bike and propped it against a nearby tree. Taller than Ang expected, she stood at least five inches above her own five-foot-four. The woman squatted on the other side of the bike, rotating the pedals, and Ang took the opportunity to once again appreciate those well-muscled legs. The woman nodded as she changed gears a couple times. The noise got a little louder and then stopped the next time she switched.

"This is a really nice bike."

Ang smiled, pleased to have impressed someone who evidently knew her way around a bike. "Thanks."

"Yeah. It's the cable connecting the shifters to the derailleurs." She pointed at the paddle shifters and traced along the frame toward the chain threaded over the gears. "It just needs to be adjusted. They can stretch a bit. I'd tighten it now, but I didn't bring my gear bag. Is this the first time you've taken the bike out this season?"

Ang grimaced. Although some of the dust had disappeared while she rode, a layer still clung to the underside. "The first time in about three seasons, actually."

The woman stood, resting her hands on her hips. "How much longer are you planning to ride today?"

"I'm headed home. I live a few blocks away. Should I walk it?"

She shook her head. "It'll be fine to ride if you don't change gears. I moved it to a mid-gear so you should be able to get anywhere close without changing. If you want to bring it to Sol Cycle, I can give it a tune-up."

Ang swiped a small cobweb from under the seat. "It definitely needs it."

She smiled again. "This is where I'd give you my card with all the information on it, but they're in my gear bag, too. I'm just out for a quick ride on my lunch break."

A brick building near the university with a mural of cyclists riding a mountain pass flickered through Ang's mind. "I know where Sol Cycle is."

The woman straddled her bike. "Hope you come in sometime."

"Thanks for the help." Ang realized she didn't know the woman's name, although it felt like they'd met before. "I'm Ang, by the way."

"I'm Krista." She slid her sunglasses slightly down her nose, and Ang beheld the most beautiful and unexpected light blue eyes she'd ever laid eyes on, and in that instance, she remembered where she'd seen her before. Almost in the same spot. On a snowy day. With a big dog. She wondered if Krista remembered her.

"What's Ang short for?"

Used to the question, she smiled. People often asked her to repeat her name. "Angelique."

Krista pushed her sunglasses back into place. "What a beautiful name, Angelique."

Unprepared for the quiver in her belly, Ang looked away. It had been a long time since the thrill of attraction had given her a tickle. Since the first time she'd met Krista, actually, and even longer before then. She watched Krista ride off. With a smile, she took in a deep breath and let it out slowly before she righted the bike and hopped on.

The gears were gloriously quiet as she pedaled home, but she wanted to change them to cause the derailleurs to go out of adjustment again, just so she could spend some more time with Krista. But she didn't have a phone number to call. She'd have to go to the shop. The question was, what would be an appropriate amount of time to wait?

Chapter Four

A lthough she'd been thinking about it almost obsessively since that morning, Krista still hadn't figured out the glitch in the accounting software, and it was closing time. Good weather meant people wanted to be outdoors, and in Denver, that meant biking for many. Her cousin Magnus and another sales associate, Kayla, were happy for her help when she got back from her lunchtime ride. Being busy also preempted any daydreams about the regrettably brief interaction with the lovely Angelique from the park. When she'd gotten back to the shop, a line had formed at the maintenance bar three deep, and it hadn't slowed down until closing, even with her help. They'd actually stayed open an additional half hour to handle the customers who'd waited patiently. Now, she was getting ready to lock up, knowing she'd likely be a little late to dinner at her parents' house that night. How had the day gotten away from her?

"Hey, cuz. I almost forgot to tell you, Raggy wants you to give him a call when you get a chance," Magnus called as he backed out of the door while Krista set the alarm. She followed him through. "He called when you were at lunch. Sorry I didn't tell you sooner."

Krista thanked him, grabbed her bike, and pressed the combo to lock the door. She sighed and dialed his number, knowing exactly why he'd called. Swinging into the saddle while the call rang through her earbuds, she kicked her bike into motion.

"Speak to me," came the answer on the other end, her grand-uncle Ragnar bellowing his usual greeting.

"What's up, my favorite Ragman? I heard you called." He was her mother's father's brother and a constant presence in her life. He wasn't just her favorite Ragman, he was her favorite human.

"Magnus didn't lie. I called. I'm not going to make it tonight," he said, sounding sad, as she suspected he would, adding the Icelandic endearment for sweetie. "Can you carry my regrets to your mamma and *pabbi*?"

His voice sounded soft and melodic, his accent stronger, the way it got when he'd enjoyed a few beers. She pictured him in one of the rockers on the deck of his cabin in the forest, his dogs, Odin and Loki, sprawled on the wooden planks at his feet. She could almost smell the Icelandic beer he always drank. He'd retired to Nederland, a small town west of Boulder, up a canyon, and tucked into the mountains. Only about an hour away. She went up there as often as she could. Admittedly, not often these days as she worked six, sometimes seven, days a week most weeks.

"I will, but we'll miss you again this week."

She would, too. Family dinners were always boring when Raggy couldn't attend. Her brother only ever talked about his medical practice, and her sister talked nonstop about grad school and all the people she counseled down at the county offices where she volunteered as part of her social work program. Her parents were supportive of all three of them, but other than making sure everything was going well, they weren't very interested in the workings of the bike shop. Sometimes, she thought they'd have been more interested in her career if she'd stayed with sports training or better yet, sports medicine. When Raggy came to dinner, she talked to him. He knew her world. Without him there, she anticipated listening to endless stories about people with medical or mental issues.

"I know, love. Me too. But the drive is getting too long for this old man."

Already missing him, she asked about his day, and they spoke for a few more minutes until she arrived at the doggie daycare where she'd dropped her boy Alfur that morning. Most days, he went to work with her, but one day a week, he got to play with other dogs all day. She clicked from her pedals as she came to a stop.

"I have to go inside to get Alfur, but maybe I'll come up this weekend," she said.

"I always enjoy your visits."

They hung up, and she retrieved Alfur, who ran alongside her bike as she held his leash for the two blocks to their house. As always, she admired him as he ran, his fluffy curled tail bobbing behind him. He'd played all day with other dogs, but he still had energy for the short run back to their house. With his thick red hair, white belly, and black mask of fur on his face, he was strikingly handsome and her best friend.

Seeing him after a day apart helped ease her disappointment about not seeing her uncle at dinner. That and the beautiful spring day. She breathed in the perfection of the moment, the wind on her face, and her good boy running next to her as she rode. She thought of Angelique, and the memory made her smile even wider. She literally interacted with dozens of people about their bikes every week. But none of them intrigued her like Angelique. Gorgeous didn't come close to describing her. There was something more. It wasn't how cute she looked in her perfectly matching bike gear, nor her top-of-the-line bike. Her air of independence and intelligence was definitely part of it but not all. She exuded something different and exciting.

Everything in her hoped Angelique would come by the shop for the tune-up they'd talked about so she could try to put a name to the something. She'd always been the type to let women come to her, but if Angelique didn't come to the shop, she might have to go to the park and try to run into her again. There was a pull there, something she had a hard time identifying. Just like the different and exciting feeling that vibrated through her when Angelique was nearby. She wondered if Angelique felt it, too.

CHAPTER FIVE

When Ang returned home from her ride, she eyed the cardboard box still untouched on her kitchen counter after a week. The grin she'd been sporting after meeting Krista faded into a long sigh. She could no longer ignore it. And not because Cleo lounged on top of it again, either.

She'd spent seven days avoiding the box containing the last decade and a half of her career. She had a mind to take it, unopened, out to the garage, shove it into one of the shelves, and forget about it. But who wanted a negative time capsule lurking in the shadows? A jack-in-the-box of horrible memories ready to surprise her sometime in the future. No, thank you.

Swiping at the sweat dripping down her neck, she kicked her shoes off, moved Cleo to the floor, and took the box into the living room. Cleo trailed closely behind, sitting next to her but not touching her, when she sank onto the floor in front of the oversized ottoman, placing the box on the floor in front of her.

She should be familiar with the contents. She'd put it all in there. But for the life of her, she couldn't remember. The whole day after she'd stormed from the meeting had been reduced to an angry blur. The details of what happened just before in the conference room, however, were crystal clear:

Robert's administrative assistant, Ann, asked Ang to meet the boss in the executive conference room for her annual review. She'd anticipated it. The company's absolutely rigid policy about providing performance evaluations on time had been driven into all managers. In fact, Ang had completed her own team's reviews just the day before.

There was little doubt in her mind about how good her review would be, especially after the quarterly reports had been released in the management meeting just a few hours earlier. Stronger than forecasted, the quarterly earnings were a direct result of her team's hard work. In fact, Robert had already sent her the summary of her review. Fives across the board. The face-to-face meeting was just a formality, really, as almost always every year. He'd tell her to keep up the good work, reveal the bonus she'd receive, and hopefully ask her to sign the promotion paperwork for the job he'd been promising her for the last year and a half. He'd probably talk about the great job he expected her to do, and he'd tell her to go out to a nice dinner using the company AmEx. Executive privilege.

Fifteen years at Lithium, twelve working directly for Robert, and she knew the drill.

Still, she had butterflies in her stomach as she stood outside the smoked glass door to the conference room. On the verge of becoming the first female executive vice president at the company, and only the second Black executive in the company's history, she couldn't suppress her anticipation. She'd worked damn hard to get there, twice as hard and twice as many hours as her peers. She'd endured the "protocol" of navigating convoluted proving grounds alongside mostly male white peers, many of them possessing half her expertise and none of the experience, for every promotion she'd ever received, including this one. But Robert had already told her she had the job.

She stood outside the conference room for a moment to calm her racing heart.

What she hadn't anticipated was Neil sitting near the head of the long glass conference table adjacent to Robert, chatting causally, when she entered the room. She liked Neil. Always a good guy and a peer she could count on, he'd proven himself as a talented retail leader, but she didn't understand his presence. Maybe his review had gone long.

"Should I come back?" she asked, her hand still on the door handle.

Both Robert and Neil smiled at her. Robert waved her in. Despite their friendly demeanors, something wasn't right. Twelve years working for Robert had given her a sixth-sense for when he was plotting something, and if you weren't part of his scheme, you might be who he was plotting against. He was definitely plotting. The question was, was she part of the scheme?

She'd taken Neil under her wing when he'd been hired two years earlier, and his performance continued to please her. She wouldn't be surprised if Robert suggested Neil take over her larger territory after she moved into her new role. Neil was her first choice, too. But she had to make sure she remained fair about the promotion. After all, some of his peers had been there longer than him.

"Robert. Neil," she said, giving good eye contact as she entered the room, a skill she'd mastered long ago.

She took the chair opposite Neil, nodding to him with a warm smile, angling herself to face Robert. Her braids pulled when she leaned back in the chair. She subtly eased the pressure and checked her watch in a practiced movement to loosen them. Fidgeting and playing with her hair broadcasted a weakness she refused to display, even to familiar coworkers.

Robert nodded, his expression the same as usual: not warm, not cold, just all business. "Angelique."

Neil smiled. "Hey, Ang."

Robert patted the closed laptop before him. "I see you already acknowledged your review file. No surprises there. Outstanding work this quarter."

"Thank you. I have to give credit to the team, though. Without Neil, Susan, José, Thomas, and Leon, we couldn't have pushed through the first quarter slump as successfully as we did."

"Outstanding work all around," Robert said with a smile. He pushed a document, facedown, toward her. "You deserve this."

She picked it up, familiar with the routine. Her bonus letter. She read the amount. More than double her last bonus, which had been generous. She tipped her head, pleased, but she didn't want to talk in front of Neil. "Thank you. Your generosity is beyond appreciated."

He crossed his arms and nodded, a paternal smile warming up his always business-like expression. "You drove the numbers home, beating projections, laying the groundwork for the sure success for the next several quarters. We continue to be happy to have you onboard."

"I'm grateful to have such a strong team and supportive peers." She nodded at Neil, who beamed back at her. She wondered when he would leave so she could talk to Robert about the promotion.

But Robert rapped the table. "Exactly why we're spinning up a new team. A new division, actually. And we want you to lead it."

Excitement rose within her. The time had finally come. But had Robert said new division? Trepidation stole in. Things weren't playing out as she'd expected. She hadn't been privy to the discussion about making this kind of change. Strange. She'd always been one of the first people to know about major structural changes in the company. She prided herself on her ability to be just ahead of the company vision, often being the one to help define it, but this threw her for a loop. A glance at Neil told her he already knew, adding irritation to the tangle of emotions battling within her.

She sat back in her chair, interlacing her fingers in her lap, a practiced posture she used when trying to ascertain a challenge. Or to uncover the plot. "Tell me more."

Robert nodded to Neil. "Why don't I let Neil tell you?"

Interesting.

Neil leaned forward, his expression almost eager. "It's exciting, Ang. You and I get to build our own division. We'll take the success factors algorithm we created for retail and apply it to each division, including operations, tailoring it to meet the needs of the various teams, straddling the entire organization. We'll basically pilot what works across the company to ensure accurate projections and support processes."

Algorithms *she* had created. She wanted to correct him, but her qualifications weren't in question. Besides, she wanted to hear the rest.

Neil went on to explain her own process to her, and she grew irritated and angry. However, she hid it well. She'd learned to hold on to her shock and disappointment when dealing with the men she worked with. This wasn't the first time she'd been given a carrot, teased with it for years, and just as it came into reach, another hurdle lurched into her path, taking the carrot out of reach again. She'd gotten used to biding her time, playing the long game. And it had mostly paid off. She just had to figure out what the next step would be.

Robert leaned forward when Neil finished explaining the broad strokes of what spinning up the new division would entail. Ang glimpsed excitement under his usual gruff exterior. "Because it's a new division, we have to prove ourselves. We haven't been given all our requested headcount yet, but we will. They'll announce the new team at the next all-hands meeting and tell everyone you and Neil will be heading it up."

If she got to pick her team, it would include Neil, so things were good so far. But it still bothered her to just now hear about this. And what did it mean about the promotion? It would be irritating if they wanted her to demonstrate what she could do in the EVP position so people would be more convinced about her abilities in heading up the new team. It frustrated her to once again have to prove herself. She supposed she should be used to it from all the times before.

She forced herself to relax. "The next all hands is in three months, so we'll have some time to get things organized."

Robert nodded.

"And we'll be doing what, exactly?" she asked. "What's your vision?"

He settled back in his chair. "You'll both report directly to me, like you do now, and you'll continue managing your teams in tech retail until we can hire new department heads to backfill them, but you'll be creating the foundation for the success factors division. Of course, you'll get to come up with the name. This is your baby."

Neil rapped his knuckles on the table, an unconscious—she hoped—imitation of Robert, and she held in a grimace. "I kind of like the sound of Success Factors. It's straightforward and descriptive."

Robert nodded and winked, "You're decisive. Exactly what we want around here."

Neil appeared pleased with himself.

Ang drifted further and further out of the loop. She leaned forward, putting her hands on the table. "I'd like to have some time to—"

"Neil will be the lead only in name," Robert went on. "Based on his program management background, but we all acknowledge who the brains are. Don't we, Neil?" Robert reached over and patted Ang's hands.

The pat felt anything but reassuring, and Ang steeled herself against yanking her hands away. What did he mean? She hadn't wanted to bring up the promotion to EVP in front of Neil, but in *her* review meeting, her patience had worn thin.

She forced herself to remain still without appearing stiff. She found it critical to appear composed and in control when turmoil rose inside her—*especially* when turmoil rose inside her—lest she lose the tenuous respect she'd worked so hard for all these years. She was used to being judged for many things, some of which she could control and others, she couldn't. But she *could* control her body language and how she expressed emotion. Not wanting to give even a small suggestion of being combative or weak, she worked hard to dispel stereotypes about the things she *couldn't* control during her rise through the company, and now, on a day she'd hoped would elevate her to a place of even more respect, helping to promote that respect to other people like her, here she sat, alarms going off in her gut and indicating she was about to get screwed over. Again.

"What about the tech retail EVP position?" she asked.

Robert waved a hand dismissively. "Don't get fixated on titles, Angelique. Why would you limit yourself there? Wouldn't you rather have a chance at something with a potentially bigger splash? There's only one path available in retail. You have an opportunity of a lifetime with this success factors gig. You get to chart your path. Try to take in the big picture."

Ang nearly vibrated with rage at his condescending tone. She struggled to keep it in check. "It sounds like you've already made up your mind for me to head up this new division," she said.

"Nothing is set in stone. But I can't imagine you'd choose retail over this."

"Shouldn't I get the opportunity to make the decision myself?"

He shifted in his seat, the first time he'd looked uncomfortable during this meeting. "I thought you'd be excited about this."

"Give me a moment to absorb. It's been all of five minutes. We've been talking about me being the EVP of tech retail for months."

He coughed into his hand. "We offered the EVP position to Carl. He accepted."

Stunned, Ang could hardly comprehend what she'd just heard. More than a year earlier, Robert had literally said the words, "I promise, the EVP position is yours," and had asked her to be patient as he "got all their ducks in a row" And did he say Carl? *Carl?* This was not happening.

The sensation of cold flowing slowly down her body fortified her.

She pressed her forefinger against the surface of the glass. "So I either accept this EVP of the success factors division, or I stay where I am and report to Carl? Carl, who has been at the company for less than half the time I have? Carl, who I put on a work plan for unwanted sexual advances toward not one, not two, not three, but *four* of our summer interns three years ago? Carl, who we had to move to operations after he threatened me for putting him on the work plan? *That* Carl?"

The whole Carl fiasco had been hush-hush to protect the company image, so she breached protocol mentioning it in front of Neil, but Robert could deal with that problem for having him attend her review session.

Robert quickly schooled his expression and held up his hands, chuckling. "You won't have to work for Carl. I expected you to jump at the opportunities presented in the new division, so I'll have to figure some things out, but you won't have to work for Carl."

Ang was absolutely livid. The career path she'd carefully cultivated had been tossed out the window. "I don't want you to 'figure some things out' for me, Robert. I've worked too hard to get to where I'm at. You promised me the EVP of tech retail. I expected to talk about it this afternoon." She unclenched her hands and adjusted the lapels of her suit jacket. "Tell me more about the EVP of success factors. I'm just shocked at this sudden shift. We've been talking about other things for so long."

"Well, about the leadership position. I already told you about the headcount. We only have one EVP approved, so this will be a lateral move at first."

Ang sat forward. "Wait—"

"Hear me out. We just have to—"

"You mean to tell me Neil and I will be moving to lateral positions while Carl moves up? Into the position you promised me?"

Robert glanced at Neil and back at her, appearing more uncomfortable than she'd ever seen him. Neil stared at a pen he fiddled with. "Not exactly. Things were moving fast. We were juggling timing, position availability, review times. A lot of balls were in the air, and some of the moves happened before we were ready. I requested two EVP positions for the new division. Neil accepted his position first. It turned out they only had one. As much as I wanted the same for you, we'll have to wait until next budget to put in the request. It's just a title. You've never been hung up on titles before."

Ang stood up, blood pounding in her ears.

"Ang. Hold up." Neil stood and had the decency to look embarrassed. "Robert, give her the EVP position. She deserves it. The new team wouldn't exist without her ideas."

Robert held up a hand. "It's already a done deal."

Ang took a deep breath. She cleared her tight throat. The thumping became so loud in her ears, she wondered if anyone else could hear it. Meanwhile, she fought back shame for losing her poise, which really pissed her off. Why did she have to maintain her cool when these assholes were not only forgiven but given promotions after waving their dicks at interns? They probably compared sizes with each other in their boy's club executive gym, laughing about it. The worst thing was, she'd been complicit. She'd known it then, and she more than regretted it now. Writing Carl up and putting a lid on it were nowhere near what they should have done. She should have called the police.

Rage at them and rage at herself erupted within her.

"Fuck you. I'm out of here. Keep the job, Neil. Robert, you can shove your grand ideas up your ass. *I'm tired of being jacked around by this company and by you. I quit.*"

Ang mostly remembered the pounding of blood in her head, and she didn't remember much after she'd left the conference room, only that she'd gone to her office, dumped several reams of paper from a box, and thrown various things into it. She remembered putting the box, along with the rubber plant she'd had for over ten years, on her office chair and wheeling it down the hall, into the elevator, down to the underground parking, and leaving the thirty-five-hundred-dollar ergonomic chair in her empty parking space when she drove away. She remembered stopping at the liquor store and buying wine with the specific intention of getting and staying drunk for a few days. But when she'd gotten home, the bottles had remained unopened, and exhaustion had consumed her. She'd fallen asleep on the couch with Cleo perched upon her chest.

Interestingly enough, Ang had slept more deeply than she had in...longer than she could remember. When she'd awakened, it had been well past midnight, and Cleo had still been curled up on her chest. She'd risen long enough to pee and move her and Cleo to the bedroom, where she'd slept just as deeply until dawn. She'd risen fresh and strangely peaceful.

The cell phone on the kitchen counter rang, rousing Ang from the memory of the day that seemed so long ago, yet only a week had passed. She considered ignoring the call, but she needed a cup of coffee to help her go through the box, so she got up, grabbed the phone, and pulled the biodegradable pods from the cupboard as she answered.

Before she said hello, her friend Geri Miyazaki took the helm of the conversation. "Yo, dawg. Kat commanded I call you to make sure you aren't curled up in a ball somewhere in your mansion, crying into a bag of braided keratin."

Ang scoffed, inserting the pod into the coffee maker. "First of all, *dawg*? You're forty-something-years-old. People in their forties don't say *dawg*."

"I am exactly forty. Don't go adding 'something' to it to age me just because I'm three years older than you and Kat. Besides, what does my age have to do with my vocabulary?"

"A woman with a PhD in science who trained as an educator should use a more refined lexicon. Braided keratin is a great descriptor, though." She poked at the Ziploc bag of hair on the counter where she'd left it after freaking out on Kat.

"What can I say? I'm around kids all day."

"But do you have to talk like them?"

"Hold up. How many times have I listened to you prattle on about your TPS reports and ROI?"

"Totally different."

"Yeah? How so?"

"It's the language I have to use to get my job done. It just slips into my everyday conversations."

"And?"

"And what?"

"And I'm waiting for you to make the connection."

"Connection?"

"God, woman. I talk to middle-schoolers all day, every day. Don't you think I'm speaking the language of my people, too?"

Ang thought about it for a moment. "I'm an asshole."

Geri laughed, and Ang could envision her sunny face and her swinging her long black hair over her shoulder in triumph. "You're just lucky infinite patience is also part of the tool kit required to do my job. Oh, and I love you. You always end up getting it."

Ang sighed. "Kat made you call me, huh?"

"She's worried you held in the horror of your new haircut in her presence because she was the one who cut it."

Ang ran her hand over her hair, smoothing over the contours of her head, which she'd come to find were actually quite lovely. "It's weird, but I'm getting used to it."

"Good. Because it looks dope, yo."

Ang held back the automatic response and poured half-and-half into her coffee along with a little monk fruit sweetener. "You think so? It's a big change."

"You've been talking about doing it for years."

"You know why."

"Screw those homophobic business types."

"It isn't just their homophobia. Don't get me wrong, that's a big part of it, but they were intimidated by me with the *long* hair. They wouldn't know what to do with themselves if I came in looking like Grace Jones in *A View to a Kill*."

"Screw them tenfold if they can't handle a confident Black woman."

Ang took her coffee into the living room and carefully took a seat on the floor next to the box. She normally wouldn't chance coffee anywhere near her white carpet and furniture, but the renegade in her dared her to; however, she still made sure to use a coaster when she put the cup on the coffee table. "Well, it's behind me now. I don't have to worry about scaring my boss, and if a haircut counts me out of any future jobs, I don't want to work there." She said it like she meant it, but trepidation about how the haircut would affect her job search started to take root inside her. Her initial response was to chide herself for feeling insecure. This wasn't her. She was in charge and confident. But being a little insecure was a normal human emotion. No one should be expected to—

She shook her head. She'd have to revisit her near plunge into the dangerous waters of self-examination at some point, but not right now. If she went there now, there was a chance she'd never return. She had to prepare herself first. In the meantime, she had to remain strong.

"Ang?"

"Huh?" She'd forgotten she had Geri on the phone. "Sorry. I got distracted by something."

"I asked what you were up to. Did you go on the bike ride you were blathering about last night?"

Ang grimaced when she remembered her drunken monologue about being free to do whatever she wanted whenever she wanted after removing the handcuffs of the corporate world. She'd gone on and on about becoming a professional cyclist, bragging about her expensive bike and the first place 5K medal she'd received from the Girls Club in fourth grade.

An image of Krista lowering her sunglasses to reveal her gorgeous eyes flashed through her mind, and she smiled. God. Her thoughts were all over the place. That was what she got for almost letting insecurity take charge. "Just a few laps around Wash Park, but it was nice to get out there without having to contend with the weekend crowds."

"What's on the agenda for the rest of your day?"

Ang sighed and took a sip of coffee, resting her hand on top of the box.

"Did I just hear a sigh of angst?" Geri asked.

"I'm not used to having so much time on my hands. It's hard to fill, you know?"

Geri's laugh exuded mirth. "I'd kill for that problem. You can keep the rest. I'll just take the too much time thing."

A blurred memory of her saying those exact words last night floated in Ang's mind. "Believe me, I used to think the same way."

"What? You're the definition of a workaholic. When you google it, a picture of you in one of your sexy business suits is at the top of the search results."

Ang sighed. She'd given her job *everything*, and look where it landed her. "I might have saved a relationship or six if I hadn't given every waking moment to a job that proved it valued me less than I valued it. Now, I have all the time in the world and no one to spend it with." She flopped backward to lie on the carpet. Cleo took that moment as an opportunity to use her as a stepping stone. When Ang put a hand on her back, Cleo stopped and fixed a look of unbridled disdain at her until Ang removed it, and then she continued her walk across Ang's midsection. The contempt was too much. "Even Cleo hates me."

"Cleo only loves Cleo. She's a narcissist. Don't beat yourself up for dedication to your job. Maybe just dial it back a little next time. Balance, baby. Balance. Are you searching for jobs?"

"Balance. Right. I'm totally a balance kind of person." Sarcasm dripped from Ang's words. Everyone knew she was an all or nothing person. And now she was nothing. "I'm not sure how to get started. Maybe an executive placement company or something." Just the thought of a job hunt made her stomach churn. What if the skills from her job at Lithium didn't translate to the needs of other companies?

"I guess it's different for you. The school district posts all job openings for all schools in one place. Do executive positions get posted on websites? Or is it who you know?"

"It's definitely a who you know situation."

"It's a no-brainer, then. You know everyone."

"Therein lies the trouble. I'm acquainted with a lot of people, but they're all in tech retail. I'm not sure I want to stay in the field. I'm tired of working twice as hard as the men. I'm tired of having to prove myself capable, when men have to prove they're *incapable*. I'm tired of getting promoted just to be given a lower salary. I'm just tired."

Geri sighed over the line. "Oh, honey. It's not just in tech. And if they drive you out of the field, it's never going to get better."

Ang sighed again. "Please don't remind me of my obligations to all the subjugated groups I represent. I'm fully aware of my personal responsibility to improve the lives of women. And Black women. And Black lesbian women. I just need you to let me whine for a bit and tell me it'll all be okay, and I can be anything I want to be, even if I decide to become a full-time cyclist."

"You would be the *best* full-time cyclist. The bicycle world couldn't grasp the magnitude of awesome if you decided to bike full-time."

Relief from the pressure building in Ang's chest lifted. Geri always had her back, even when she was being a baby. "Thank you, Ger. You just proved why you're my best friend."

"Really?" The earnestness in Geri's voice caused Ang a twinge of guilt. Just like her romantic relationships, she'd mostly prioritized her friendships after work. That was going to change starting now.

"Always," she said.

"Can I tell Kat?"

"She's aware. You were here long before she was. But let's not remind her."

"It's our little secret," Geri said, whispering dramatically. "But I'm gonna have a T-shirt made. I'll wear it in the house and smirk privately when Kat calls and has no idea I'm wearing it."

Geri could always make her laugh. "You do you, girl. You're practicing your smirk now, aren't you?"

"Maybe. But back to you. You're not looking for a new job right now, you're going a little stir crazy with all the time on your hands, and you're ignoring your duty to forge new paths for Black lesbian women with short hair. That's a lot for one day. I'd take a nap."

"Since I'm biologically incapable of napping, I'm just about to go through the box I took home from the office, and I'm going to throw away a bunch of baggage. Afterward, my calendar is completely open, but I've been contemplating a good binge session of *American Horror Story*."

"Can I be a voyeur on the line as you go through your box?" Geri snickered. "That sounded dirty."

"Yes, it did. I think Regina would be proud of you."

"Oh, come on. No one can live up to the level of depravity my wife wields."

"True, but you did outdo yourself just then."

"It's a gift. Open the box. Let's get this party started."

"Yes, ma'am." Ang lifted the top off the box and peered in. She lifted out a couple of five-by-seven picture frames. One held a snapshot of her holding Cleo, and the other displayed a picture of her, Geri, and Kat on the beach in Cancun last spring. She thought of the two excursions she'd been looking forward to but had missed because of a crisis at one of the stores. "There's not as much in it as I thought."

"Didn't you pack it yourself?"

"Yeah, but I have stress amnesia, and I wasn't really paying attention." She did a mental inventory of her office. "I left some stuff behind. I suppose I'll have to go back for it at some point."

"Make them ship it to your house."

Not a bad idea. "I imagine I'll have to go in to drop off my badge and laptop. I can just grab it then." She hadn't answered the half dozen calls or listened to the messages from the office. She sighed and rolled the tension from her shoulders. "Or I can just ask Ann to box it up and send it. I'll figure it out."

"As long as you do it your way. You don't owe those assholes anything. So what else is in the box?"

"Mostly office supplies. I just dumped my drawers."

Geri snickered again. "She said, 'Dumped my drawers.'"

"Okay, Cartman. You just canceled out the points you got for the box comment."

"Please. My comedy would have my seventh-graders rolling on the floor."

"Well, this thirty-seven-year-old just rolled her eyes." She spied the fancy fountain pen her parents had sent when she'd made vice president, still in the box because it was too fancy to use. "I just found the present my parents gave me for my last promotion." She picked it up.

"What did they give you? Let me guess. A monogramed valise? A bust of Aristotle? A pearl-inlaid globe?"

Ang laughed because they were all gifts her parents would give, tasteful with an air of intellectual importance, i.e., ostentatious and good for show. "Close. A Montblanc pen."

Geri sucked in a breath. "Tell me it's the Little Prince."

Ang examined the box. "It is. A red one. It's very pretty."

Geri whistled. "Very expensive, too."

"It's lost on me, to be honest, but I think this will be my new journaling pen."

"Leave it to me in your will. In the meantime, you'll produce prose of epic meaning with such a fancy pen. Any other fun things in there?"

"Just an electronic picture frame I never took out of the box and a file folder of emails I printed out to cheer me up on stressful days."

"Did it work?"

"The picture frame?"

"No, the emails. What did you print out? Kitten and puppy memes? Dirty jokes?"

Ang grimaced.

"I can hear you making a face all the way over here," Geri said.

"It's embarrassing. Just notes from people saying nice things, attagirls from my superiors, good news, a few reviews."

"Why's it embarrassing? Why wouldn't you want to save reminders of your awesomeness?"

"I shouldn't rely on others to tell me I have value." She sounded like one of the memes Geri had mentioned.

"Get over yourself, Ang. Everyone likes to receive praise once in a while."

"I'll take your word for it." She put all the odds and ends back into the box except the framed pictures and the Montblanc pen. Cleo had laid claim to the picture of the two of them, anyway, as she'd sprawled out on it.

"Now that you're done with that, opening day is next week. You ready to break your Rockies Jersey out?"

"Are you kidding? I can't wait. The past two days, with all the sunshine and perfect temperatures, has me longing for long afternoons at Coors Field."

They spoke about meeting up for the game and hung up shortly after, and Ang scratched under Cleo's chin, instigating a chainsaw purr from the lounging cat.

She wondered if the contents of the box were a metaphor for her career. The only things worth keeping being moments with her friends and gifts from her family? It made her wonder if any of it mattered, and if not, why should she spend time mourning the loss?

CHAPTER SIX

Krista leaned back in the desk chair and tossed the hacky sack into the air, caught it, and tossed it again. After digging through accounting software all day, the answer as to why the totals weren't matching up dangled right outside her grasp, and her frustration only grew worse. Swifty kept offering to help, but it wasn't fair to him, and besides, if the numbers were even remotely correct, she might have a tax problem, and she didn't want to add to his worries. As the owner of the store, she should have a handle on her accounting.

It didn't make sense. There were at least a dozen custom bikes noted just in the last month, all of which showed delivered by the vendor records and then returned in her books, and since she was the only one who could approve a sale that big, she knew that had to be an error. Besides, the transactions resulted in a wash, with no real money changing hands since the bikes, if they were ever even shipped, which she doubted, were returned to the vendors. The books didn't zero out, though. It made her wonder what other paperwork might be wrong. If she couldn't count on the transactions lining up, she couldn't trust any of the other stuff being correct, either. Aside from doing a physical inventory, she couldn't think of any other way to clear the books and pinpoint the error.

A hand on her shoulder pulled her from her thoughts.

Krista rubbed her forehead. "I was totally in my head just then."

Swifty laughed. "I figured as much when I called your name from the counter, and you didn't respond."

"Just working on the books."

"Why don't you trade with me for the afternoon? You take maintenance, and I'll figure out the books. I can probably get it figured out in an hour or two."

"Thanks. I think I'm almost there, though," she lied. "Don't you have to take Dirk to his appointment this afternoon?" She checked her watch. Swifty's husband Dirk's chemo appointments were every other Wednesday afternoon, with only two left, including the one today. She kept track because she planned to have a bottle of champagne sent to their house to celebrate the last infusion milestone. "Only one more after this week, right?"

The expression on his face told her something changed. "The doctor admitted him Monday night. His counts dropped over the weekend, and he spiked a fever. They're going to skip this week to let him get his counts up."

"Oh, man. I thought this round would be easier on him. How's he holding up?"

"It's Dirk, he always rolls with the punches." He looked like he could cry. "This time, though, he's been in bed since the last infusion two weeks ago and just keeps getting weaker. He can't eat because of the sores in his mouth. So they admitted him when the blood work in the emergency room showed all his numbers out of whack."

"I wish you two could get a break. It's been one thing after another."

"Him being in the hospital is a good thing, actually."

"I guess they have more things to help him recuperate. IVs and such." Ang couldn't imagine what Swifty was going through. Just more reason for her not to let him in on her worries about the accounting discrepancy. He relied on the insurance she provided, and he shouldn't have to worry about losing it if the business was in trouble when he needed it the most.

He nodded. "Also, he's not at home all day alone while I'm here."

"You know you can take as much time as you need, Swifty. We'll make due here."

"I can't afford to not work."

"I told you we'd work it out."

He waved a dismissive hand. "It doesn't matter now, anyway. He gets better care in the hospital. Besides, in-patient billing is better for insurance reasons because they cover more of it. I'm hoping they'll keep him for the next infusions, too, since the chemo is covered better in-patient. Outpatient is way more expensive."

"I can imagine," she said, but she couldn't. Not really. Insurance remained a mystery to her, even though she'd compared plans when she renewed for the shop every year. Seeing the tables and lists in sales documents was different than dealing with referrals, copays, in and out of network, approvals, and all the other things she'd heard him talking about on the phone through the last year. "Please tell me if I can help at all, okay? Seriously. I'll give you everything but Alfur." She couldn't be more serious.

He smiled at her weak joke, rubbing the back of his neck, no doubt uneasy at being on the receiving end of generosity when he was always the first to offer help when others could use it. "We're good, kiddo. But thanks."

"Hey, not to change the subject," she said when that was exactly what she was doing. "It's about inventory and deliveries. There were some special orders on the books, including a couple of Pinarellos. I don't remember having them on the racks."

He perked up, appearing uneasy. Maybe he suspected her of changing the subject to get his mind off things. "Oh yeah. It's because they never got delivered. There's a glitch in the ordering system. If you check, you'll notice they were credited. I never said anything because I caught them before they were shipped and got it all straightened out."

"It's weird, though. It looks like it happened a dozen or so times."

"It took them a little while to figure out the glitch. In fact, I'm not sure they have. It's one of the reasons I watch the books so closely, so I can catch it when it happens, and so we can get the credit before invoicing. Um, are you having any issues with it? Like I said, I can figure it out when you're ready."

She waved him away. "See? Another reason why you're the best. I have it. Now, go hang out with Dirk. I have the counter."

Chapter Seven

Ang lifted the bike from the back of her BMW and rolled it down the sidewalk toward Sol Cycle. Music spilled from the open doors of the shop. It didn't surprise her with the good weather. Colorado residents never took late March weather for granted. It could be in the seventies one day and snowing the next. After the cold winter, every sunny day meant going outside.

Inside the store, the smell of bikes reminded her of her college cycling days. She paused to let her eyes adjust to the darker interior and marveled at the number of cycles on display throughout the large space. Very different from the stores she ran, the aesthetics of which leaned toward minimal product on the sales floor. This crowded sales floor held rows upon rows of bikes with many hung from racks suspended from the ceiling. A half dozen customers wandered the floor, some talking with sales associates. No one currently stood behind the desk near the front of the store, and there was no sign of Krista. A pang of disappointment shot through her.

She took a moment to scan the wall of framed photos behind the desk. Most were snapshots of customers and employees throughout the years. Many of them appeared to be from decades earlier.

A simple sign with the single word, MAINTENANCE, hung above a wide counter in the back of the store. Ang threaded her bike down the aisle, seeing new gadgets and gear she wanted to check out before she left. Her retail-trained eye mentally rearranged the shelves to move parts closer to the maintenance area, accessories grouped by function, putting together eye-catching endcaps with small gadgets closer to the register so customers would be more apt to make an impulse buy. Retail succeeded with attention to detail and flow.

She took a place in line behind two other people, neither of who pushed bikes, so she assumed they were there to pick something up.

"I thought it might be you I spotted walking into the store."

Ang turned toward the voice. Krista approached carrying a couple of take-out beverage trays filled with to-go coffee cups. Ang didn't have the right to the little buzz of excitement she got from seeing the woman she'd talked to less than twenty-four hours earlier.

Without a hat or sunglasses, Krista looked even younger than she had the day before, and Ang guessed her to be maybe twenty-five, another reason it wasn't right for her heart rate to keep rising the closer Krista moved toward her. This time, Krista wore a loose-fitting T-shirt with a sasquatch design, a pair of gray cargo shorts, and hiking sandals. She wore her blond, almost white hair in a single braid pulled over her left shoulder, with a bandana across her forehead tied behind her head. She exuded that outdoorsy Colorado vibe Ang always admired. In comparison, her white linen shorts and acrylic-blend pullover with a floral pattern were stuffy. Where Krista wore woven bracelets, Ang wore a silver Tiffany bracelet. Even the running shoes she wore, expensive and designed specifically for her feet, were boring. Ang could confidently say she'd never been half as cool as Krista. And, God, those legs.

She mentally shook herself. *Focus, Ang.* She gestured at her bike. "I figured I should get it tuned-up sooner rather than later. And there's the whole derailleur thing." A dull response, but it fit the reason for her being there.

"For sure. We're supposed to have a few more days of sunshine before the weather turns for a day or two next week. Gotta get the rides in when we can, right?"

"Exactly. Um, I just wanted to say thanks again for helping me yesterday."

Krista tilted her head. "It's nothing. Hey, wait here while I set these drinks down in the back, and I'll help you check this beauty in." Krista veered toward the end of the counter and nodded at the place she wanted Ang to wait while she ducked through an open doorway. She reemerged seconds later with two drinks, one of which she handed to the tall man with a beard behind the counter; the other she took a sip of.

Feeling conspicuous for skipping two others in line, Ang hid behind a wide wooden beam at the end of the counter. There'd been a time when she would have appreciated the deference, but with her life upside down—and without the identity provided by having a high-powered job—she felt like a poseur, undeserving of the extra attention. "They were here before me."

"You get to skip the line when you make an appointment." Krista winked. "Besides, I'm technically on my break, so I'd just be kicking it in the back sipping my latte. You're not taking me away from helping someone else."

"I don't want to impose on your break."

"I wouldn't do it if I didn't want to, Angelique. Besides, I work through my breaks most days. Let me have a good reason for doing it this time."

Krista winked at her again, and Ang chided herself for the heat crawling up her neck. She loved the way Krista used her full first name. "Well, thank you."

Krista smiled and came around the counter with a clipboard. "Let's see, there's the adjustment of the gear cable and of course, the tune-up." She checked some boxes as she inspected the bike and wrote a few things before pointing at a list of services posted on laminated sheets of paper taped to the counter. "Your bike is in good shape. I recommend the basic tune. It includes tightening the derailleur, and the deep clean comes complimentary with all the services we provide. Everything else is good. Do you have any concerns you want us to check out?"

Except me? Ang almost laughed out loud at the thought. "I think we covered it. You'll call me if anything comes up?"

Krista handed her the clipboard and indicated what information to fill out. "Definitely. We'll contact you before we do anything we haven't already discussed. Sound cool?"

"Perfect." Ang admired Krista's smile, how perfect and white her teeth were. Honestly, she could have been a model in an outdoor catalogue.

"...will that work?" Krista asked with an expectant rise of her eyebrows.

She'd missed something. "Will what work?"

Krista grinned as if she knew the content of Ang's thoughts, and Ang tried to maintain her composure. "I asked if picking up your bike on Friday around noon would work for you."

"Sorry. Um, yes. Friday's good."

"Great. I guess I'll see you then."

Ang turned to leave, almost feeling the imprint of Krista's gaze upon her back. She was grateful she didn't knock over a row of bikes on her way out. Not until she got into her car did she remember she'd wanted to check out some of the bike gear she'd seen. Why did Krista distract her so much? There were so many reasons why being attracted to her wasn't a good idea. The age difference alone was normally enough to dampen her interest, and she'd never been into women with tattoos and piercings, not that Krista had a ton of them, but still, how did kissing someone with a lip ring work? Besides, Ang was into professional women, women who understood what it was like to work a corporate job. They didn't have to be vice presidents, but knowing the ins and outs of leadership gave them something to talk about while they got to know each other. It just didn't make sense that a twenty-something woman probably working her first job out of college—if she even went to college—was a good fit for her.

But...there was definitely something there, and Ang liked the little charge of excitement it gave her every time she was around Krista. She was already looking forward to Friday.

CHAPTER EIGHT

The lilac bush near the gate in Krista's backyard displayed signs of leaf buds, which always made her happy because it carried the expectation of spring. The grass was a little greener, as were the trees, which were showing signs of budding. She blamed it all on the warmer weather over the last few days, which also played a big part in why she sat in the chair swing in her yard instead of in the office at the shop, working on the books. Concentration eluded her as everything around her caught her attention, except the laptop balanced on her crisscrossed legs.

Staring at her flower beds, she planned what to plant and how to get the most use of her small garden, when a pair of bushy-tailed fox squirrels ran across the top of her fence, jumped onto the box elder tree, and scurried up the trunk, only to stop a few feet later to chatter at Alfur, who mostly ignored them. He'd learned long ago that he'd never catch one, so he didn't waste his time; instead, he peered through one of the two dog windows she'd installed in the fence, waiting for someone to walk down the alley behind the house, preferably someone with a dog.

With a sigh, she woke up her screen again and stared at the numbers continuing to perplex her. Still frustrated, she thought she might take Swifty up on his offer and let him give it a shot. If she had an accountant, as her father had often advised her to get, the issue would already be resolved. But if she was going to hire someone new, it had to be a store manager. There just wasn't time enough in the day to do all the administrative stuff and also help manage the staff. When the college students left for the summer, she'd be down half her sales team, so her first priority would be filling those slots, followed by writing the schedules, managing breaks, keeping the sales room clean, and closing the register every evening. In addition, she worked with the marketing agency for advertising; kept up with sales licenses, taxes, payroll, inventory; scoped out new equipment, and did all the mundane tasks a successful bike shop owner did to keep things running. She'd worked six or seven days a week for months, and she needed a break. If she could cut her hours down to just five days a week, she'd be happy. She loved the store, but if she kept this up, she knew she'd eventually grow to hate it.

Like right now. She hated changing to the new software and wanted to throw her laptop across the yard.

Thankfully, her phone rang to prevent her from doing it.

"What's the good word, turd?" she asked, seeing her sister's name on the caller ID.

"Not a lot, camel toe," Asta said, completing their customary greeting. Camel toe had once been Camelot to make it rhyme, but over time, and with mysterious logic, they'd evolved it to its current form. "Mom wants to know what's going on with Uncle Raggy. He hasn't come to family dinner in a couple of months, and she's worried about him. She thinks he's existing on hot dogs and beans if he's not drinking his dinner."

"He's fine," Krista said, not sure of it at all. She only repeated what he told her every week when he called to say he wasn't coming, but she hadn't seen him since the last time they'd all seen him for family dinner. Now she had guilt for not having gone up to visit him more often like she used to. "I'm going up this weekend. Probably Sunday. Wanna come with?"

"I would desperately like to come with, but I have study group."

Although bummed, Krista was glad she'd have one-on-one time with her uncle. She loved going up to his place. Just a small one-bedroom cabin in the woods, it held memories of some of the best days of her life: playing in the forest, swimming in the little lake, riding her bike on the trails. But lately, who had time? She hadn't seen Raggy in a couple of months, and she hadn't been up to his cabin since before the winter holidays.

"Thanks. I'll tell Mom," Asta said. "I'll go up with you next time."

"Why's Mom asking you about this anyway? Why didn't she ask me at family dinner?"

"I don't know. I'm around more than you. I do laundry over there and have dinner with them three or four times a week."

Her sister wasn't being snarky, but the comment still stung. "Work has been a bit crazy. I'm going to hire a store manager to get some things off my plate."

Her sister laugh-snorted. "You could hire twenty new managers, and you'd just find more work to do. You love the shop. If I didn't drop by to hug on Alfur, I would never see you."

Okay. Maybe Asta was being snarky. Truthful but snarky. Krista deserved it, though. She lived blocks away from her parents, and she only ever spent time with them lately at family dinners. "I'll make a better effort to hang out with you and them."

"Good, because I miss you. I'm in desperate want of some sister time."

"Everything going okay?"

"Yeah, just missing you."

She said she missed her right back, and they talked for a few more minutes before hanging up. Krista closed out the accounting software and stopped daydreaming about her flowerbeds. Instead, she did a search on sales manager job descriptions and started to put together a job posting. It didn't matter if she could afford one. She needed one. She'd figure it out. She always did. It was just that being a successful business owner wasn't filling her days with as much joy as it used to. It wasn't bad, but it just wasn't...*enough*. Enough what, though? And did she even have time for more? She sighed. She wouldn't be able to find out if she didn't get another manager in the store.

Several minutes later, she'd finished drafting the description of the position when a Zoom call from Swifty came through. She laughed as she answered. When Zoom calls became popular, he'd fallen in love with the application. She never talked to him on the phone anymore.

"Good morning," she said when his image rendered.

"Don't you mean afternoon?" He smiled, but his face appeared gaunt, and he looked exhausted.

She checked the time in the status bar of her computer. "Dang. The morning flew by. What's up?"

"Two things. I want to replace the entire derailleur assembly on your 'friend's' bike." He made air quotes, and she snorted. As if. Angelique existed way beyond her league. "You told me to tell you if there were any issues with the bike before I called her."

"She *is* just a friend, funny guy. I met her a couple of days ago in the park. Don't call, just replace it. I'll comp it. Use the Shimano Dura-Ace."

"You got it, boss. Only the best for your 'friend.'"

She shook her head. The more she corrected him, the more he'd push it. "What's the second thing."

"Yeah. I have to leave early today. Dirk has to have his port moved. It's blocked again. It's a minor surgery, but they have to put him under, and I want to be there when they bring him from recovery. You know how bad he is with anesthesia."

"Of course. I'll be there in less than thirty minutes. If you leave before I get there, tell Magnus he's in charge."

"I don't need to be at the hospital until two thirty, so take your time."

About to hang up, Krista thought of something else. "Hey, I'm gonna pull the trigger on hiring a sales manager. Have you changed your mind?" She wondered if the cost of treatment he'd been complaining about would make him reconsider an earlier discussion where he'd said he'd rather eat a hotdog than work in sales again. For a vegetarian, that declaration said a lot.

"I'm very sure. A couple of dollars more an hour is not compelling enough to make me want to sell bikes to people who can't tell the difference between disc brakes and caliper brakes."

"Okay. I get it. I just wanted to make sure before I open it up. Magnus doesn't want it either, Kayla is too new, and Rajib and Hill are leaving for summer break in June."

"I'm more than sure. I like fixing bikes, not selling them. If you make a maintenance manager position, then we can talk."

He kidded, but she wished he didn't. She couldn't afford two new managers. She really wished she could.

After they said their good-byes and she promised to bring in coffee, she closed her laptop and considered taking the long way into work through the park. Maybe she'd run into Angelique. There was no way Angelique would be interested in her, but it didn't hurt to daydream a little.

Chapter Nine

The store bustled with customers on Friday when Ang went to pick up her bike, and just like Wednesday, all of the sales clerks were busy helping customers. As she walked through the shop, she overheard snippets of conversation, and it inspired her to spend more time on her bike, although after so much time out of the saddle, she considered herself a novice compared to all these people. Again, her casual but neatly ironed shorts and polo shirt were out of place among them.

A pile of fluff lying on the floor in front of the desk caught her attention. When she approached, a furry head popped up, and the dog she remembered from months ago greeted her with his tongue hanging from his mouth.

"I remember you, Alfur. Aren't you the cutest, fluffiest thing I've ever seen?" She knelt, letting her fingers dip into the soft, thick, red and white coat. He put his paw on her arm and pulled her hand to his face, so she scratched around his face and ears. She wished women were as easy to please...*and* as direct.

A head in a yellow knit cap appeared over the edge of the counter. "Alfur's a chick magnet."

She recognized the same man from when she'd dropped her bike off. He looked exhausted compared to just two days before, and she wondered if the owner of the store worked the staff too hard. She remembered Krista said she worked through her breaks a lot.

"He's just the cutest," Ang said, laughing when the dog licked her hand. She gave him another good scratching and stood. The man leaned against the counter. The nametag hanging from a lanyard around his neck read Swifty.

"You're Krista's friend," he said. "I'll get her."

"If she's not busy," said Ang, getting a little tickle in her stomach when he called her Krista's friend.

Swifty smiled. "Krista asked me to tell her when you came in. Hold on just a sec." He bobbed his head as he walked, reminding her of the hippie from *The Muppet Show*, and disappeared into the back room. A few seconds later, he reappeared with Krista and Ang's bike.

"Hello, Angelique. Your little beauty is all set. She gave us very little trouble. A model patient, in fact." Krista brought the bike around the desk and patted the seat. It practically gleamed.

"Wow. I don't think she's ever been this shiny, even when I bought her," Ang said, eyeing her bike.

"We do a deep clean on every maintenance ticket. It's a nice little way to say we appreciate your business."

"I love it. Do I check out here or at the front counter?"

"The front counter. I'll walk you up."

Alfur trailed after them as Krista wheeled her bike up to the desk, and she leaned to pet him as they walked. When Ang glanced back, she noticed a small line forming at the maintenance desk, and another clerk joined Swifty at the counter.

"Is the store always this busy?" she asked.

"We have peaks and lulls, and it's definitely seasonal. We were dead up until about a week ago. We'll probably stay busy from now until fall, but the crowds will dip a little when the college lets out for summer break."

Ang noticed the help wanted sign displayed at the front desk, and her retail brain clicked into gear. This time, she paid attention to customer service, process, inventory, and flow. Above everything, Sol Cycle impressed her with their customer service. While there were a few things she would do differently, she didn't notice anything major. Of course, there could be critical things to be addressed behind the scenes, but she probably would have seen more evidence in the visible areas; weak areas usually eroded even the best of facades.

All of this passed through her mind while Krista rang her up. Krista handed her credit card back with the receipt.

"I think you made a mistake on this. You must have forgotten to run the card," she said, noticing the service total.

Krista just smiled. "It's on me."

"It's sweet of you, but—"

"But nothing. I wanted to do it."

"Well, thank you. You'll have to let me repay you somehow."

"How about you let me take you to lunch?"

The offer took her by surprise. "You mean now?"

Krista grinned, and her bluer than blue eyes sparkled. "I'm about to take my lunch break, so, yes."

"Um, okay. But only if you let me pay. It's the least I can do."

Krista laughed. "We can discuss it when we get there."

Ang had no intention of Krista paying for lunch after comping the bike service. "Do you have a place in mind?"

Krista winked. "Do you like sandwiches?"

"I've been known to eat them, yes." The slow roll that occurred in her belly at the wink Krista gave her was a nice surprise—a *very* nice surprise.

"Pinky's deli is across the street. They're excellent. Have you been there?"

"I haven't."

"You're going to love it. Let's get your bike to your car first."

Krista told several anecdotes about the local shop owners as they walked, ordered their food at the counter, and took a table on the outside patio. Ang nearly had to tackle Krista to let her pay, though. But in the end, Ang was able to get her card to the amused man behind the register. Ang enjoyed the playful fight to pay. Used to always picking up the tab, she liked that Krista wanted to pay like it was a date. It wasn't, but it felt like it. Another slow belly roll made her smile wider.

As they took their seats, she peered at the sign, which looked to be an original from before either of them was born. She'd driven by it countless times but had never stopped.

"The scoop of ice cream in the 'y' on the sign always reminds me of an ice cream shop," she said.

"It used to be. The owner kept the sign when he bought it because he couldn't think of a better name."

"Do you know the owners of all the businesses around here?"

"Most of them. It's a fairly connected neighborhood. We all cater pretty heavily to the university, and we watch out for one another. Sol Cycle has been around longer than most of them, so I guess we're considered a fixture."

Ang swallowed a bite of her BLT. "I remember Sol Cycle from being on the cycling team in college. We got a discount. I never went into the store before this week, though. The owner came to the school." Ang laughed at the memory. "We called him the Yeti. I probably shouldn't have said anything since he's your boss."

"The Yeti is my Uncle Raggy," Krista said before she bit into her Rueben.

Ang covered her mouth. "I'm so sorry."

Krista swallowed her food and snorted. "For calling him the Yeti? He loves it, thinks it's funny."

Ang laughed. "We definitely meant it as a term of endearment."

"He really enjoyed working with the college cycle team. You were on the team?" Krista asked. "Me too."

Ang liked that they were both alumni. "Probably a few years before you were, but yeah. Small world. My best friend Geri and I shared a room in the Towers."

"I missed a lot of the typical college experience. I graduated high school from South and going to college at DU simply meant my commute became shorter. I grew up in the neighborhood and lived at home while attending. Are you a Colorado native?"

Ang shook her head. "I grew up in Massachusetts, just outside of Boston. I had the full college deal at DU, dorms for the first two years, and then a house near campus with four roommates. I couldn't wait to leave home."

College was a wonderful time for Ang. Not only did she meet Geri there, where they became what had turned into life-long best friends, but she was finally away from home, and when she joined Lithium right after she graduated, it gave her an excuse not to have to return to Boston where she was born and raised. She loved her parents, but having distance from them was good for all involved.

"I wanted to live in the dorms so badly, but it didn't make sense when I already lived so close to the school. I spent a lot of time there, though." Krista took a sip of her drink. "You said you were only a few blocks away from your house when I met you at the park. Do you live in the Wash Park neighborhood?"

Ang nodded, swallowing her last bite. "Just a few blocks east of the park."

"How long have you lived there?"

"About ten years. After I left DU, I lived in LoDo for a few years."

Krista's eyes grew dreamy. "As a kid, I wanted to live in a loft downtown. It seemed like it would be fun."

"It is. For a while. But I got tired of always being on the go. I wanted to chill out at home more often. Ironically, my life got busier when I bought my house. Until recently. Anyway, I loved the neighborhoods around DU, so here I am."

"Here you are." Krista's eyes always seemed to sparkle, as if she were just about to smile, which she did a lot. Ang loved looking at them. "And we're both DU alumni." Krista gathered their trash and put it in a nearby garbage can.

"The gazillion alumni emails remind me all the time." Ang liked how excited Krista seemed about their common school experience. Her delight was infectious and made the sunny day seem brighter. It was a nice change from moping around her house, and she didn't want their time together to end. "Have you always lived in Colorado?"

Krista nodded. "I'm a second-generation native. I live a few blocks south of the store on Downing. My folks have always lived in the University Park area, so I grew up around here. They teach at the college, and I didn't move far when I bought my own place.

I seriously have not lived outside of a two-mile radius, if you can believe it."

Ang was pleasantly surprised that Krista owned her own house. Maybe she wasn't as young as Ang had first guessed. She carried herself as if she could be little older, aside from the way she dressed. It wasn't as if it meant anything anyway, even if Ang was attracted to her—and she couldn't lie, she was—she wouldn't do anything about it. They were so different. Besides, Krista probably wasn't interested in her that way.

"I love this area," Ang said. "Not too far from downtown where I work, but far enough out so I don't have to deal with all the event traffic and crowding. Plus, there are the parks and bike trails and neighborhood businesses."

"You work downtown?"

Ang took a sip of her drink. Damn. A small knot of anger tried to take hold, and she didn't want it to ruin the time with Krista. "Did I say that?"

Krista nodded. "You did."

Ang considered lying. After all, Krista wouldn't know the difference. Would she even see her again after this lunch? She hoped so.

Krista ducked her head to get into Ang's line of sight. "Sensitive subject? Are you a secret agent? An assassin?"

Ang laughed, a little embarrassed by the unintentionally long pause. "Nothing so exciting. I quit my job at the company I worked for a couple of weeks ago, which was downtown, and I'm still getting used to not working there."

"What did you do?"

"Retail management." Ang didn't want to get into why she left, so she kept it high-level.

"Oh, yeah? Like managing stores, making schedules, and inventory?"

Ang smiled. "Yep. Only, I did it at the corporate level for a lot of stores."

Krista's smile dimmed a little.

"What?" Ang asked.

"I almost asked if you wanted a job."

"You mean at Sol Cycle?" Ang said, amused.

"Yeah. But I guess it would be a big step down."

Ang was flattered. They were merely at different places in their lives. Everyone started somewhere. "I noticed the help wanted sign. What are you looking for? Sales clerk?" Ang occasionally thought about those years and longed for the reduced responsibility and lower stress. As a floor clerk, with only herself to worry about, her primary challenge had been to meet her individual sales goals. At the end of the day, work was over until her next shift. Such a carefree life. A tiny part of her wanted to help Krista out. Boredom threatened to kill her, and she didn't expect to go back to corporate work immediately. She needed time to figure out what she wanted to do with her life.

Thinking about going back to a corporate job literally made her nauseous.

"We have plenty of sales clerks. We work with the college to get part-time seasonal employees. We also have two full-time employees besides me. Swifty works the maintenance counter, and Leticia is our sales manager, but she went on maternity leave at the end of last year, which turned into a leave of absence when she decided to take off the first year with the baby. When she comes back, it'll be part-time as a regular sales associate. What we really could use is another manager. Someone who can do the schedules and inventory stuff. I do it all now, but I'm drowning. It's getting old working six and seven days a week.

Krista being the store manager made sense. It explained how she could afford her own house. But the hours she worked made Ang want to tell her boss or her uncle or whoever owned the shop that there were laws, not to mention ethics, against making her work so much. But Kat invaded her mind saying, "It ain't your lane, girl." And would be right. At the same time, maybe she should consider the position, supposing Krista was serious, which she found ridiculous. Krista had no idea what her situation was or her capabilities. One thing she knew for certain was that she'd have the shop performing better than ever with her expertise. They'd be lucky to have someone like her. It wasn't false bravado or arrogance, just the truth.

Okay. Maybe a little bit of arrogance.

It had nothing to do with how much she liked being around Krista, she told herself. It would be ridiculous to take a job just to be around a woman she'd just met, right?

"Maybe I could help you out for a little while, a few weeks, until you find someone. As a friend. Keep the salary. I'm going nuts at home already, and it's been less than two weeks," she heard herself saying. What?

Krista appeared as surprised as Ang was.

"There's no way I'd let you do it for free." She paused, appearing to think. "It *would* be awesome to have someone sharp while we searched for someone more permanent. If you decide to do it, obviously."

"How about we both think about it?" Ang said. Seriously? Was she really considering it?

"If you decide you want to do it, we have an online application you can fill out on our website."

Krista probably thought she would turn it down. Hell, even she did. A week ago, she wouldn't have even considered it. But her expertise *was* in retail. And it could be fun.

Chapter Ten

The numbers were starting to make sense to Krista, but she still hadn't pinpointed the issue. She saw a correlation to the tax and rebate totals, which made her nervous because she never wanted to mess up taxes, but she told herself not to start worrying until a real reason presented itself. Quite different from the rest of her family, she and Uncle Raggy were the laid-back ones, and she'd taken Uncle Raggy's often given advice, *thetta reddast*, to heart when just a little girl. It *would* all work out okay. She just needed to get to the bottom of it. It didn't make sense yet, but it would.

Closer to a solution, Krista stopped trying to figure it out, at least for the evening. She was tired, but she couldn't go to bed yet. Not before seven o'clock. If she went to bed now, she'd just be up at 3:00 a.m. Besides, she'd just put a frozen pot pie in the oven, which would be done in a half hour, and she needed to call Uncle Raggy.

She picked up her phone, hoping he wouldn't be too far into his beer yet. The last few times she'd talked to him, he'd been drinking in the middle of the afternoon. Who knew how many he'd put away by now?

"Hallo," his voice boomed over the line after a couple of rings.

"Hallo, Uncle. It's your favorite niece."

"Ah! Hallo, Sigrún."

"Not Sigrún."

"Then Anna."

"Nope."

"It must be my third favorite *systurdóttir*, Krista," he said, using the Icelandic word for niece. "Yes, it must be. I recognize the voice even though I'd given her up for dead. Does she call?"

"Hey, I call you all the time. I spoke to you just a few days ago."

"I called *you*, if I remember correctly."

"True. Well, it's your lucky day, I called you just now, and one of the reasons I'm calling is because I want to come up on Sunday. Are you free?" she always asked, but he would be free. He always was.

"In fact, I'm not free this Sunday. I'll be in Lyons helping a friend repair their deck."

This was a surprise. "Have I met this friend?"

"It's a new friend I met snowshoeing a couple months ago."

"Since when do you snowshoe?"

"I picked it up just this winter. The sporting goods store gave free rentals on equipment to handsome mountain men. Naturally, they meant me, so I gave it a try."

She could envision her eighty-year-old grand uncle snowshoeing. He'd always been outdoorsy and fit, thanks to all the years of biking. "Let me guess, you were a natural, and it's now your favorite thing."

"I hated it. I'll stick to ice fishing in the winter and my bike the rest of the time."

She laughed. "Well, you made a new friend from it."

"True. Sorry I'm not free on Sunday. How about next Sunday?"

"Sure. I've missed you, and I want to make sure you're not eating only hot dogs and beans."

She heard the air he blew between his teeth, a thing he did when something exasperated him. No growl followed, so she figured he was only slightly annoyed. "Did your mother put you up to this? She said the same thing in a message she left on my machine not too long ago. I don't desire you women checking in on me, you know. Visit? Yes. Check up on? No. I'm good at taking care of myself. And if I fail? The dogs will grow fat on my bones."

He laughed at his often-told joke, and Krista squirmed. She hated to think about what she'd do if anything happened to him. The hot dog and beans thing sounded like something her mom *would* say. "She told Asta to call me. The fam is worried since you've missed family dinner so much lately. But she made me realize I hadn't been up to visit you and the pups in way too long, and I started missing you." The truth always worked with him.

"You're making me feel bad for teasing about Helga and Anna being my favorites."

"I thought you said Sigrún and Anna."

"Just testing you."

"Seeing as they don't exist, I didn't take offense."

"Does this mean you're taking more time off then?" he asked.

"Who's checking on who now?" she teased. "But, yes, I'm working on it." It was a small lie, but she didn't want him to lecture her, and if she said it enough, maybe she could manifest it. He was a big believer in willing things to happen, so she would give it a try. And maybe if she was lucky, a certain amber-eyed woman would follow up on the discussion they'd had at lunch.

"I never would have sold the shop to you if I knew you were going to become a workaholic. Your youth is meant for fun and tomfooleries. You'll have time to build your fortune later on. Besides, I am still holding out hope for you to find a rich woman and settle down. Heaven help me, but you're making me nostalgic for your tom cat ways. Before the store, there were a lot of lady friends. You haven't spoken of one of your ladies in quite some time."

The tom cat comment stung a little, but she didn't want to bore him with the details of her nonexistent love life. The few months she'd taken off from it had turned into a year, and surprisingly enough, she didn't miss dating. *Not* surprisingly enough, she hadn't figured out why she couldn't seem to settle down. She wanted to find her happily ever after, but where would she start? Besides that, she didn't want to keep hurting people along the way. In the meantime, she didn't want to talk about it, even if he understood her better than anyone else. "Well, it's been quite some time since there's been time to date. But you're not one to judge, Mr. Dedicated Bachelor. Maybe I inherited the single gene, too."

"I hope not, *mitt krútt.*"

He sounded sad, a thing she never thought she'd hear from him about this particular subject. He'd always been proud of his lothario ways. She decided not to press him on it.

"Well, I'll bring lunch when I come up next weekend."

"Sounds good, my favorite *systurdóttir*. I look forward to it. Most of the snow is gone, so maybe we can go for a hike."

She ended the call and dropped her phone next to her on the couch. Uncle Raggy sounded good and not at all drunk, to her relief. And his getting out with friends made her hopeful. Retirement had been difficult for him at first. She'd had to ask him to stay away, as he'd still come in almost every day, even after she'd taken it on. It had been hard to tell him to stop telling her how to run the business, but she had to learn how to manage things on her own. He'd taken it well, though. She could tell he still found it hard sometimes, but he was doing better. She couldn't believe he, of all people, thought he should school her on taking time off, though.

Speaking of taking time off, she logged into the staffing software to look for a new manager. She wished Angelique was serious about wanting the job, if only for a few weeks. It would give her some time to hire someone more permanent, and it wouldn't be awful to have her around. Not to date but just to get to know her. There was something about Angelique. In the past, Krista would have called it attraction, and it was. Krista wasn't dating, but she wasn't dead. There was something more. She wanted to really know her. But even that didn't describe what it was like to simply be around her. Part of her didn't want to because defining it might make the extraordinary more ordinary, and she liked to think of what she felt about Angelique as extra-extraordinary.

CHAPTER ELEVEN

Cleo took a seat on Ang's hands, which happened to be typing on her laptop. With a full twelve pounds of hairless flesh propped on her hands, she wasn't able to move her fingers to type, let alone view the screen with the Sol Cycle website on it.

She laughed. "Everything has to be on your terms, huh?"

Cleo simply began to groom her paw. With no choice but to sit there until Cleo decided to move, Ang told her cat about her day. It was therapeutic, and less than five minutes later, when the automatic feeder dispensed her kibble, Cleo let her know she'd listened long enough and jumped down. By then, Ang's left hand was asleep, and she'd had some time to think about her and Cleo's relationship. She'd come to a hypothesis. Maybe, just maybe, Cleo was mad at her because she'd spent so much time away from home while working, and the cat required time to forgive her. Ang couldn't force Cleo to love her, but she could let Cleo set the rules for forgiveness.

Ang contemplated her epiphany while she shook out the pins and needles. Maybe there was a path forward for them after all. She could hope.

When the sensation came back in her hands, she went back to what she'd been doing and navigated the Sol Cycle webpage. She should at least be familiar with the job posting before she turned down Krista's offer.

"They should revamp this site," she mumbled as she searched for the job posting page and finally found it under the About Us link at the very bottom of the homepage. The posting described the position very much as Krista had, and Ang was correct. She could perform the job in her sleep.

She realized she was imagining herself working at the shop and wondered why she was even considering a job she was extremely overqualified for. Was it because Krista was cute? Because if so, it was the stupidest reason ever. First of all, Krista *was* cute but probably fifteen years younger than her. Second, there was no way she could date someone she worked with, assuming Krista was even interested. Sure, Krista had asked her to lunch, but it didn't mean anything. Did it? No. It was stupid to even think about.

Third of all, she didn't need the money. At least for the time being. She'd eventually have to find another job, but there was enough savings to tide her over for a while. Fourth, although she'd been a cell phone luddite when she'd started with Lithium, they didn't require extensive training like bikes, and she was hardly an expert there. Sure, she really enjoyed riding and planned on doing a whole lot more of it now with all her free time, but was it enough to draw her to the job? The employees at the shop appeared to enjoy working there, which was good. But did she know enough about bikes to sell them? She could name most of the parts, how they worked, and could tell low-end equipment from high-end. Besides, the internet was a wealth of information. And as far as Ang was concerned, bikes were infinitely more interesting than cell phones, gaming consoles, and tablets.

She hit the apply button. It wouldn't hurt to do an interview. If she didn't like it, she could always turn it down; that was, if they actually offered her the job. Which would be temporary. It might be fun to try something different. It wasn't like she had to include it on her resume when she decided to hunt for a real job.

The application was short and simple. She completed it within ten minutes, attached her resume, and sent it off, hoping she could stop analyzing why she was even considering it. That done, she went into the kitchen to figure out dinner. While she stared into the refrigerator at the sparse contents, realizing she was going to have to order in again, the phone rang. She closed the refrigerator, picked it up, and pulled the menu from her favorite Portuguese restaurant from the drawer under the coffee pot. Empanadas sounded good.

"Hello?"

"Is this Angelique?" a woman's voice asked.

A telemarketer. No one called her Angelique except her mother and stepfather.

"May I ask who's calling?" She'd never been able to just hang up on telemarketers. As much as she despised talking to them, everyone had to earn a living.

"This is Krista. From Sol Cycle."

Krista! Ang lowered the menu. Sparkling eyes filled her mind's eye. "In that case, this is Angelique." Oh my God. Did she sound breathless? She squeezed the bridge of her nose.

"You're really interested in the sales manager position?"

"That was quick. I just submitted it. Like a minute ago."

"I happened to notice the notification as I was about to log off for the night, and I thought I'd call. I haven't even read your resume."

"You're working late."

"I took a nice long ride after work and thought I'd get a jump on closing out the month's books while my dinner cooked."

Ang let the refrigerator door swing closed and leaned against the counter. "I was just figuring out a dinner situation myself."

"I'd invite you over to share mine, but it's a single serving pot pie. Homemade, though. My mom makes them to freeze and gives them to all of us for winter comfort food. This is my last one." Krista paused to laugh. "But you don't care about my dinner plans. We were talking about the job. So you're interested?"

"I thought about what you said about filling in until you could find a permanent manager. I'm going crazy at home. I'm talking to my cat, and I'm afraid she might start talking back. I think it would be fun until I figure out what I want to do when I grow up or until you get a new manager, whichever comes first. If you're still interested in hiring me." As she said the last, Ang was surprised by how nervous she was and realized how embarrassed she'd be if she was turned down. Part of it was ego. No small business could afford the rates she normally earned, and the advice she could give them would be gold in their hands. But a small part of her trembled at the possibility that her expertise was with very large tech corporations. Was arrogance blinding her to her complete ignorance of what would work for a small business? Her heart beat in her ears while she waited for Krista's response.

"I'm definitely interested." Krista breathed out loudly. "Although, I think you're way, way, *way* overqualified. I'm scanning your resume. Are you sure you'd be happy here? You read the description, right?"

Ang's relief made her knees weak, and she tried to cover a laugh that came out almost shaky. "I read it. And I *am* overqualified. But aside from you needing the temporary help and me being temporarily bored out of my mind determining my next career move, I love riding bikes, and I want to rekindle my passion for it." Some of her confidence returned as she spoke. "I think this would be a great way to do it. It won't be difficult, but it'll occupy my mind. I probably shouldn't admit this, especially to a potential employer, but I think I'm having a midlife crisis. I have no idea who I want to be when I grow up." She said it in a cheerful way and with a smile, but when she said the words "midlife crisis," a pang of anxiety shot through her. It was a much-used description, usually accompanied with humor, but she found nothing humorous about how she felt: untethered, useless, identity-less. But why was she telling this to Krista?

"At the risk of violating human resources policies, you are way too young to be having a midlife crisis. In fact, you're too young to have accomplished all the things on your resume."

Ang absorbed the compliment, feeling a little better about blabbing about her identity crisis. "I won't turn you in to HR, but I am. Old enough. I'm thirty-seven."

"If you're really interested, we do this thing where we have a group interview with some of the others to make sure it's a good fit. Are you up for it? You'd have another chance to reconsider. What am I saying? I'd be a fool to let you slip away."

"Maybe you'll reconsider before I do." Ang laughed again. She laughed a lot with Krista. Maybe that was what made her comfortable telling her things she didn't like admitting to, even to herself. Had she seriously told her she was having a midlife crisis?

"How does Tuesday at three work for you?"

Ang didn't bother to check her calendar. It was empty. "Three works for me."

A bell sounded over the line. Krista chuckled. "My pot pie is ready. I guess I'll see you on Tuesday, Angelique. I can't believe you're even thinking about this. Have a great weekend."

"You, too, Krista."

Ang hung up and stared at the menu for a minute before she realized she wasn't concentrating on it. Did she really have a job interview? Nervousness churned in her stomach. She liked Krista. She was young, but she was smart and interesting. She owned her own home, which spoke of stability. And she was attractive, but if they were going to work together, it didn't matter. Nothing was going to happen anyway, what with the age difference.

She was getting way ahead of herself. She didn't even know if Krista was interested. She also reminded herself that she didn't have the job yet. She tossed her head back and took a deep breath. The absence of braids swinging down her back was still novel. Leaning against the counter, she texted in an order with Maria Empanada.

Before she set the phone down, a new worry crept in. What could she wear for the interview? The rest of the staff dressed just like Krista, super casual and with a cool flare, like they really didn't care about what they wore as long as it was comfortable.

Ang's wardrobe was *not* cool *or* comfortable.

She walked to her room and stepped into a walk-in closet filled with suits and business casual clothes, nothing that would fit in at the cycling shop. Not a single pair of long baggy shorts or a funky T-shirt to be found. Even her shorts, mostly linen, mostly cuffed, mostly ironed, came off as overdressed. She opened a drawer where she kept her workout clothes. It was all stretchy yoga wear, and she wasn't about to wear yoga pants to an interview.

She had no choice. She was going to have to go shopping if she got the job. In the meantime, she pulled out a pair of khakis and a white button-up. Still uptight mom clothes. She sighed. They would have to do for the interview.

CHAPTER TWELVE

Monday was nuts, especially for a snowy day. The snow hadn't started to stick yet, but the forecast was calling for several inches over the next few days, which usually meant business would be slow. However, customers kept coming in. The team was hopping, and Krista was on the floor with them, trying to keep up.

She wasn't about to complain about good sales, especially since it looked like she hadn't held back enough to pay the tax bill if the numbers in the new system were correct.

When she'd taken over the shop, she'd never thought she'd be spending so much time working on the books—even without the issue with the new software. If she *had* known, she would have still done it, but she reserved the right to complain about it. Owning Sol Cycle was a dream she'd had since she's started hanging out as a kid watching Uncle Raggy sell bikes to all the interesting customers. Now here she was, the owner. Living her dream.

It would be even better when she had a manager, which made her think about Angelique. Why she was even considering the job was a mystery. Krista just knew she'd be a fool not to jump at the opportunity to hire her, even for a few weeks.

"You look deep in thought," Swifty said, coming toward the front counter from the back.

She leaned forward, propping herself on the glass surface. "Just taking a breather." It wasn't a total lie. "How's it going in the back?"

"Not as busy as the front, I'd say. We had a steady stream of drop-offs this morning, but it fell to almost nothing right before lunch, letting me get ahead on the actual work. We won't have to schedule a week out anymore."

"Oh yeah? What are we looking at now?"

"Three days for most work orders."

"Great." She was impressed.

"Yeah, especially since I have to ask if I can take the rest of the afternoon off. I can come in later to make the time up."

"Is Dirk okay?" She hated that he felt like he needed to ask. She'd told him multiple times that he could take as much time as he needed. "You don't need to make the time up." She saw an argument flare in his eyes and made a sweeping motion with her hand. "Actually, do what you need to do."

His eyes lost the argument, but they were still haunted, which broke her heart. "The new port isn't staying clear. They're going to put a new one in. This time in his arm."

Damn. It's always something. "Poor guy. I hope this one works better."

"Well, the good news is the chemo is working. This course is more effective. We're cautiously optimistic."

She wanted to jump around, it was such great news. "Get out of here. Go take care of your husband."

"Thanks, boss." He turned away and then back. "Oh, I'll call off deliveries and have them come tomorrow. You're too busy to deal with them today."

He was always watching out for her. "If it's not too much hassle, I'd appreciate it."

"No problem. I'll do it from the car on my way to the hospital."

She couldn't have asked for a better person to work with. Swifty was just so self-sufficient, and she never had to worry about him taking care of things, even when he was dealing with a husband battling cancer.

The afternoon flew by. Customers were in the store almost an hour past closing, finishing up their purchases. When the last one finally left, Krista said good night to Rajib as he left and locked the front door behind him, turning off the bright overhead lights. Alone in the store and happy to have Alfur with her, she made her way to the back office to put the day's cash and receipts into the safe before heading home. Anywhere else, she didn't have a problem with being alone or in the dark, but in the shop, she imagined the eerie eyes of the hidden people Uncle Raggy used to tell her about. She knew now that they were just Icelandic folk tales, but she still felt their mischievous eyes watching from the shadows.

She was just closing the safe when a thump at the delivery door made her spin around, heart racing, and Alfur, who never barked, woofed loudly, twice, before standing between her and the door, growling. She should have checked that it was locked before everyone left, but she'd gotten complacent with the low crime rate in the neighborhood. Was she going to fall victim to the little that did happen?

The door opened, and she searched for something to protect herself with, picking up a standing tire pump. The intruder stopped just inside the door, shaking snow from their shoulders, and Alfur ran forward, but instead of attacking, he wagged his tail. When they lowered their jacket hood, Krista was relieved to see Jerome, one of the delivery drivers. Relief flooded through her, and she lowered the pump.

"Hey, Krista."

"Hey, Jerome. You scared me to death. Swifty said he called off deliveries today."

Jerome appeared confused, peered at his phone, then shook his head. "Aw. Yeah. He sent a text. I've just been trying to keep up today, so I haven't paid as good attention. You want me to come back tomorrow?"

"Since you're here, it's okay. You must be really behind."

"Naw. It's been crazy, but I managed to keep up. I normally come at this time on Mondays. Swifty said it was better for him."

Strange. It meant a long day for Swifty, who usually came in just after her and left at the same time she did every night. He would have to come back to the shop if Jerome was there over an hour after closing. She didn't put it past Swifty, though. He often came in after hours to keep the schedule from getting pushed out too far. Maybe there was a similar method to his madness going on with deliveries.

Jerome slid the dock door open, and the back room instantly went cold. She slipped on a zippered hoodie from her chair. Jerome propped the back doors of his truck open.

"How many do we have today?" Krista asked.

He studied the packing list and handed it to her. "Looks like twelve."

She scanned it, searching for Trek and Cannondale. She'd sold several today and needed to replenish her stock of mid-grade cycles. "Good. We needed a few more of exactly these," she said, setting the list on a bench.

He went into the truck and handed her boxes while she stood on the platform and pushed them into the shop. Soon, all twelve were lined up inside the door. She signed the slip, and Jerome slid the bay door shut and left.

Krista wished she'd put gloves on to help. Her fingers were stiff with cold, so she stuck her hands in her armpits as she scanned the list again. She hadn't checked all the brands against the slip, but she'd made sure the quantity and shop name matched. She noticed two Colnago bikes on the list. It had to be a mistake. She would have known if they'd sold a Colnago, which ran into the tens of thousands of dollars. There was a chance Uncle Raggy had something to do with it, since he still had contacts in the racing circuit and occasionally used the store's wholesale channels to get the racers high-end gear at a discount. Swifty would probably know.

She almost called him but decided against it. Dirk's surgery was enough for him to worry about. She'd talk to him about it tomorrow.

Chapter Thirteen

The barista handed Ang her steaming Americano in a
ceramic mug rather than the to-go cup she expected, so she
took it as a sign to stay instead of heading directly back home in the
snow. There would still be snow when she left, just like there would
be snow over the next two days, according to her weather app, but
there was nothing pressing after the interview at Sol Cycle, and it
would be nice to enjoy her coffee and relax. She couldn't remember
the last time she'd slowed down enough to gaze out through steam-
bordered windows watching individual snowflakes drift from the
sky. Maybe never. Cleo was probably happy for a couple of hours of
alone time, anyway.

Most of the tables were occupied, so she took a seat on the
weathered leather couch in the corner of the café, dropping her
bag on the low table before her. She breathed a long breath out and
settled into the seat, cradling the cup, absorbing its comforting heat.

The interview had been an interesting experience. She'd
expected to meet the owner of the store, but it was only Krista,
Swifty, and two sales associates, Kayla and Rajib. Krista called the
interview a round table, which was insanely accurate since the five
of them sat around an actual round table on mismatched chairs and
chatted. It hadn't felt like an interview at all.

Krista had introduced her to the others, and Swifty had
asked where she'd worked before; she'd told him, but most of the
discussion had featured where they liked to ride and good hiking

trails. Before she knew it, the group had gone back to work, and the interview was over. She'd shaken hands with everyone again, and Krista had walked her to the front door and said she'd give her a call later in the day.

Ang hadn't gone in with any real expectations, but the interview was almost anticlimactic in its lack of substance, so instead of heading straight home, she'd crossed the street to Monsieur Beans while thinking about Krista in her sweater, cargo pants, and knit beanie. She made casual appear so adorable. If Ang ended up working with her, she'd be distracted all the time.

A familiar voice roused her from her thoughts. "Hey, you."

Speaking of the devil in cute cargo pants, the very woman stood a few feet away holding a to-go cup. An inexplicable sense of being caught doing something she shouldn't fell over Ang, and she almost stood to explain why she was there.

"Long time no see," she joked, forcing her internal unease not to show.

Krista laughed. "It's been forever, I know."

Ang raised her cup. "The weather calls for a warm drink."

Krista raised hers in turn. "I'd like to blame the weather, but it would be a lie. It's almost pathological how often I come here."

"Have a seat." Ang gestured to the chair across from her. "Or do you need to get right back?"

Krista sat and propped her feet on the low table between them. "The snow keeps the hordes away on days like this. I guess I could start on one of the piles of paperwork I have on my desk, but I have all weekend."

"You work too much." Ang couldn't believe those words had come from her mouth, having been on the receiving end of them so many times herself.

Krista cocked an eyebrow, looking amused. "Hopefully, it'll change in the near future now that interviews are over."

"Was I the last one?"

Krista chuckled. "You were the only one. I was going to wait a bit to give you a sense of actual consideration and to not seem too eager, but the others loved you. You have the job if you want it."

It surprised Ang how relieved the words made her. Even if she didn't need the job, finding it was hers for the taking was nice. Also, the more she got to know Krista, the more she liked her, so getting to spend more time with her was a plus. If she could just get past her tiny crush. She'd decided to give an answer by tomorrow afternoon, but she was curious. "Did no one else apply?"

Krista picked at the sleeve around her coffee cup. "There have been a few applications, but I've been too busy to set up interviews."

"But you set mine up immediately."

"The difference is, I know you. Well, I don't *know you*, know you, but we've met, and I like you, and then your resume was..." She waved her hand dismissively. "Anyway, it was easy to set up an interview with you. And the others really like you. So it's yours if you want it."

Ang thought her rambling was cute, and the pink spreading across her cheeks was amusing...and also cute. As someone who'd had to interview people for countless jobs, Ang could confidently say that employers were often at the mercy of the job seekers, yet job seekers believed they were at the mercy of employers. Granted, there was the nature of supply and demand, but it often depended on who needed it more than the other. She didn't *need* the job, and she got the impression Krista didn't need *her* in particular, so it was an unusual situation. She could probably decline, and it would be fine, aside from not getting to see Krista all the time.

"Great. When should I start?" Her answer surprised her. So much for saying she'd get back to her. The delighted smile on Krista's face erased her concern. It was only a temporary thing, anyway.

"Excellent. I should give you a week or so before you start, but the crappy weather for the next two days is a good time to ease you in, and we could give you some training without it being so busy. Which do you prefer?"

"I literally have nothing going on. Tomorrow would be great." Did she really just become employed? On the outside, she might have looked like this was something she did all the time, but on the inside, incredulity swirled like a cyclone.

They agreed on a time and chatted for a few more minutes before Krista rose to leave.

"Um, Krista, before you go. I have a weird thing to ask."

Krista sat back down. "Sure. What's up?"

Self-consciousness swept over her. "You're aware that I've spent my entire adult life in the corporate world."

"Yep."

"Suits are what I'm used to wearing to work every day."

"Uh-huh."

"So, I, uh…well, I have biking clothes. Cycling shorts and jerseys."

"Which are very nice on you."

Heat raced up Ang's neck. "Um, thanks."

An expression of understanding spread across Krista's face. "Are you asking me what you should wear to work?"

"Well, sort of."

Krista shrugged. "Just casual stuff. Mostly shorts and T-shirts unless it's a blizzard, and then maybe throw on pants."

Ang wasn't sure how to express that the kind of casual displayed in the shop was a specific kind of outdoorsy, a chill kind of fashion with a specific kind of cool. She'd call it a young look, since most of them were much younger than her, but Swifty was a decade or so older, and he dressed like them. Their vibe was something she didn't know how to express, least of all replicate, and should she even try? How could she explain it without sounding like a nerd or possibly judgmental? Her thoughts tumbled inside her head, and she decided not to try to explain. "My idea of casual is different than your idea of casual."

"Well, what did you wear before you landed your corporate job? Like, when you were going to school? Surely you didn't dress like the super savvy business lady you are now."

"School was so long ago, and I guess I was a T-shirt and jeans kind of person."

"That's just fine." Krista's eyes sparkled, and she snapped her fingers. "I have an idea. Do you trust me?"

Ang lifted an eyebrow. "Why am I frightened?"

Krista appeared amused. "You have nothing to be afraid of. You rock your look. But I do have an idea. Can you hang out here for ten or fifteen minutes until I get back?"

Ang agreed because she was curious. She envisioned everything from Krista bringing a friend back for a *Queer Eye for the Corporate Chick* thing, to them going through some catalogues from the store. By the time Krista reappeared ten minutes later with a couple of large paper bags with the Sol Cycle sun logo on the side, she still couldn't imagine what Krista was up to.

"I guessed on your size, and to be honest, sizes run all over the place on specialty clothing, but there has to be some stuff in these bags that you'll like. You can bring back anything you don't want."

Ang peered into one of the bags at a stack of clothing. She supposed the other was more of the same. "Is this from the store?"

"My sister has an online clothing shop. Well, she did. It was more than she could handle with school and her busy social life, so she shut it down. These are all samples. They're from leading outdoor clothing retailers and a few local specialty shops. They didn't want them back when she closed the store, so she's been storing them at the shop until she figured out what to do with it all."

"So would I pay you or her?" Ang wasn't used to being on the receiving end of help, and it filled her with equal parts gratitude and embarrassment.

"Neither. She's going to end up donating them."

"Well, she can donate what I don't pay her for."

"She already took it as a write-off, so it's essentially already been paid for."

It took a few minutes of convincing, but she finally accepted. "Tell your sister thanks for me. Really. And if she'll accept payment, I'm serious. I want to."

"My sister would give away the shirt off her own back. I am one-hundred-percent sure she'd want you to have these."

"Well, thanks. I hope to meet her in person one day to tell her."

"She comes by the store after school a lot, so you probably will."

CHAPTER FOURTEEN

Krista and Alfur left for work earlier than usual Wednesday morning to neaten up the store before Angelique's first day. A ball of excitement was already sparkling in her stomach when she woke up, and she wanted Angelique's first day to be awesome. A lot of it had to do with Angelique's expertise in retail, but she had to admit that she wanted Ang to enjoy her experience at Sol Cycle... and being around Krista.

Between her and Swifty, the store was usually very clean, but lately, with Swifty dealing with Dirk in the hospital and with her preoccupied with accounting anomalies, some of the basic tasks had fallen to the side. Most people probably wouldn't have noticed, but Krista did.

When she arrived, she was surprised to find Swifty already hard at work on a bike in the maintenance area. Although it was still snowing, the back door was propped open to let in fresh air, and Pearl Jam was dialed up on the satellite radio. Swifty let out a comical shriek when Alfur came up beside him and pressed against his legs. Krista couldn't help but laugh. Swifty turned and joined in, although his laugh was a little shaky.

"You two scared the heck out of me," he said, reaching to give Alfur the pets he wanted.

"You're in early."

Swifty glanced around the room. "I just wanted to get a head start on some of the work orders. Get the backlog down to two days again."

"How's Dirk doing?"

"Antsy as hell. He wants out of the hospital and keeps threatening to leave against advice. He can barely hold himself up, though. He's so weak from having no appetite. The doc says his numbers are getting better, though. A few more days and he can take the next infusion."

"Won't another infusion just make his numbers go down again?"

"Yeah, but they can bolster them faster by keeping him in-patient."

"Will he be in the hospital until then?"

Swifty shook his head. "They're hopeful he'll go home for a few days before the final infusion. Fingers crossed."

Krista tried to discern how he was taking all of this. She'd normally ask him directly, but lately, he just said he was fine to every inquiry, even when she knew he wasn't. It hurt that he didn't lean on her. Maybe it was because he'd always been more like an uncle, but she wasn't a little girl anymore, and she wanted to be there for him. "It seems like the plan changes day to day. I can't imagine how you deal."

"Dirk would rather be at home, but he realizes he has to have the in-patient treatment to get stronger. And I have nothing to complain about. Just a little longer and this will be over. It's just hard to watch him get worse before he gets better."

"It sounds like the chemo is harder on him than the lymphoma."

"It sort of is, but it's working, and he has a really good prognosis once it's over, so the short-term effects are worth the long-term results. At least, that's what I keep telling myself." His voice broke, and he struggled to compose himself.

He worked so hard to keep up his strong front, and even though she'd been waiting for him to open up to her, it killed her to witness him crack. She'd never been close to someone going through an extended illness, so she wasn't sure what to do other than going to the hospital to see Dirk on occasion and reminding Swifty that his job was secure no matter how much time he needed to take. "I know, Swiftman," she said rubbing his arm. "You said you were worried about the medical bills. Is the hospital working with you?"

"We finally hit the out-of-pocket limit for this year, so we're not racking up many expenses now, but with what we have racked up, it's gonna be tight for a while. I'll be slinging coffee over at the Bean before coming here when we open at ten. I've been meaning to tell you."

"Steph said she was giving me your employee discount yesterday, so I put two and two together."

He straightened up the tools on the bench. "I started last week. I wasn't keeping it a secret. It just hadn't come up yet. Today's my day off at the café, but I'm already used to getting up early to be there by the ungodly hour of five-thirty, so I just came here."

Krista's heart went out to him. The pile of work orders was unusually small, so he was working out his stress by staying busy, she guessed. "Hey, I've told you it's okay if we get behind, especially now. We still turn bikes around faster than most of the shops in town, and our customers will understand. They love you, Swiftman. Also, I can get Raggy down here for a couple of days to help out. He's always offering."

She was surprised when tears fell down Swifty's cheeks because he avoided most displays of emotion, but he wiped them away and rubbed his glistening eyes quickly. If he wasn't so prickly about things, she would have hugged him. Instead, she fussed with a few papers on the desk next to her. He cleared his throat. "I think I can get caught up today, but thanks. I'll definitely let you know if we should call Raggy. I miss the old Sasquatch."

Krista laughed. She missed having him in the shop, too, especially since he'd stopped telling her how to run things. "I'm going up to visit him this Sunday. I'll tell him you miss him."

"Thanks. I'll bring in some beer for you to take up to him."

"He'll love it. If it makes it to him." She winked.

"It's an IPA, and you'll hate it, but I'll bring you a stout."

"Yes, please," she said, giving him a quick hug before going to the back door and swinging it shut. It was okay to hug him if it was out of happiness. He didn't need to know she was hugging him for comfort, too. "It's freezing back here." She peered around the room and noticed the delivery from Monday night had been inventoried and put on the floor or was hanging in stock, but she didn't see the custom bikes. "Oh, hey, did you find anything out about the Colnagos?"

"Turns out they were part of a private sale, and the buyer shipped them here for assembly," he said as he continued to work.

She was relieved. With the cash discrepancies on the books, she didn't want to be on the hook for almost a hundred thousand dollars of inventory she hadn't ordered, even though they could return it. "Weird, we always get a heads-up, and custom bikes usually come fully assembled."

Swifty paused in the spoke adjustment. "They were. I meant to say for inspection. They were in perfect condition. Very nice bikes."

Krista finally noticed the boxes broken down and bundled near the recycling pile. "Who's the buyer? Must be serious cyclists buying premium racing bikes." It made sense. Lots of Olympic hopefuls from around the world lived in Colorado for high-altitude training.

"Never met them before. He told me his name, but I forget. Starts with a J, I think. Since it was just an inspection, I didn't charge him or write a work order or anything. Just verified the bikes were in good shape and gave him all the paperwork. I bet they'll become regulars since they had the bikes inspected here."

"Sounds good. But next time, we should probably at least write a work order. For liability."

Swifty finally looked up from his work and gave her thumbs-up. "You got it, boss. Um, so, hey, I need access to the inventory system. So I can place the next order."

"Why don't you just put it in the old system, and I'll import it. I still haven't worked out the discrepancy, and I don't want to introduce new data until I figure it out."

He sighed and dropped the wrench he'd been using. "It's a pain in the ass dealing with two systems. I don't want to complain, but it is."

His response surprised her. Swifty didn't usually express frustration like this. Besides, nothing was different for him. They were still using the old system. It was just her in the new one, mapping the data and learning it so she could train everyone else on it when they officially switched over.

With everything going on with him, it probably wasn't even about the system.

He wiped his hand down his face and scratched the stubble on his neck. "It's just…I used to do all of it, and now you're doing it, and I worry you didn't like the work I was doing."

Aha, that was his worry. Stress must have really been getting to him if his normally healthy self-esteem was fracturing. It hurt her to think he was worried about work things in addition to everything else. "In case I don't say it enough, I like the work you do. You're the best, Swifty. I promise, I'd tell you if I had any concerns. Me keeping the new system separate is just for now. I'll get this wrinkle ironed out and hand it all over to you soon. Besides, nothing's changed. You're still in charge of the old system."

"I guess it's…I hate it when you're annoyed, and it's probably something I'm doing to muck up the books. You should just let me figure it out. You shouldn't have to deal with my mistakes."

"I'm not annoyed, just frustrated. I tell you what, if I don't figure it out by next week, I'll ask for your help. Okay?" It would have been comical, the juxtaposition of him feeling bad because he thought he caused the issue and her feeling bad because she'd been the one to hype up how great the system was, if not for the additional stress it put on him. Pangs of guilt flared through her for causing it.

He didn't appear completely pleased, but Krista thought he seemed happier with the answer. Even with all the things on his mind, he was committed to keeping up with his work and worried about her frustration. He was a good guy, and she thought again how lucky she was to have him in her life and at the shop.

CHAPTER FIFTEEN

Ang's first day of work was both exciting and a challenge to both her patience and ego. Going from being the person with all the answers to the person searching for answers was more than a little humbling. While she enjoyed learning, she did not like the ungrounded sensation. Alfur must have picked up on her discomfort because he stuck close to her all morning, leaning against her leg, grounding her, and she loved it. She'd never considered getting her own dog. It hadn't seemed fair because she was never home, which was no longer true. Maybe a dog would be nice.

Working the floor when she was used to working at a desk didn't bother her.

Her discomfort was more about not knowing the product very well. It would come to her, though. She reminded herself she wasn't letting anyone down if she didn't know an answer; she just needed to know who to go to when it happened, and it happened a lot.

"You're a natural with customers," Krista said as she watched Ang finish a sale.

"I'm learning from the best." Kind of flirty, she had to admit, but she didn't want to bore Krista by telling her she could do sales in her sleep. They'd talked enough during the interview, and she'd just be rehashing information. Besides, she liked the pink crawling up Krista's neck.

When Krista told her she was happy with how quickly Ang had picked up the basics of what to do behind the counter, it was all Ang could do to not give her pointers on how to improve the process. No one liked a know-it-all new hire. There would be a time and place to provide suggestions, so she'd give it some time.

The real learning came through watching Kayla and Rajib when the discussion turned to features of equipment. Ang's background with bikes was dated and had never been particularly strong. They really knew their stuff, and by the end of the day, Ang's notebook was full of questions about the products. Some of it she could find on the internet, but some could only be answered by the other employees.

For part of the morning, Swifty took her under his wing while Krista made calls, and there weren't any customers. She was impressed with the depth of his knowledge and how he incorporated it into the maintenance flow, but she was amazed at how quickly he was able to get most of the work orders turned around. She wondered if it wasn't just Krista that the shop's owner took advantage of.

Ironically, she was critical of the extra hours the employees of Sol Cycle worked when she'd always kept long hours herself. By lunch, Ang was too exhausted to worry about it anymore. It wasn't the physical exertion but from being in constant learning and customer service modes. It was a good kind of tired, though.

She was tidying up a shelf of reflectors when Krista came up beside her. "Hey, new kid. Can I buy you a sandwich? The afternoon shift is here."

The suggestion came at the exact right time. Ang had already finished dusting and refacing the sunglass display case at the front sales counter. She stretched her back. A glance at her watch told her it was almost one o'clock. Her stomach rumbled loudly.

"I'd kill for a BLT with extra mayo right now," she said.

"Pinky's it is. Grab your coat."

The spring snow was falling thick and heavy as they navigated the slushy sidewalks and crossed the boulevard to get to the sandwich shop they'd eaten at last week.

"How's your first day treating you?" Krista asked as they draped their coats over their chairs at a table after ordering.

Ang plopped down, happy to be off her feet. "Good. I'm learning a lot."

"You're really good with customers. I could tell you were a natural people person. I sensed it the first time we met."

"You did? I was in a mood that day."

"I couldn't tell. Who wouldn't be when they're having bike issues?"

"I meant when we met the first time."

Krista paused in the unwrapping of her sandwich. "We met before? I would have remembered."

"Not officially. We spoke for a minute one day in the park when Alfur decided to chase a bike."

"Alfur chased a bike?" Krista's expression was one of confusion before it changed to one of dawning understanding. "You were the hottie on the park bench."

Ang's mouth dropped open. "What?"

Krista slapped a hand over her mouth. "What I meant to say is, I remember. You were striking. Dressed all in black. You had long hair, though."

Ang ran her hand down the back of her head. "I had braids for a long time."

"They were gorgeous, but I like the short hair just as much, if not more."

Heat crept up Ang's neck. "The short hair is new."

"I can't believe I didn't remember until now. You're right. You weren't smiling, at least, not the beautiful one you have now, where your eyes sparkle. I like this smile."

Ang grimaced, but she was still pleased to hear Krista liked her smile. "My girlfriend had just broken up with me."

"Yikes. Sorry to stir up bad memories."

"It's fine. It was definitely for the best. Even the second time we met, I don't think I was very friendly. I was hungover from my friends helping me drown my sorrows after I quit my job."

"Sounds like there's a story or two there."

"The breakup, the job, or the hangover?"

"I guess all of the above."

Ang laughed.

"The breakup was nothing interesting. I worked too much, and she didn't like it, and I wasn't invested enough to change things. Pretty much how most of my relationships end. As for the job thing, I'm still trying to wrap my head around it, so I'll have to get back to you on that. And the hangover? All I can say is, I'm not in my twenties anymore. Ouch."

"We'll have to talk more about the relationship thing, but I sense it's gonna take more time than we have for lunch. But let me guess." Krista sat up straight and squinted, studying her. "You're a strong and capable woman. Very dedicated. I'll bet you don't ask for help very often, and it made your girlfriends insecure."

Ang felt seen for the first time in a very long time, but it also made her feel exposed. The combination was almost unbearably uncomfortable. She didn't know how to respond. Thankfully, the counter called out that her latte was ready. Krista put down her sandwich and got up before she could.

"Did I get it right?" Krista asked when she came back, sliding the latte toward her.

"A little," she lied. *Try all of it.* "Are you a secret therapist or something?"

"Nope. My sister is, though. I majored in sports medicine."

"You wanted to be a doctor?" Changing the subject was a relief.

Krista shook her head. "My parents would have been pleased. My big brother is the doctor. I kind of kicked around being a trainer for a sports organization for a while."

"That's why you're good at fitting people to bikes."

"It helps, for sure. We were talking about you, though. What part did I not get right?"

Ugh. Back to her. Ang took a bite of her sandwich. Krista had a way of enveloping her with her gaze. She didn't hate it. It did make her self-conscious, though. "You pretty much got it. I do have a hard time asking for help, but I usually get it even when I don't ask for it."

"Not surprising. You draw people. I've watched how they respond to you. People want to please you."

Ang arched an eyebrow. "Maybe you should go into comedy. You're hilarious."

"I'm serious. I've known Swifty most of my life. He's great with customers, but he never tries to engage them before they approach him. He did with you. I'd blame it on him being a guy and you being a beautiful woman, but he's gay. You draw people. Like you drew me to you at the park when we met. Both times."

Ang was speechless. Beautiful? Drawn? She wanted more information about why Krista was drawn to her, but she was off-limits now that they worked together. "I like Swifty," was her non-response, awkward as all get out. "When do I get to meet the owner of the store? The website doesn't say anything about them."

Krista laughed and took a bite of her sandwich. "You've met them. They're me."

Ang was stunned. "But...what...I didn't..." she sputtered. "The store has been around for so long, I just assumed the owner would be older," she finally got out and then winced. Could she sound more like a jerky ageist ass?

Krista merely laughed. "My Uncle Raggy *is* super old. He's my mom's uncle. I bought the store from him five years ago when he retired."

Ang tried to do the math, but she was even more confused now. It shouldn't matter, but it did. It meant that Krista was responsible because she had a business to run. Her focus was probably on more than just having a good time. That changed things. She hated that it mattered, but it did.

Krista set her sandwich down and grinned. "You're trying to figure out how old I am, right? If I bought the store five years ago? I'm twenty-seven, but I look younger. It's probably from being around college students all the time."

"I wasn't, I mean, it didn't really—" She hung her head. "Okay, fine, yes. I was, and yes, you do, and I'm a jerk."

"You're not a jerk."

She *was* a jerk. "Number one rule for interviews: research the business. It's not on your website, but I should have dug a little deeper." *And not been an ageist ass.*

"It's really no big deal. It's not like you would have acted any differently, right?"

Would she have done anything differently? Ang wasn't sure. Maybe she'd have asked Krista out by now. No. No. No. She couldn't go there. "Probably not."

"So forget about it. You're just used to corporate honchos swinging their enormous power all over the place. I'm a simple small-business owner. All my power lives in the bodies of the people who agree to work with me. My success depends on them and the customers who buy my goods."

Krista was right, and it applied to both small and big business. Ang's domain was the corporate world, where bosses and owners were like royalty, wielding all kinds of power over their empires. It was going to be interesting learning from the small-business perspective.

She smiled. "Well, when you put it like that..."

Krista laughed. She really liked it when Krista laughed.

CHAPTER SIXTEEN

K rista pushed her chair back. She was almost there, but the answer was just out of reach.

After digging into it more, the only thing she could ascertain was that her taxes and rebates were higher than they were supposed to be based on sales, but the sales numbers tracked with the historical totals she sent to her tax person. There was definitely something off, but she couldn't find where the error originated from. Maybe Swifty could figure it out like he said he could. In the meantime, after her initial fears over cashflow, the business bank account was healthy, so whatever the discrepancy was, it probably wasn't as worrisome as she'd initially thought. Thank goodness.

But she couldn't stop thinking about how all the time she'd spent trying to find this discrepancy was really showing her how she should be better at running her business. Especially after seeing what a natural Angelique had been that day.

Angelique had started work that morning with so much confidence and knowledge, Krista had been impressed. She'd known she was more than qualified, but Krista had expected her to become a little uncertain or lost sometime during the day. Instead, she'd faced each new challenge and tried to work things out, and when she couldn't, she'd turned to others without showing any insecurity or fluster. Krista wished she had a fraction of that confidence and ability.

"Hey, Krista, I'm gonna take off, okay?" Angelique said, poking her head into the back.

"I thought it was just me and Alfur left," Krista said, assuming everyone had gone home when Kayla locked up.

"I was at the maintenance desk going through old work orders Swifty asked me to organize and lost track of time. I could hear you talking to yourself, so I just kept working. But I better get back home to fix my queen dinner."

At the mention of a queen, disappointment coursed through Krista. It was almost enough to distract her from finding out she'd been talking to herself. "What was I talking about?"

"I couldn't hear the words, but you sounded frustrated."

"I'm working on a bug in a software program." Relieved she hadn't heard specifics, Krista's mind returned to the queen comment. She'd assumed Angelique wasn't involved with anyone. They'd never talked about it, though. Why would they? They hardly knew each other.

Her expression must have hinted at her disappointment because Angelique straightened up. "I can stay if you want. I'm familiar with sales and inventory management systems. Cleo can wait a little while. I'll just have to endure her cold shoulder and maybe a slap or two."

Krista was appalled. "Your girlfriend slaps you for being late for dinner?"

Angelique laughed loudly. "My *cat* does. Any time I'm even a few minutes late with Cleo's food—and often when I'm not—she whacks my hands when I put the food in her bowl. But since it's a big part of the meager attention she *does* give me, I endure it. She has me trained."

Krista couldn't help but laugh. "I can relate. If I don't give Alfur his breakfast by seven, he jumps on the bed and starts licking me. My last girlfriend left me because of it."

"I guess they have us both trained. Wait. What? Your girlfriend left because Alfur wanted breakfast?" Now, Angelique appeared appalled.

"She left me because I wouldn't tell her I loved her, but I like to pretend it wasn't me. Besides, she did hate Alfur jumping on the bed."

"It's not my place to judge, but good riddance. Any woman I date comes second to Cleo, as much of a snooty witch she can be. But she's *my* snooty witch, and I love her."

"How can you not, with all the charisma you described?"

"Exactly," Angelique said. She turned halfway around to leave and swung back. "Oh, hey. Do you happen to have tomorrow night open? It's Friday night, so you probably have plans, but I have an extra ticket to the Rockies' opening game. Even if you don't like baseball, it's a good time. They give out things at the gate and have fireworks after."

"Sure." The surprise invitation caused butterflies to take flight in Krista's stomach. She wasn't particularly interested in baseball, but she was interested in going to a game with Angelique. "I've been meaning to go one of these days."

"You've been meaning to go to an *opening* game or *any* game?" Angelique asked.

Krista shrugged. "Any game."

"What?" Her eyes showed shock, and all Krista could do was laugh.

She lifted her hand. "I know. My uncle is a fanatic about baseball and goes all the time, but for whatever reason, it never worked out for me to go with him."

"Well, I'm honored to take you to your first game. My friends, Geri and Kat, and I split the price of a four pack of season tickets each year, and this year, I get the extra season opener ticket. The seats are just behind the home team dugout, close to the plate, so all the action is up close. You'll love it. Plus, it's supposed to be in the seventies. It'll be nice after the snow this week."

"Sounds fun." Krista was tickled about the invitation and was trying to figure out a chill way to say thanks when her cell phone buzzed. It was Kayla. "Kayla's asking about you. She said she forgot to check in on you before leaving, and she doesn't have your number. Oops. She asked me not to tell you about the forgetting part."

Angelique flapped her hand. "You can tell her I'm fine. But speaking of numbers, should I get yours, you know, so I can call if I can't make it in or something? I should have saved it when you called me about the job."

Something about asking for her number made Krista's stomach flutter. Her stomach was having a heyday with butterflies and flutters, and she reminded it that Angelique was now an employee, and it wasn't appropriate, but her stomach didn't seem to care as she sent her number. Angelique's phone pinged, and she nodded at it. "You have my number now."

The sound of the back door cypher lock disengaging interrupted their conversation. Swifty came in, stomping the snow from his boots. Much of it was already melted, but the back of the shop was in perpetual shadow, and quite a bit remained back there.

Alfur hurried to him, tail wagging, and Swifty searched the room until his gaze settled on Krista and Angelique. "Hey, ladies. I didn't expect you to still be here."

"Just finishing up some admin stuff," Krista said, feeling self-conscious even though the fluttering stomach thing was probably not visible.

"I just finished going through the work orders you gave me." Angelique sounded self-conscious, too. Interesting.

Swifty watched them with a serious expression, and Krista wondered why he'd come back. "I thought you were headed to the hospital."

"I went, but Dirk shooed me away. Said he was going to sleep and I'd only be listening to him snore."

"And you came here?" she asked. He was spending entirely too much time at the store, even if it was to keep his mind off all of the stuff going on at home. How could she tell him without upsetting him, though?

"I forgot my phone." He went out to the maintenance desk and came back holding it. "See you tomorrow."

After the door closed behind him, Krista made sure it was locked while thinking how her fluttery feelings toward Angelique had her spun up a little. Between wondering if it was a bad thing to feel attracted to her new employee and feeling a little insecure that Angelique was probably better at this job than she was, her thoughts and emotions were all over the place.

She and Angelique collected their stuff and left. They discussed plans about the game the next evening, and as Krista walked Alfur home, dodging frozen puddles of snowmelt, part of her wished she'd accepted Angelique's offer to drive. But after one glance at Alfur's wet feet and Angelique's shiny BMW, she'd said no. It was only a few blocks, but she liked that Angelique didn't care about dog hair in her fancy ride.

Chapter Seventeen

It was hard to believe over a foot of snow had fallen just a couple of days earlier as Ang peered out over the baseball diamond in Coors Field. The grass was bright green, the diamond was pristine, and the sun was shining brightly on her and her friends. She glanced around and sighed. It was good to be back. Nothing compared to watching a live baseball game in the Colorado sunshine.

"Cheers, my dears," she said, holding up her plastic cup of beer. "We couldn't have asked for a more beautiful opening day."

Kat and Geri tapped their cups against hers. Kat took a sip and motioned toward their fourth seat. "Who'd you ask to come to the game?"

"My new boss. She has to close the store, but she said she'd be here in time for the national anthem." Ang had told Kat and Geri about the job at Sol Cycle, and they'd been a little surprised but supportive.

"What? And miss batting practice?" Kat rolled her eyes when she said it because she normally skipped all the pregame activities. Today, she'd only come early because it was the first game of the season, and the stadium was giving out jerseys to the first five hundred fans.

"I don't get it," Geri said. "Who wouldn't want to watch all these fine athletes in tight pants? Fresh from spring training. Toned muscles. Fresh tans. The bounce in their steps." She shivered as she ogled the batter taking practice swings. "I mean, except for you two."

"Is Regina aware you come here to salivate over the players?" Kat asked.

Geri arched a perfectly shaped eyebrow. "She's more than aware, and she loves the heat it brings to the bedroom when I get home."

"I'm mildly turned-on. Bi chicks are so weird," Kat said, shaking her head.

"But you still love me," Geri said, putting her hand on the side of Kat's head and pushing her playfully.

Kat just laughed.

It felt so good to be at the ballpark with her two best friends. Ang couldn't help smiling. This was the most relaxed she'd been in a long time. How many times had she come to a game, only to be interrupted by a crisis at work? She'd come to anticipate the emergency calls, and it was blissful to know it wouldn't happen this time. She felt close to her friends. They were in their collective happy place, enjoying the spring weather, the ballpark, and each other. Happy anticipation washed through her knowing Krista was going to meet her there, too.

"How's the new job going?" Geri asked.

"Good. Different but good. I thought it would be a little easier than it has been, but I think it's just been a while since I worked the sales floor. I'm exhausted by the end of the day."

Kat smirked. "Are your *wittle* feet *huwting?*"

Ang wanted to say yes because they did, but she didn't need Kat teasing her for being a desk jockey. "My feet are fine. It's just the learning curve. I screwed up the schedule the first time I did it on my own, and I moved some merch into the endcaps based on what I thought was higher volume sales but really wasn't. It's fine. Nothing major, but it kind of takes the wind out of your sails when you're used to being the expert, you know?"

"Totally," Kat agreed.

"What's your new boss like?" Geri asked.

Ang opened her mouth to reply when a new voice piped in from behind them. "She's a real hard-ass. A top-notch shrew, in fact."

They all turned. Krista sat in the empty row behind them holding one of the giveaway jerseys and a giant purple foam hand with the forefinger sticking up. Her sundress gave her a whole new appearance. Ang liked it. She liked it a lot. It was her hair, though, that intrigued her. Her platinum hair was loose from the braids she usually wore and hung, shiny and smooth, all the way to her hips. She was gorgeous, and Ang hoped the attraction surging through her wasn't visible. She'd never hear the last of it from her friends, and she really, *really* didn't want Krista to pick up on it. It would be so embarrassing to have to admit she had a crush on her much-younger boss, who could have any woman she wanted, one who wasn't some stick-in-the-mud professional who had to change her clothes four times before she found something casual and without starched creases to wear to the ballpark.

"And a sneak," Ang said with a chuckle when she found her voice. She pointed to her friends. "Geri, Kat, this is Krista, my boss."

Krista came around to take her seat, and as she did, Ang caught both her friends checking her out. Who could blame them? Krista was beautiful. Geri had the grace to look chagrined to be caught. When Kat raised her eyebrows, Ang imagined the dozen questions she was dying to ask.

Krista took the seat next to her, and Ang was aware of a pleasant scent, something a fragrance maker might call "linen" or "fresh cotton." She liked it. It suited Krista.

"I'm glad you could join us," Kat said, leaning forward to peer around Geri and Ang.

"Did Angelique tell you I've never been to a Rockies game before?" Krista asked.

Kat's jaw dropped open. "Do you watch on TV?"

Krista shook her head. "I prefer to play sports rather than watch them."

Kat eyed her up and down. "You're a Sporty Spice."

Ang dropped her head into her hands, wondering if she'd made a mistake asking Krista to the game but was relieved when she laughed. "I hope you don't get too bored," Ang said.

Krista glanced around in awe, resting a hand on Ang's leg. Ang liked it more than she should have. "Are you kidding? This place is fantastic. Just being inside the stadium fills me with a sort of electric energy." Ang felt it, too, but it wasn't the stadium doing it to her at the moment.

The piped-in music gave way to announcements, followed by the national anthem while the Colorado Air National Guard did a flyover.

During the first inning, Ang enjoyed the casual way Krista's arm brushed hers while she filled Krista in on the team. When Geri reached around Kat to tap her shoulder, Ang wasn't surprised to be asked to go on a nacho run. They hadn't made it up ten steps before Geri squeezed her arm. "Girl, she's smokin'. How could you not tell us?"

Ang glanced over her shoulder. Kat and Krista were laughing together. As if she sensed Ang's gaze, Krista turned with a smile and waved. Ang returned both and kept walking, ignoring Geri's smirk.

"Well, now I understand why you took a job you're overqualified for."

"She's not why I took it. I was bored."

"Sure. If you need to rationalize it," Geri said, clearly not buying it.

When they arrived at the concourse at the top of the stairs Ang turned to her, crossing her arms. "Are you psychoanalyzing me, Doctor Miyazaki? Because I'm not going to pay you."

"Oh, you'll pay. One way or the other." Geri turned toward the nacho stand. "You can't deny she's an attractive woman."

"I'm not denying it. It just isn't why I took the job. She said she could use some help. I was going stir-crazy without a routine, and I have certain retail skills she could benefit from. It's a win-win situation. And it's only temporary until she finds a new manager."

"And you find a new job?"

"That, too." Ang forced the anxiety that came with that thought away.

Geri ordered the loaded nachos and leaned against the counter while the kid behind it piled chips and all the fixings into a paper dish. The scent of processed cheese, hotdogs, and giant pretzels prompted Ang to order two of each, plus a couple more beers. If Krista didn't want any of them, Kat would take them.

Geri gave her the side-eye. "Double win for you, I'd say. How old is she, anyway?"

Ang transferred her weight to her other foot. "Twenty-seven."

The vendor pushed their order toward them, and Geri handed some to Ang. "Ten years, huh? You normally go for women a little older than you, but it's not as bad as I thought. I was thinking she was closer to twenty than thirty."

Ang stopped herself from explaining something she was trying to figure out herself. "It's not a thing even if the difference in our ages was twice that because nothing's going on."

Geri clucked her tongue, and they finished gathering the food and drinks. She clucked a couple more times as they shuffled to the condiment station. A response was brewing, and Ang waited patiently.

"You might want to tell her," Geri finally said.

Ang scoffed. "Yeah, right."

"Oh, stop. The girl is crushing on you hard. And while you deny it, there are definitely sparks flying between you two."

Ang pulled her head back and gave Geri a look, but Geri just ignored her, scooping jalapenos onto her nachos. "Your vice-presidential glare holds no power over me."

Ang rolled her eyes before grabbing napkins and condiments, and they headed back to their seats. The usher motioned for them to wait at the top of the stairs until the current play was complete.

As they waited, Ang whispered, "Okay. I might have a little crush on my boss. But nothing's going to happen." It surprised her how much relief there was in admitting it.

Geri gave her another side-eye.

Ang shook her head. "Seriously. Nothing *can* happen. For a few reasons. Besides, she's never indicated interest in me. And there's her age."

The crowd stood as a player rounded third. Geri bumped Ang's arm, ignoring the field. "Oh, honey. The girl is more than interested."

The crowd continued to yell and high-five all around them as the usher motioned for them to continue. Ang was about to deny Geri's statement but noticed Krista watching them descend.

Ang couldn't help but return the smile Krista gave her.

"Yeah. Nothing's gonna happen but steamy, sweaty lady sex," Geri laughed.

If Ang's hands hadn't been full, she would have given her the one finger salute.

CHAPTER EIGHTEEN

K rista topped off the gas tank in her Jeep and tore the receipt from the front of the pump. She'd stopped in Boulder to get gas and pick up some of Uncle Raggy's favorite elk jerky, and as she climbed back into the Jeep, she remembered he'd asked her to call when she left Denver. She was almost to his cabin, but if she didn't call, she wouldn't hear the end of it, so as she pulled out of the service station, she dialed him up through the Jeep's Bluetooth.

"Talk to me," Raggy answered in his typical fashion.

"I'm in Boulder and about to head into the canyon."

"Already? I told you to call me when you left."

"I am. I'm leaving Boulder." Technically, she was right.

"Don't be clever with me." He laughed. "Now I have to rush to get the place picked up."

She returned the laugh. "I can say you don't, but you will anyway. You have half an hour to make the bed and wash the dishes. Do you want me to stop at the co-op for anything?"

"No. I got everything I need. Just bring yourself along. I'll be here waiting for you."

Although the roads had been plowed and anything left on the pavement had melted, there was still quite a bit of snow on the side of the road the farther up the canyon she drove, and she hoped the dirt road Raggy lived on was in good shape. He would have told her if it was unpassable, and regardless, her Jeep could get there. By the time they got to the reservoir, Alfur's tail was beating a steady rhythm against the back of the front passenger seat. A few minutes later, she pulled into Raggy's long, pine-tree-lined driveway and followed the tire tracks until she arrived at his cabin. As she suspected, he was standing on the wraparound porch, flanked by his dogs, Odin and Loki, Alfur's litter brothers.

She killed the engine and leaned across the Jeep to let Alfur out. He bounded from his seat the instant the door was open, and all three dogs met to frolic in the yard. Krista waved at her uncle and climbed from the car, lugging all the stuff she'd brought with her, and Raggy hurried down the steps to help. She followed him into the house, noticing his shaggy white hair was combed back and wet.

"Why were you standing out in the cold with wet hair?" she asked as he dropped all the stuff on the bench by the door. "You could get pneumonia, and that's bad for young men like you." He answered by smothering her in a long hug. The aromas of fresh soap and aftershave brought up all the good memories from her childhood, when she'd visited him at what used to be his mountain getaway but was now his year-round home.

"I couldn't sit still waiting for you. It's been months since I set these eyes upon you."

"It all comes with the cold water," she said and laughed. It was a favorite of her uncle's many sayings, meaning good things came to those who waited.

He laughed his deep-chested rumble and held her at arm's length. "You appear healthy."

"I'm riding every day."

"Are you letting the others do their jobs?"

He always asked the same question, and it drove her crazy. Like she had any choice. "I'm trying to take the weekends off."

"Good. Good." He gathered the bags again and led her through the front room and into the kitchen, which was neat and clean as always, with a fresh tablecloth on the small breakfast table. He always kept a clean house, and when she'd teased him about making the bed and doing the dishes, she knew he'd already done it all.

"I also hired a sales manager."

"Oh? When did you do this?" After setting the bags on the counter, he took a seat at the table, gesturing for her to do the same. There was nothing like sitting at his table, talking over a strong cup of coffee. She basked in the sun shining through the windows and the aromas of brewing coffee and the toast he'd had for breakfast. Every bit of it represented love and comfort to her.

"She started this week," she said smoothing the linen placemat in front of her.

He leaned forward, his huge hands stacked on the table. "What does this sales manager do?"

"She does the hiring and recruiting, the schedule, figures out how to maximize sales, keeps the staff educated, manages inventory. Those sorts of things."

"What do you do?"

She hated it when he got into the details of managing the shop. She'd told him not to give her advice, which he'd been very good about since then, but it had been a while since they'd spoken about the shop, so she hoped he'd honor his agreement. "The books, payroll, manage the business plan, and help the sales manager do all of their work."

"Swifty has done inventory for fifteen years. Is he tired of it?"

"He hasn't said so, but he needs a break."

"Has he asked for a break?"

"No, just the opposite. But he has too much to deal with taking care of Dirk." She waved her hand. "He got a second job. I'm afraid he's going to burn out."

"Yes. He told me about the job."

"You spoke to him?"

He nodded. "Maybe once a week on the phone."

"Then you know he's struggling. What does he say about the shop?"

He leaned back and looped one arm around the post on the back of his chair. "He says it's doing well, business is good, even off-season. People are happy. Even him. But not as happy as he could be because you took over inventory. Also, you brought in a new system."

She sighed. She was starting to regret it, too, since she hadn't figured out the issue with the reconciliation. "I updated the accounting system to automate inventory. I've had trouble getting it to reconcile, though. Once I get it straightened out, no more manual inventory. It'll all be scanned in, and the system will track and automatically do the ordering."

"If Swifty is willing to keep it up, why change things? Is it overkill? We're just a small shop."

"We?" She smiled at him, thinking it was a good time to remind him he'd turned the store over to her, and she got to run it the way she wanted to.

He shrugged and put his hands palm up on the table. "Sorry. Habit. But isn't it?"

"Is that what he told you?"

"No. I assumed. He doesn't complain. He's just worried about how much you work."

It was hard to be mad when he was just watching out for her. "It's funny you think I work too much. Swifty is the one who should stop working so hard. He can't right now because he needs money for medical bills, but at least I can try to make things easier for all of us. Don't worry. It'll be okay."

"Yes. He will have to bite the molar for a little while longer. Dirk will get better, and then he'll put it behind. That's how life is." He made a sweeping gesture to indicate he was done with talking about it, and she was relieved. "Anyway, it sounds like you have it under control, *mitt krútt*. Let's not talk about work anymore. What did you bring me?"

"Swifty sent beer, and Mom sent *skyr* she found at the butcher shop, of all places, and she made some homemade *kleina*." She smiled at the way his eyes lit up at the mention of the Icelandic yogurt and doughnuts he loved so much. "Of course, there are pot pies. Always pot pies. And elk jerky. I found the kind you like at the service station."

Raggy rubbed his hands together. "You're too kind to your old uncle. The coffee is fresh. Let's have some kleina."

Krista put the skyr and the beer in the refrigerator and the pot pies in the freezer while he put two small plates and things for coffee on the table. It appeared he'd recently gone to the store. Where there was normally only condiments and beer, she spied leftovers, which meant he was making himself meals instead of heating up canned soup. There were even leafy greens in the crisper. Of course, there was still beer, but there would probably always be beer. At least he was eating healthy.

"Tell me about this friend in Lyons. Did you get the deck fixed?" she asked.

He nodded as he poured the coffee. "Just a small repair."

They talked about Frozen Dead Guy Days, an annual festival in Nederland, which had happened last month. She'd missed it for the first time ever because of work, which had been a disappointment to both of them, since it was their thing. But he said he went with a friend, which was nice. Then there was fishing and the goings on about Nederland to talk about.

When they finished their coffee and kleina, they went for a short walk along Alpine Drive since the slushy snow under the trees was too wet to comfortably walk through. She was relieved to find Raggy healthy and somehow younger-looking than the last time she'd visited him. Because he hadn't been coming down for family dinner, she'd feared he might not be doing well, but it appeared she was wrong. He was clean-shaven, which contributed to the younger appearance, but there was something else. Something was lighting her eighty-year-old uncle from inside.

When she was getting ready to leave, he told her to tell her mother he'd be coming down for family dinner this week, which made her very happy.

CHAPTER NINETEEN

The morning air was a little chilly on her bare legs, but Ang was happy to ride her bike to work on Monday morning. It only took a few minutes of pedaling before the chill didn't even register, and she noticed the small signs of spring taking hold of Denver. She was about halfway to work when her phone rang, interrupting the music she was streaming. Without thinking, she tapped her earbud to answer.

"Ang? This is Ann. Have I caught you at a good time?"

The chill rushed back over her at the sound of Robert's assistant's voice. She'd always liked Ann, but she hadn't spoken to anyone at Lithium in nearly three weeks. Not that they hadn't called but because she refused to answer any calls from the company prefix. She expected to talk to them eventually but wasn't expecting it to be a surprise. Part of her couldn't believe she'd found it so easy to put fifteen years behind her, but another part knew it wouldn't remain easy.

"Hi, Ann. I'm just riding my bike. What can I help you with?"

"Well, first of all, I miss you."

Ang's emotional barrier toward all things Lithium melted a little. Ann was one of the good ones. "I miss you, too, Ann."

Ann paused. "Robert says you won't answer his calls."

"It's true. I've been avoiding him." She didn't have to pretend otherwise. When was the last time she'd been able to talk so directly at work? *Former* work, she reminded herself. She didn't have to play games anymore. It was liberating.

"He asked me to give you a call and arrange a meeting with you."

Ang coasted to a stop on the side of the bike path. "A meeting? I don't work there anymore. Shouldn't I be talking to HR?"

"He wants to talk to you first. He thought a couple weeks off would help everyone get some perspective, and then you two could talk."

Ang didn't answer right away. It was odd Robert hadn't notified HR. Suddenly, things were complicated again. Strings hadn't been cut as cleanly as she'd thought. Her stomach clenched at the knowledge that she was still attached to the job and people she'd walked away from. Anxiety crept in. She'd started to get used to not being connected to Lithium, and now all of the emotional and psychological weight she'd shed by quitting fell back onto her. "It's been three weeks, and I'm not sure if there's anything to talk about. I quit. Tell him I'll call HR later today to get the paperwork finalized."

"He wants to talk to you about reconsidering."

Ang dropped her chin to her chest and shook her head. Was he out of his mind? "Is he standing there listening to this conversation?"

"No. No. I mean, he wanted to, but I told him I didn't think it would be right. He's in his office."

"Did he tell you what he did?"

She made a humming noise, the one she made when she was trying not to blurt out what was on her mind. Ang had always appreciated her composure. "No, but I have an idea. I processed paperwork for other people."

"Right. Well, you can imagine how I can't work there anymore and maintain my self-respect."

A sigh came over the line. "To be honest, I was damn proud of you for standing up to him."

That support meant so much to her. She'd felt so isolated in her efforts to justify her continued employment at a place that forced her to work so hard to make the tiniest of advancements. She'd never suspected that others could see the things she went through. "Please tell him I won't meet with him. I'll talk to HR."

Ann's voice lowered to a whisper. "I'm on your side. I'm glad you're standing firm. I'll miss you, but if anyone can make this company change its…well, you know what I mean."

"Thank you. Your kindness means a lot to me."

They hung up, and Ang kicked her bike into motion again. Despite the confidence she'd displayed when standing up for herself three weeks ago—as well as the encouraging words from Ann moments ago—a heavy sense of doubt settled over her. Was it the right decision? What was she doing with her life? She'd thrown her career away and had no idea what she was going to do going forward.

A fox ran across the path several feet ahead of her, and she slowed to watch it run. This wasn't something anyone witnessed from their office twenty floors high in the city, and if she'd still been working at Lithium, that was where she'd be, probably in a meeting; the last thing on her mind would be a fox running through her urban world.

The cloud of dread disappeared, and a sense of being in the right place at the right time struck her. It was a beautiful day, and she was riding her bike in it, going to a job she found interesting and enjoyable. She thought about Krista and the others—especially Krista—and anticipated her day.

Within minutes, she was at the shop, arriving at the same time as Krista. Alfur ran next to Krista's bike as she coasted to a stop.

"Amazing. He just runs alongside? He doesn't try to pull you over? Oh, jeez!"

Krista steadied Ang just as she was about to fall over, having forgotten to click from her pedals before coming to a stop. "They take getting used to," Krista said, letting go of Ang's arm when both feet were on the ground.

"It was second nature when I was on the cycling team. I don't know how I lost the habit so completely," Ang said, dismounting. Embarrassed, she happily accepted the distraction when Alfur leaned into her and then lay down to show his belly. She swung her foot over the seat of her bike so she could give him a scratch. "He's amazing. Makes me want a dog." The thought surprised her. But having said it aloud, she found she really meant it. "Preferably one just like Alfur."

Krista unlocked the door to the shop. "I got lucky with him. I found him and two of his litter mates at the Dumb Friends League. My uncle took two of them, and I kept Alfur. But seriously? You want a dog?"

The blurt was born mostly from wanting to redirect the conversation, but when Ang thought about it, she was surprised that she actually meant it. Cleo would have something to say about it, but she'd just have to get used to it. She peered up at Krista's smiling face. "Totally serious. Does Alfur have more siblings? He's just about perfect. What breeder did you get him from again?"

"The Dumb Friends League is a rescue center."

Ang stood and followed Krista into the store, pushing her bike toward the back room. Alfur padded close behind. "Maybe I should go with that. I haven't had a dog since I was a kid, and we got Trip, our German Shepherd, from a pet store. I have a hairless cat I got from a breeder at the advice of my allergist. I'm not allergic to dogs, though, so I can go wherever I want for one."

Krista turned and stared at her with a smile Ang thought might turn into a laugh at any minute. "Cleo is hairless? One of those Sphynx cats?"

"She is."

Krista's eyes sparkled with amusement. "I'm sorry. I've never actually seen one. Just in memes and I associate them with—" Krista dropped her head forward and shook her head. "I'm sorry. Never mind."

"With what?"

"Um, well, it's ridiculous, but I always think of a turtle without a shell. Even though turtles *are* their shell. But I'm not making fun of your cat. I swear."

Ang laughed. "It's okay. You can laugh. Cleo is absolutely the most ridiculous cat. And I never thought about it, but you're right. She does look a little like a turtle without a shell."

"I have to meet your Cleo."

"You'll love her. She kisses up to everyone but me. She just bosses me around."

Krista rolled her eyes. "Somehow, I doubt it."

Ang held her hand up. "It's the honest truth. She rules the house and treats me as a feeding apparatus and a heating pad. You'll see."

"I can't wait. If you're serious about getting a dog, you should check out the Dumb Friends League. Maybe there's a match for you there. I'll go with you if you like."

Ang smiled. "I'd like that."

Ang's phone rang, and she realized she still wore her wireless earbuds. When she instinctively touched one, she accidentally answered. Slightly panicked it could be Robert, she pulled out her phone for the caller ID. Damn. It was Lithium.

"Hello, Angelique. This is Janelle. From Human Resources. We've spoken in the past. About Carl Davies."

At least it wasn't Robert. HR wasn't much better, but maybe they'd called to get the paperwork going. "Yes, I remember. Can you please hold for a few seconds?" Ang said, lifting her bike and hanging it from the spare hook next to Krista's. She mouthed she'd be back in a minute and retraced her steps outside so she could take the call in private. She leaned against the outside wall when the door closed behind her, her guts feeling like she'd swallowed glass. The calls from Ann and then HR weren't a coincidence. This was the beginning of her having to finally actually deal with her decision to leave Lithium. Amazingly enough, her fear of being free wasn't as bad as she'd imagined. She was ready to move on. She just wanted to wave a wand and make it so. Dealing with people was going to suck.

"Hi, Janelle. How are you?"

"I'm well. Thank you for asking. And you?"

"Doing well. What can I do for you?"

The inane pleasantries caused Ang to pinch the bridge of her nose. How many times had she exchanged the same stock phrases when walking into meetings or answering calls? It occurred to her that she hadn't uttered those words in three weeks, and they came just as easily now as ever.

And why all the tenseness? She hadn't done anything wrong. She was justified in her feelings and actions. So why did she feel like she was going to be punished?

"Robert gave me a call this morning. He said you abandoned your job, and I wanted to reach out to you to talk about it. If you want support, I'm here to help you through this."

First, confusion rushed through her and then anger. "Those were his words? He said I *abandoned* my job?" *That* was why she was tense. Robert was going to try to punish her. Well, he'd better get ready for a shock. She wasn't going to go down without a fight.

"Those were his words, but he wasn't being—"

"Let me be clear. I quit my job. I did not abandon it." Ang realized she was clenching her teeth. She deliberately unclenched them and rocked her head back and forth to release the sudden tension in her shoulders.

"I'm sure he didn't mean anything with those particular words."

She blew out a breath. "And I'm sure he did."

"He did mention you were taking some time off to decompress. He was hoping—"

Ang wasn't interested in anything else Robert had to say, and she wasn't going to consider going back. She wanted to make that clear. "Did he tell you why I left?"

"He said you were disappointed about the pending reorganization."

Ang laughed even as the tension settled between her shoulder blades again. How had she lived with it for the last fifteen years? It was like poison sitting there, eating away at her.

"I was not just disappointed. I was pissed. Pissed that he gave the position he promised me—the position he'd been grooming me for and talking to me about like it was mine for over year—to Carl without so much as talking to me first. In addition, he promoted Neil to a similar position in the new department and expected me to make a lateral move to the new department to work in the same capacity as Neil without the benefit of the title or the raise. Does that sound fair to you, Janelle?"

"I don't handle job administration, so I wasn't aware of it."

"But does it sound fair to you?"

Janelle paused, and Ang was sure she was trying to remain neutral while she gathered the facts. Her duty was first and foremost to the company. "I think I should get more clarity around all of this before I can answer. I think you have every right to be upset based on what you described."

"Look. You have to protect the company. I don't have any intention of suing, although I have friends telling me I should. I just want this to be over. I'd like you to get the paperwork done so I can tie up the loose ends."

"Can you come into the office in the next day or two to sign the paperwork?"

"Can we do it remotely? I'd prefer not to come in if I can help it."

"I understand you still have things in your office."

"I was hoping Ann or someone could just pack it up and send it to me."

"I'll see what I can do. I'll give you a call later today with details." Janelle paused, and Ang was about to hang up. "I wish this wasn't happening. I'll investigate what you told me. It surprised me when Robert took Carl off the work plan, and this further confuses me, but I'll—"

"He what?"

"He took Carl off the work plan. He said you were aware."

"This is the first I've heard about it."

"Well, Carl certainly would not have been offered a promotion—" Janelle stopped. "You know what? Never mind. I misspoke. I will investigate what you told me, and I'll get back to you soon, okay?"

"Thank you."

Ang stood outside for a few more minutes and processed the conversation.

Robert was lying because he was trying to cover his ass for promising her a job he gave to someone else. She was sure of it. It was a classic Robert move, and he usually asked someone else do it for him. Even she'd "managed optics" for him on a few occasions, although she would have never agreed to cover something like this up. There was something else going on, though, and Carl factored in on it. Part of her was curious, and part of her just wanted to be done with everything related to Lithium.

She closed her eyes and took a couple of deep breaths before she went into the store. She returned to the back room and smiled when she walked in on Krista giving Alfur a treat for doing a trick. What a huge difference it was to work here. When she started looking for a new job, she wanted it to be more like Sol Cycle than some corporate cubicle farm.

CHAPTER TWENTY

Krista came back from Monsieur Beans with five drinks and was headed to the back room when she came upon Swifty and Angelique in a heated discussion at the maintenance desk. It was at low volume, and there were no customers around, thankfully, but their body language said they were both angry. She watched for a moment, curious if they would resolve it, but it soon became clear that neither of them was giving in.

"Hey, you two. Come get your coffee." She entered the back room without waiting. They followed. When she set the drinks on the table, they both wore expressions of thinly disguised anger. Swifty was never quick to anger. She'd witnessed him like this only a few times, always after a customer had laid into him. But she'd never seen Angelique angry, and she decided there and then that she never wanted to be on the receiving end. She was surprised Swifty hadn't already backed down.

She handed them their drinks. "What's going on?"

Angelique turned to Swifty. "Do you want to tell her?"

He crossed his arms and tilted his head. "I've said what I wanted to say."

Angelique turned back to Krista, visibly impatient. "I wanted to have a conversation about the services the shop provides and the related pricing, trying to understand. However, Swifty not only refused to discuss it, he provided me with a long list of reasons why I shouldn't be here and how I was going to destroy the soul of the business."

Krista had a hard time seeing Swifty be so harsh, especially when he'd never displayed any kind of animosity toward Angelique. "Is this true, Swifty?"

"Of course it's true," Angelique said.

Krista stared for a moment before responding. She could understand Angelique's irritation, but she didn't appreciate her tone. Maybe it was normal in a corporate setting, but not in her shop. Either way, she definitely didn't like it pointed at her. "I don't doubt what you said. I just want to listen to Swifty's perspective."

"She wants to start charging for the deep clean," Swifty said.

Krista raised her eyebrows.

Ang crossed her arms. "I didn't say as much, but, yes, that's the direction I was headed."

"Did Swifty explain how the deep clean is our signature service?"

"Not in those words but in essence."

"Why do you think we should charge for it?"

"I didn't say we should. I was trying to find out more about it before making a recommendation. Work orders indicate some customers come in for very minor repairs, and Swifty spent minimal time on the requested service, yet he spent half an hour performing the deep clean, effectively giving us a negative return on investment."

"I understand your concern. On the surface, it's negative ROI, but over time, it goes positive when the customer comes to us for other services or to buy a bike. It's an indirect positive affect to the ROI."

"I suspected as much, and when I told Swifty I just wanted to look into it by going through the work orders and sales invoices to verify if those customers are truly making those follow-up purchases and not merely coming in over and over again to take advantage of the free bike wash without another purchase, he told me I should stick to things I know more about."

Krista turned to Swifty, who seemed to be barely containing his anger. "Is that what you said?"

"Yes."

She sighed, put her coffee on the table, and slid up to sit on the table next to it. "I'm not saying we shouldn't look into it, but I can tell you that very few, if any, of our customers take advantage of the free bike wash and don't follow up with a substantial purchase or maintenance request. I'd bet good money." She watched a flare of renewed anger in Angelique's eyes, and she didn't like it. Mostly because she didn't want Angelique to be mad at her, but also because Angelique hadn't been there long enough to be getting angry over a suggestion not being immediately accepted.

"The decision is yours to make. I would hope you'd at least want to check and see if the idea has merit, but you call the shots." And with that, Angelique turned and left, leaving Krista with a sense of having been dismissed, a sensation she did not like one bit.

"Is it just me, or is she the most arrogant person you've ever met?" Swifty asked, apparently thinking Krista was siding with him, and it just made Krista want to defend her. First, regardless of the way in which Angelique had approached the topic, Krista had no doubt that she'd had a solid reason for bringing it up. Second, even though Krista didn't like being on the receiving end of Angelique's anger, she wasn't being arrogant. It was a name people often called women who were confident, and it wasn't fair. Third, and probably most importantly, Krista suspected that the call Angelique had taken earlier had more to do with her demeanor than anything else, and despite Krista asking if she was okay, Angelique had refused to talk about it.

Krista was more disappointed in Swifty's attitude. Angelique was just trying to do her job, and he wasn't being helpful at all. It wasn't her fault she wasn't up to speed with the customs of the shop yet. "I think you're being unfair. You could have at least offered to talk it through and maybe do the investigation she asked for. But until I figure out the software issue, I can't run the reports to do it, anyway."

"Unfair? I thought we hired her to make schedules, work on staffing, and do advertising. But instead of taking the time to learn how we do things, she wants to change things in areas she doesn't know anything about."

"Why did you give her the work orders to organize, then?"

"To be honest, I was tired of her questions about the kinds of inventory we carry and how different components work."

"So you're angry she's making suggestions for changes because she's too new, yet you gave her a mindless task to avoid teaching her the things you don't want to talk about?"

Swifty scratched the stubble on his neck. "I guess."

"I'm a little confused, Swifty. You're usually happy to talk shop with people. Most of the time, you're a chatterbox when it comes to how bike parts work together. What's your hesitation here? Do you regret not taking the manager position? Are you having a hard time with having someone else in the role?"

"I've never wanted to be a manager. I like fixing bikes. But I've been here a long time. I guess I don't like someone coming in and changing things. We've been doing just fine for a long time."

"I get it. Now tell me this, do you not like Angelique? You were positive about her in the interview. You've been pleasant to her until now. You've said nothing to indicate you have any concerns. She says nothing but good things about you. Yet you went from zero to one hundred on the anger meter just now, and I'm very surprised about how you spoke to her. Do you think she deserved it?"

Swifty hung his head, staring at his boots. "No, and I'm not proud of it. I do like her. I just didn't like her using her cold corporate tone with me. It rubbed me the wrong way. I'm an asshole."

Krista could see his point. The corporate Angelique was not her favorite person either, even though it gave her a little sexual thrill when she glimpsed it, it rubbed her the wrong way when it reminded her that Angelique could probably run circles around her if she was given free rein over the shop. She knew it was insecurity on her part, and she suspected Swifty felt a little of that, too, minus the sexual thing.

"You're not an asshole." Angelique stood in the doorway. "I'm sorry. I want to apologize for storming out. What you said about my cold corporate tone, I'm aware I switch it on when I think someone is brushing me off, and I'm used to people jumping when I say jump. I don't like it about myself. It would rub me the wrong way, too, and

I'll try not to do it. I'm used to just jumping in, but I can wait a little longer to understand the business better before making suggestions to change anything. I didn't intend to step on toes, and I'm sorry."

Swifty's expression said he took her words to heart. "You're right. I did brush you off, and I'm sorry. I'll try to be more patient and give you a heads-up if I'm having a hard time with anything before I go off half-cocked."

Angelique's apology felt genuine, and it gave Krista a glimpse into how Angelique probably managed her teams, competently and with kindness. Swifty's response was a lot closer to who she knew him to be. She glanced between them, proud. The butting of their heads had been surprising, but it was good to watch them work it out so quickly. And to be honest, the ease with which Angelique had been able to admit her fault was even sexier than the corporate Angelique.

Oh, God. Krista was in trouble if she thought she was going to keep her crush from getting worse.

Chapter Twenty-one

The bag of dog food slipped from Ang's hands, but Krista caught it before it hit the sidewalk.

"Thanks. I cannot believe I have a dog now," Ang said for what must have been the dozenth time. Grateful for the help, she juggled the folder of adoption paperwork, a bag of dog toys she'd purchased from the shelter, and a leash attached to a very curious, thirty-five-pound bundle of black and white fur making zigzags and pulling her up the sidewalk to her front door.

"Hey, when a match is made in heaven, there's no denying it. Rupert and you were made for one another."

"But I just went to look and check out my options. I'm the type who takes months to make decisions like this."

At Ang's front door, they both peered at the dog who sat patiently at their feet and staring up at Ang with big blue eyes. Just like in the shelter, he gazed at her as if he was seeing her very soul. Everything in her melted when he watched her, like she was the love he'd been searching for all his life.

"I'm not sure you had a choice. I think he made the decision the minute he set eyes on you. There's no way to resist those eyes."

Ang smiled at the memory. It was true. Rupert had come right up to her like he'd always known her and had stood there, wagging his whole back end, until she'd crouched to pet him. He'd snuck a kiss from her, quick and polite, before he'd placed his head on her knees and had leaned into her. He'd been so earnest and gentle from the first moment, ignoring everyone else. She'd been chosen.

When she'd found out he was available, the adoption went quickly, and here they were. Rupert was about to enter her world. Ang looked at Krista. "It feels like it's been longer than just a couple of hours. The first time our eyes met, I just knew he would be awesome. It just exuded from him. Am I being weird?"

"Not at all. It's how I was when I first met you." Krista's face turned red, and she pursed her lips as if she'd said something she wished she hadn't, but then she shrugged. "I don't make it a habit to stop in the park to talk to random people, especially when I'm doing a speed run, which is what I was doing the second time we met. I had this powerful suspicion you would be an awesome person. And you are. It was strange."

Ang's stomach did a little flip. "I felt something, too. Normally, I refuse to appear like a damsel in distress, but it didn't bother me with you."

Krista snorted. "Damsel in distress? I don't think anyone would ever mistake you for one of those."

So many things rushed to Ang's mind, but before any of them could solidify into a coherent thought, a whine distracted her, and the moment was broken. Ang looked at Rupert, who was watching her raptly. She knelt in front of him and ruffled the hair on his neck.

"You want to go inside, Rupert? I have to warn you, I don't run this house. You heard me talk about Cleo when they asked me a thousand questions about the house you'd be moving into? Well, Cleo is the boss, and you're going to meet her in a minute. I expect her to do one of two things. She's going to ignore you completely, or she's going to put you in your place. You ready?"

Krista wore an amused smile. "I can't wait to meet her. I guess we're about to test Rupert's training and Cleo's tolerance, huh?"

Ang lifted her brows and nodded with a shrug, even though her stomach was a swarm of anticipation. It was Cleo she worried about. The shelter's paperwork on Rupert said he was eight years old and had been raised as a companion to an older man who'd recently passed away. His disposition was gentle and devoid of any type of aggression, and because the man had cats, too, he was used to being around them. On paper, Rupert was the perfect fit for Ang, who was nervous about getting a dog and not very confident about her training capabilities.

Cleo was going to make or break the situation. Ang wasn't sure what she would do if it went badly. Rupert didn't appear worried. She gave his head another pat, sighed, and stood, glancing at Krista before opening the door. She'd already unlocked it via an app on her phone when they drove up.

"I hope Cleo likes me. It's hilarious because I'm invested, and I've never even met her," Krista said, bouncing on her toes while balancing the bag of dog food on her shoulder.

Ang's nervousness about introducing Rupert to Cleo the Boss took a back seat to Krista being in her house for the first time. Normally, she was proud of her home, proud of what she'd been able to provide for herself. But this was different. Krista wasn't the type to be easily impressed with material things. She worried her house would come off as sterile and lack personality. The word ostentatious flitted through her mind. An image of her mother did, too. She stuffed it down. It was too late now. They were here.

The door swung open to the high-ceilinged foyer and the sweeping staircase leading to the second floor she rarely ever went up to. Ang set all of Rupert's new stuff on the floor and walked him into the living room. Without her having to shorten his lead, Rupert stayed at Ang's heel, sniffing furniture but staying close. Krista put the food down, shut the door, and followed. Ang was glad to have Cleo and Rupert's first encounter distracting her so she didn't have to focus on her concern over Krista's perception of her home.

Cleo was in her normal lounging place on the high wooden table next to the window, lolling on her side in a square of sunlight. A constant heat seeker, her back was to the window, soaking up the sun's rays. Her large, indifferent eyes opened, following them as they approached the center of the large room. As soon as Cleo's eyes landed on Rupert, Ang stopped, holding her breath. Cleo pushed herself up, yawned, and arched her back in a lazy stretch. Ang's shoulders relaxed when she realized Cleo was going with the ignoring option.

She glanced at Krista and let out her breath, waiting for Cleo to flop back down. Instead, the cat yawned one more time and jumped from the table. Ang's shoulders crept up to her ears as Cleo slinked serenely up to Rupert, stopping about a foot away. Like a queen at inspection, Cleo calmly assessed the new guest for a moment. Rupert lowered his head and sniffed a few times but remained sitting, and to Ang's surprise, Cleo walked right up to him and leaned into him. She rubbed her head against him as if they were long-lost friends.

Ang couldn't believe it. "Never in a million years."

"So this is Cleo, huh?" Krista crouched next to Rupert, who sat quietly sniffing.

"I seriously can't believe it. No hissing. No ignoring. This is amazing."

Krista offered Cleo a sniff of her hand before running it along the cat's gray-skinned back. "She has blue eyes. They're beautiful."

"Not as beautiful as yours," Ang said without thinking. Heat rose up her neck.

Krista just laughed. "You must have a thing for blue eyes. Rupert's eyes are blue, too."

"I guess I do."

Krista glanced up with a crooked smile. "Well, I have a thing for amber eyes."

Ang let the comment sink in and decided Krista didn't mean it like it sounded, like maybe she liked Ang's eyes, like maybe she was flirting a little.

Krista ran her fingers over Cleo's back again as the cat continued to rub against Rupert, who appeared to enjoy the attention.

"The shelter said to keep him on leash until he gets used to the house, but it seems like he's at ease. Do you think I should let him go?" Ang asked, scanning the room, trying not to fixate on Krista's comment.

Krista stood. "They said he's house-trained, so I think it's safe." Rupert peered at them, tongue hanging from his mouth. It looked like he was smiling, as if he understood exactly what they were talking about.

"I might have lucked out with Rupert." Ang unfastened the leash, and he stood. He licked her hand and carefully walked around Cleo as he moved into the living room, sniffing at everything. Cleo stayed near him, wending through his legs as he explored.

"You have a beautiful house," Krista said.

Ang smiled, the insecurity rising again. "I'm thinking of redecorating."

"In what way?"

Ang looked around. "I never really spent a lot of time at home before, and I realized my house doesn't really reflect my personality."

"What do you mean?"

Ang paused, thinking. "I've channeled my mother's aesthetic. Not my own."

"What aesthetic is that?"

"Pretentious."

"It's not pretentious."

Ang appreciated Krista trying to be kind. "Sure, it is. It's the current version of plastic covers and carpet runners people used to put in their living rooms. It's to be appreciated but not used. White furniture and carpet? And none of it comfortable. I sit on the floor when I hang out in the living room. Stainless steel accents and appliances? Come on. Fingerprint city. I furnished a museum. No. A mausoleum. I need to do an exorcism."

Krista laughed. "What changed?"

"I'm home more often. I got rid of my housekeeper because I have more time to clean, and I found out I like to do it, but the things I clean bring me no joy. Also, I don't want to worry about muddy paw prints." She ruffled Rupert's neck fur.

Krista walked toward the back of the room. Floor to ceiling windows with a view into the backyard and French doors opened to a multi-level deck with built-in planters where some of the annuals were starting to come up. "Your backyard is fantastic. I'll bet you have the best summer barbeques."

Ang didn't want to say she'd designed the backyard for big outdoor gatherings but had never had one. The yard was tidy now because she'd been bored a few days earlier and had put the patio furniture out, but she wanted Krista to see it in the summer, when it was vibrant with leaves, flowers, and vines. The trees were starting to get buds, and the bulbs were starting to sprout green in most of the border beds. It looked great, even though the most use it ever got was the couple of times a year when she, Kat, and Geri enjoyed a glass of wine out there before a Rockies game or a concert. Most of the time, she went to their houses, which were warm and inviting with lots of colors and textures. There had been times when Ang had pretended to be a little drunk just so she could stay at one of their houses. They felt like home.

"I've been meaning to get a barbecue."

Krista turned to her, mouth agape. "What? You don't have a barbecue? We have to rectify this immediately. You also need an elf house in your garden."

"An elf house?"

Krista looked at her, eyes wide open. "Where else would they live?"

"Considering they aren't—"

Krista put a finger across her lips. "Shh! You don't want the *huldufólk* to feel unwanted."

"*Huldufólk?*"

"Elves," Krista said as if it was obvious.

"Is this a delusional thing I need to be afraid of?"

"It's an Icelandic thing. They bring good luck. Don't worry. We'll get you an elf house, and you'll see."

Ang smiled. She wasn't quite sure if Krista was serious, but she liked this glimpse into her.

CHAPTER TWENTY-TWO

When dusk fell, Krista and Angelique were out on the deck trying out the new grill. Music played over hidden speakers, and Angelique sat watching, cross-legged on a cushioned wicker footstool, near where Krista cooked. Krista snuck glances at her. She was beautiful. It might have been the soft cotton button-up shirt she wore, the kind that looked like a man's dress shirt, but when untucked and flowing on a woman, looked like a pirate's shirt, sexy and a little wild. Or maybe it was the expanse of soft skin exposed in the unbuttoned vee, making Krista long to run her fingers across its surface. The golden light framed Angelique in soft edges, and Krista felt it hard to breathe.

"I wish Alfur was here instead of camping with your sister. I think he'd like Rupert," Angelique said, scratching his ears. "What would you be doing today if you hadn't gone to the shelter with me?"

Krista focused on the veggie kabobs and scallops she was tending on the grill as she concentrated on breathing. Tightness wrapped around her midsection. Was it anxiety? Or was Angelique's proximity causing her to forget to breathe?

"I work a lot. The shop is open seven days a week, so I try to take Sundays off, but I usually go in on Saturdays. When I don't, or if I leave early, I like to take long bike rides. I also like to go up to the mountains. But I tend to work more often than not." She found talking about work made it easier to breathe.

"Is it stuff you weren't able to get to during the week? Or is it other stuff?"

"Mostly stuff I didn't get to during the week." Krista didn't want to talk about work. She wanted to ask Angelique about her childhood, what her favorite color was. She wanted to get to know her better. God, it was hard not to touch her.

It hit her then. Her trouble breathing, the tightness in her stomach. This was the thing missing with all the other women. This was the feeling of promise and hope and the beginning of something that could be more. *This* was what she'd been looking for when she met someone. She'd been feeling it all along. She wanted more. She wanted whatever was happing between them to grow, to last. Did Angelique feel it, too?

"Do you think it's a staffing issue? Or is it work only you can do?"

Krista almost missed the question. The feelings of falling and flying at the same time made her almost giddy. She turned a kabob and breathed in.

"I think it's stuff *you* could do in your sleep."

"Is that so?" Angelique appeared pleased.

"Things like inventory analysis and process stuff. You know, assess how current processes are working and if there are things we could do better."

Angelique nodded, and Krista noticed how she tilted her head to the left when she concentrated. "It's my bailiwick. I usually have teams working on much of that for me, but I am well-versed in it. I called it Success Factors. Everything should have a purpose, and the purpose should always be to support a specific goal. If you can't describe how an activity supports the goal, it's probably something you don't need to do or something you need to do but haven't identified properly."

The way Angelique talked about work was sexy. Confident and sexy. Krista didn't think about business goals that way, and it was obvious Angelique was better qualified for it, like she was at so many other things related to a successfully run store. It gave her a little more insight into Angelique's interest in things like the deep cleans and product placement. Her knowledge and passion for it made retail seem exciting.

The veggies and scallops were done. Happy for the distraction, Krista moved them to the outdoor table that Angelique had set with a tablecloth, linen napkins, plates, and silverware, along with a Caprese salad, sliced baguette, and a bottle of wine. The spread was absolutely amazing. Although, Angelique could have used paper plates, and she would have loved it, too.

As Angelique arranged the food, she walked around Krista and ran a seemingly casual hand down her arm, making her shiver.

"You're cold," Angelique said.

Just the opposite. "I'm fine."

"Hold on. I'll be right back."

Krista plated their food and poured the wine while Angelique went inside. When she came back, Angelique was wearing a light sweater and handed Krista a zip-up sweatshirt with a Rockies logo. She thought it might be the one Angelique wore to the game last week; when she put it on, it smelled like Angelique. God, she was in trouble.

"Thanks."

"It's always cooler in the evenings, especially in the spring."

Krista nodded as she sat down to their meal. "I usually bring a jacket if I'm out in the evening, but I didn't expect to be here all day."

Angelique, who was watching Rupert curl up on the cement under the table at her feet, glanced up. "I didn't intend to keep you all day."

"I'm having fun." A pang of insecurity swept over Krista. "Have I overstayed my welcome?"

"Not at all. I'm having fun, too."

"What do *you* usually do on Saturdays?" Krista asked, secretly happy with Angelique's response.

Angelique tilted her head. "I used to catch up on email and run reports to get ready for the coming week at work. Last weekend, I took a morning ride down to Cherry Creek Reservoir, and when I got home, I set up my old record player and pulled out a box of vinyl. It was decadent to spend so much time just enjoying music."

"My uncle gave me a bunch of old records he brought over from Iceland. I've always wanted to spend a day listening to them." Just looking at the covers brought back wonderful memories of dancing to the records at Uncle Raggy's house. She wanted to share the good memories and feelings with Angelique.

Angelique closed her eyes, moaning. "This is so good," she said after her first taste of the scallops.

A shiver went down Krista's spine. The sound was earthy and raw, almost lusty. Something Krista never expected, but she liked it—she liked it a lot. She swallowed hard. "Um, it's Martha Stewart. I found it online, and now it's a go-to barbeque dish. Lemon juice, olive oil, and a little salt. It's super simple." She didn't add how she usually made it when she was trying to impress a date. That wasn't why she'd suggested it, though. Well, not really, but maybe a little.

"Do you have a record player?"

Krista cleared her throat. "Uncle Raggy keeps telling me he'll dig his out of the basement to give to me."

"You can bring them here."

"That's sweet. Maybe." She was trying not to sound too eager to spend more time with Angelique, but now she worried she sounded too unaffected. What was wrong with her? She never got anxious about first dates, not that this was a date, but she sure wished it was. Thank goodness, Angelique didn't appear to pick up on anything she was thinking.

"You're going to have to teach me how to make these scallops. They're so good. I didn't know you could make them on the grill."

"Martha Stewart pan cooks hers. But the grill is the *best* place to make them. Otherwise, they stink your whole house up."

As if they'd done it a thousand times, they talked about their day while they finished dinner and then took the dishes into the kitchen, Rupert following closely as if afraid he might be left behind. When Krista began to rinse the dishes and put them in the dishwasher, Angelique stopped her.

"I'll have my housekeeper do them in the morning." Angelique laughed. "By housekeeper, I mean me. *I* will do them in the morning."

Krista wondered why Angelique had agreed to work with her. She was lucky to have her, but being her boss was a wrinkle she didn't know how to navigate. Especially because she wanted to kiss her so badly, it was a distraction that made it hard to act normal.

With dinner finished and no dishes to help with, she was about to thank Angelique for the fun day and try to make a graceful exit, but Angelique poured herself another glass of wine.

"I haven't fired up the pit in long time. Do you want to sit out back?"

Krista was torn between not wanting to overstay her welcome and not wanting to go home to a house even quieter than usual since Alfur was in the mountains with Asta. As if sensing her dilemma, Cleo made a figure eight through her legs, and Krista reached to pick her up. The cat pushed her head under her chin and purred loudly. Cleo's loose skin had been strange the first time she'd touched her, but she'd gotten used to it. "It sounds great, actually. But are you sure? I've kinda monopolized your day."

Angelique smiled at the cat tucked into Krista's chin. "Cleo obviously wants you to stay."

"Well, it's settled." Krista said. A smile of delight flashed across Angelique's face and Krista hoped it wasn't entirely because Cleo was getting her way.

Angelique poured her another glass of wine, grabbed a lap blanket from a basket near the couch, and turned off most of the inside lights. They went out to the firepit, the centerpiece of a cozy seating area. Angelique fired it up with a flick of a switch, and the warm glow pushed back the shadows. Krista settled into the cushions with Cleo, who continued to purr under her chin. Angelique draped the blanket over her and Cleo and dropped onto the other end of the couch. "She gets cold pretty easily."

"The blanket is nice. My legs were a little chilly."

Angelique rubbed her own thighs. "Yeah. I might go in to get another."

"There's room here," Krista lifted the edge of the blanket, absolutely astounded that she found the courage and that it sounded casual, when she felt so *not* casual.

Angelique hesitated for a second, before scooting over, and Krista laid the blanket across her lap. Rupert jumped up on the cushion on the other side of Angelique and snuggled in.

"It was a big day for him. He must be exhausted," Krista said, smiling at how comfortable he looked with his head on Angelique's lap.

They watched the fire as the gas-fueled flames leapt among the pieces of decorative glass lining the bottom of the pit. Krista enjoyed the rumble of Cleo's purr against her chest as she sipped her wine. The moment was sublime in the comfortable silence.

When Cleo shifted, Krista thought she was going to get up, but the cat stood and repositioned herself, half on her and half on Angelique, wrapping her front legs around Angelique's arm, pushing her nose into her chest.

"Well, hello there, baby girl."

Angelique sounded incredulous, and Krista watched her, ready to ask her to explain, but the light from the fire made Angelique's face almost ethereal, especially with the flames dancing in her eyes, and Krista couldn't bring herself to interrupt her moment with Cleo. When a tear slid down Angelique's cheek, though, she couldn't ignore it. "Are you okay?"

With one arm held captive by Cleo, Angelique tried to wipe her face with the hand holding her glass of wine. "This is the first time Cleo has ever shown me any sort of real affection."

Krista put her glass on the table and did the same with Angelique's before leaning closer and wiping the rest of the tear and its path away. "You can't be serious."

Angelique's gaze held her eyes for a moment before she gave a small sound that wasn't quite mirth and peered at the cat. "Oh, I am. She's been aloof since I brought her home. It never really bothered me until we started spending more time together, and I expected her to warm up to me. She only ever uses me for warmth."

"What's changed, do you think?"

"Oh. Definitely me. I'm home a lot more."

"Is it possible you're more relaxed?" Krista wondered if she should have said it, but she'd happily noticed Angelique seemed more at ease in the last week, and she was learning a new job, albeit a job she said she could do in her sleep. She couldn't imagine how tightly strung Angelique had been at her high-powered corporate job.

Angelique paused and then turned back to her. "It could be. Maybe she's been tuned into my stress level, like it was an invisible electric fence or something."

Krista watched her face in the firelight, the shadows of her high cheekbones, her delicate brows, how her mouth moved as she spoke, how her eyes sparkled. She noticed her own hand resting on Angelique's shoulder, where she'd left it after wiping away her tears, how her thumb stroked the edge of the collar of her sweater, just barely moving across the skin of her collarbone. It was so quiet. They'd stopped speaking and were just staring at each other.

"Are you wondering if you should kiss me?" Angelique asked. Krista realized she was. "Should I?"

Angelique leaned in, answering the question with her warm lips and after a few seconds, her soft tongue. Krista wasn't surprised that Angelique was a good kisser, but she was surprised at how well they fit together when they kissed. She'd never put much thought into kissing before; it was just something she did with someone she desired. But she didn't simply *like* kissing Angelique, she *savored* it, taking in every sensation. It wasn't just a touch or a taste or a feeling. It was everything. It was an *experience*, and it eclipsed everything she'd ever known about kissing. First kisses were usually tentative, a slow progression of nonverbal questions and answers, usually exciting, sometimes a bit frantic, but always more of an exploration than a connection.

This? This was a union of energy, of heat, of souls from the first press of lip against lip. It spread through her, lighting her up inside. Krista took in every movement, every touch, in crucial intensity, and they hadn't moved closer except to meet each other's lips, making auras pulse brightly beneath Krista's closed eyelids.

When Cleo jumped down, they paused, breathing heavily. Krista watched the regal cat stroll into the house and disappear through the open glass door. Rupert followed but lay near the door, probably so he could keep an eye on his new mother.

Krista wondered if Angelique could sense the storm of sensations crashing through her, but she didn't need to ask; it was reflected in Angelique's eyes.

"So that's what kissing you is like," Angelique said, her voice full of wonder.

Krista would have laughed if she hadn't been thinking the same thing. "You took the words from my mouth."

Angelique nodded slowly, never breaking their gaze. "I can't describe it. I was worried that it would be difficult to navigate with the lip ring, but it wasn't. I really like it."

"Oh yeah? You don't have to be gentle," Krista said, turning so she could wrap an arm around her waist, sliding the other hand to the nape of her neck, pulling her in, pressing their bodies together, kissing her again. Angelique's arms went around her. The perception of being enveloped flooded over her. But it wasn't enough. She pulled Angelique toward her as she leaned back against the cushions, pulling Angelique on top, never breaking the kiss. The kiss became deeper, and Angelique took her at her word about not having to be gentle, ratcheting up Krista's desire.

When the weight of Angelique settled on her, she moaned, wanting more, and she slid her lips down Angelique's jaw to her neck, tracing her tongue along the skin as she went. Her body was on fire. She focused on the kiss and the press of their bodies, especially the thigh Angelique had between her legs. She wanted to grind against her, let her hands explore, but she didn't want competition for her attention to the kissing, and she knew that as soon as her hands found skin and warmth, she'd want more. A lot more.

"Can we go inside?" Angelique whispered. "I'm about two seconds away from doing something private in public."

Krista realized the houses on either side had a view into the backyard. She didn't notice anyone watching, but she was sensible enough to listen, although a small pang of disappointment threaded through her when she thought maybe Angelique wanted to stop.

"I guess I should—"

Angelique put a hand over Krista's mouth. "I don't want you to leave. I want you to stay. Can you? Stay?" Angelique's eyes searched hers. She nodded. Angelique stood and pulled her up and toward the house, turning off the firepit as she went.

Just inside, as the door lock clicked into place, Krista wrapped her arms around Angelique and kissed her. She meant the kiss to be deep and powerful, and it was, more insistent, more demanding than before. But there was something else. A need. She sensed it surging through both of them. The length of Angelique's body pressed against her spread heat through her from head to toe. Angelique returned the kiss with her own demands and insistence and passion, telling Krista that what was about to happen was inevitable and would likely consume them both. She was ready for it.

Seeming out of breath, Angelique swiftly led Krista through the living room, down the hall, to open double doors. Krista sensed the largeness of the room but didn't care about anything except Angelique and getting them to the huge bed piled high with comforters and pillows, which was as soft as it looked when they both fell onto it. They rolled into one another, hands searching, bodies rubbing, lips tasting.

Without breaking the kiss, Krista hooked an arm around Angelique, rolling on top, and as she did it, she pulled the Rockies jacket, her T-shirt, and her sports bra over her head, barely pausing their kiss. The cool air of the bedroom made her nipples rise, and she focused on Angelique's clothes, peeling off her sweater and unbuttoning her top. With the buttons undone, Krista kissed the mounds of skin quivering above the cups of Angelique's bra.

Angelique wrapped a leg around Krista and with a surge of her hips, levered on top. Surprised and more than a little turned-on, Krista lay on her back with Angelique astride her. The heat between Angelique's legs penetrated her. Angelique pulled her top off and reached to undo her bra, and after Krista helped slide it down her arms, she beheld Angelique's unbound breasts. Her mouth watered to taste her dark nipples, her lips craving the soft warmth between them. As if reading her mind, Angelique leaned forward, moaning when Krista took the tip of one rigid nipple into her mouth, sucking softly at first and then a little harder. Krista cupped the other, enjoying the soft heaviness in her palm and the impossibly soft skin against her fingertips. Her sex pulsed, and she reached to slide her shorts and underwear down, finishing disrobing with a couple of kicks.

Angelique lifted her hips. "Take mine off, too."

Krista did as she was told, first with her hands, then using her feet. With Angelique completely naked above her, Krista wrapped her arms around her torso, pulling her close, and kissed her, relishing the unimpeded contact of skin between them, the interlacing of their legs bringing them even closer together.

Krista rolled over to be on top and pushed herself up on her elbows above Angelique, who looked as though she was trying to suppress laughter. When Krista cocked an eyebrow, Angelique let the laugher go. "I'm not surprised we're both used to leading when it comes to this." She peered between them, making Krista look, too. She took in how their breasts were pressed together, their chests heaving. It took her breath away, and she couldn't help but shimmy, enjoying their skin sliding between them.

"I won't lie. I'm usually pretty direct in bed. Will it be a problem?" Krista said, kissing Angelique's neck, then propping herself up to gaze into those beautiful eyes again. They smoldered, ratcheting up Krista's desire.

"Let's put it this way, I normally lead when I'm on the dance floor, but if my partner is a strong lead, I can follow."

"I'm pretty strong," Krista said, finding Angelique's wrists and holding them. Angelique sucked in a breath, tensing. Krista kissed the inside of each wrist before letting go. Angelique remained tense. "But I can let go, too."

Angelique slid a hand between them, and Krista hissed as a finger slid through her wet folds. The finger paused over her clit, hovering, not quite touching, the heat telegraphing its nearness. Krista waited for the pressure, but it didn't come. Instead, with the mere suggestion, she swelled like a balloon, ready to pop, as if there was a current flowing over her most sensitive skin. She fought the urge to bear down on Angelique's hand. She'd come instantly, but she was pretty sure Angelique could spin her up for a second round with little effort. She stared into Angelique's eyes, her breath hitching, letting the current build between Angelique's finger and her clit, pulses rolling through her body, not yet an orgasm but very, very close. She silently urged her hips to remain still, even though she wanted desperately to rock them. It was an eternity, the stillness, her body filling to the absolute limits with Angelique's power.

Angelique reversed the trail of her finger through Krista's now wetter folds and slowly withdrew her hand, caressing Krista's torso as she did. Krista wondered how she knew how to keep her on the edge. All she had to do was remove her finger or apply even the slightest pressure to make Krista cry out in frustration or writhe with release. Instead, she was aching for Angelique, wanting to explore every inch of her, needing to inflame her to the heights where Krista currently hovered.

"How do I find out what you like?" Angelique said, sliding the finger into her mouth. A pulse beat along Krista's clit.

"Everything. I'm open to almost anything as long as you enjoy it, too," Krista said, barely able to breathe.

"I could feel how open you are." Angelique smiled and sucked her finger. "I'm the same. I'll let you know if I'm uncomfortable with anything. Gently. There's one thing I want very badly, though."

"Anything. I'll do anything."

"I want you inside me when I come the first time, and I want to come fast."

Krista was glad Angelique wasn't touching her then, or she would have come, and she wanted it to last. As it was, a wave of pure energy rolled through her, and she did exactly what Angelique wanted.

CHAPTER TWENTY-THREE

A ng slowed her bike and swung her leg over the seat, careful not to kick Rupert, who was sitting patiently in the carrier Krista had installed on the back. He was strapped in, but she was pretty sure it wasn't required. He was such a chill dog. All the time they'd spent over the weekend had only reinforced what a good dog he was.

As she unharnessed him, she thought about Krista and smiled. Despite the absolute rightness of asking Krista to stay the night, once she'd left on Sunday, Ang had gone back and forth about it. Was it wrong to sleep with her employer, even if the job was short-term? Mostly, though, she thought about how good it had felt. She wondered how all day at work without touching Krista was going to be. A thrill of anticipation warmed her from the inside. In a few different places.

Her phone rang, and she tapped her earbud to answer.

"I'm running a little late this morning," Krista said after they exchanged greetings. "I stayed up late working on the books and forgot to set my alarm. *Someone* kept me up this weekend, and I slept longer than I normally would." Krista's voice definitely had a teasing tone, and it made Ang's stomach flutter. "Would you mind opening and setting up the outside display for me today? I'll be there in about an hour."

Ang smiled at the reminder of their night together, and her body warmed in response. "Take your time, boss. I'm already here.

I left early to make sure Rupert was comfortable on the ride in. I've got it covered. See you when you get here." Ang worried that she wouldn't be able to keep her desire for Krista to herself and then she wondered how Krista felt. The same? Had she been on Krista's mind since their first touch, too? How could she ask without sounding needy?

"Hey, I just wanted to ask, um, are you okay with, um, this weekend?" Krista asked.

The question surprised her. She thought she'd been very obvious in her enjoyment. Multiple times. "I'm more than okay, actually," Ang said and listened to Krista let go of a breath. She smiled. She wasn't the only one overthinking the weekend. "How are you?"

The pause after the question made her anxious. Was Krista regretting their night together? But she finally answered. "The same. I want a lot more of it, in fact." There was another pause, but this time, Ang was too titillated to let any worry slip in. "Which is new for me. I don't date a lot. But I want to date *you* a lot."

"I find that difficult to believe," Ang said, wondering if it was a line.

"What? That I want to date you?"

"Not so much that part, but now that you ask, yes, a little. But more about the *not* dating a lot."

"It's true. Commitment eludes me."

This was a very unusual conversation. In fact, it was usually her talking about applying the brakes. "Then you're lucky. I don't usually get married after the first orgasm...or three, in this case. So how about we just take it one day at a time? See where it takes us?"

"That sounds perfect." There was a smile in her voice. "How'd Rupert do on the ride in? I can't wait for Alfur to meet him."

Ang smiled. She smiled a lot when it came to Krista. She had also bonded with Rupert over the weekend, which just made Ang adore her even more. Everything about Krista was making her adore her more, which seemed almost impossible until it kept happening. She was definitely in trouble. "Great. We did a practice run through the park yesterday after you left, and then we fired up the barbeque again afterward and played a little ball in the backyard." She didn't mention that she would have biked to Krista's house if she knew where she lived.

"With your backyard, I wouldn't blame you. I'd spend all of my time out there. Especially if you were with me."

Warmth spread through Ang's chest. "Well, having been introduced to the wonder of the perfect char, I might never cook indoors again. Although, I appreciate it more when beautiful women are doing the cooking for me. And just in case you're wondering, I mean you when I say beautiful women."

"Oh, that was smooth." Krista laughed. "You can continue to demonstrate your appreciation with future invitations to cook for you. I will happily be of service."

She loved the idea of Krista servicing her. As well as the other way around. "You just want to spend time with Rupert and Cleo, admit it," she teased.

"Is it obvious?"

Ang snorted. "Please. I felt like I was intruding on your lovefest with them earlier."

"What can I say? Dudes and chicks dig me."

"Well, this chick does, and she has to set up cycles. Be safe on the way in. I can't wait to introduce Rupert to Alfur." She couldn't wait to steal a few kisses, too. It would be hard to keep her hands to herself after they'd stayed up all Saturday night learning how each of them liked to be touched. Ang had even learned some interesting things about herself, such as how much she liked letting someone else set the pace once in a while. When she'd learned that Krista was just as much of a leader as she was, she'd said she could let go only because she'd wanted Krista so badly. She hadn't been sure she could actually do it. But Krista had shown her how good it felt to let someone else take over once in a while. Just thinking about it made her wet again.

They ended the call, and Ang, just a little distracted, went to work moving the bikes out front. She was almost finished when Swifty strolled through the front doors. She introduced Rupert to him.

He looked confused to see her. "You're here early," he said to her, petting Rupert.

"I left earlier and got in faster than I thought I would."

"I promised a friend I'd meet him to pick up his bike this morning." He glanced around. "Where's Krista?"

"She's running late. She'll be here in about forty-five minutes."

"Good. Good," he said distractedly and went back to the maintenance area, coming out with a bike. It looked like one of the high-end road bikes from last week that they'd returned. Ang had almost bought one herself until she'd seen the price. Even with an employee discount, they were pricey. She could afford one, but she'd decided to be more conscious about spending until she figured out her job situation. With her current ambivalence, it could take a while to find the right fit, whatever path she decided to take. She thought she'd be more worried about it than she was. Krista was the reason for that. She was a good distraction.

"Special order?" she said.

He scratched the back of his neck and studied the bike. "Um, just a repair. My friend who brought it in is out front. I'll be back for my shift."

He left, and Ang shook her head with a chuckle. After the confrontation last week, they had repaired the rift, but he usually kept to himself in the mornings and was generally easygoing by early afternoon. Some people were just not morning people.

Ang rolled the last display bike out and was locking it to the others when Alfur came running around the corner of the building, dragging his leash behind him. Krista must have been close behind, and butterflies lifted off in Ang's stomach.

"Hey, buddy," she said, bending to pet him. Rupert was inside the store and Ang wanted to introduce them but watched the corner for Krista. A few seconds passed, and Krista didn't appear. "Weird. Did your mom send you ahead?"

Alfur took a few steps backward before dashing back around the corner. He didn't even acknowledge Rupert, who was pressed to the inside of the glass door. Krista had to be very close. Ang laughed and went into the store. She expected Krista and Alfur to follow, but they didn't.

Strange. She stepped outside to wait. As if her thoughts conjured him, Alfur rounded the corner again, but still no Krista, and when she peered around the corner, Krista wasn't in sight

She turned to Alfur, who was staring at her, prancing in place, still ignoring a curious but patient Rupert, who was tentatively sniffing him. Alfur loved meeting new dogs at the shop. He was always well-behaved, but he was always interested. This was not right.

"Where's your mama, bud?"

He gave a short bark, causing her and Rupert to jump. Another thing unlike him. He nosed her leg and then took off down the street again. A weird foreboding filled Ang's gut. She locked the store, and she and Rupert went to find Alfur.

An ambulance turned the corner behind them and sped down the street, turning left at the intersection. The sense of foreboding in her gut turned to dread. She began to run, and Alfur appeared again from the direction the ambulance turned and then ran away. When Ang rounded the next corner, a discordance of flashing lights overwhelmed her. A small crowd was gathered near them, and Alfur dashed into it.

Ang ran toward him, scanning the area for Krista, and just as she came parallel with the ambulance, the scene stopped her in her tracks. Krista's bike lay in the street amid a small scattering of plastic and glass, and while she couldn't see the person lying on the pavement, she recognized the shoes. Without thinking, she pushed past the crowd to the side of the paramedics.

Krista wasn't okay. All the blood.

"Stand back! Stand back," an officer shouted. Ang shrugged away from grabbing hands. She knelt next to Krista, ignoring the rough gravel on her bare knees.

"I know her. Please tell me she's okay. What happened?" The officer took hold of her arm, pulling her up, making her step back. She tried to pull away, but the cop held on. "I need to stay with her."

"You need to let the paramedics do their job," the officer said.

The officer didn't pull her far away, just a foot or so, giving the emergency crew room to work. Ang repressed the urge to vomit. She swallowed hard. Blood pooled under Krista, and her body was twisted grotesquely. Her leg bent in an awkward angle and, worst of all, she wasn't responding. Her eyes were half-closed, and her head rolled to the side as one paramedic applied pressure to a blood-soaked patch of Krista's shorts, and the other paramedic worked to stabilize her neck. One arm lay extended, and Alfur whined, pressing his muzzle into her palm.

This was not happening. Ang felt as if the whole scene had been staged, that it wasn't real. But it was. Krista was on the ground. The paramedics were pushing Alfur away. She tried to pull from the officer's grip. "Is she okay? Is she okay?"

"The paramedics are working hard. We have to give them room."

Ang was hardly aware of the tug on her arm while she watched the pool of blood spread. Rupert whined, straining against the leash, sniffing at Krista's foot. Voices were speaking all around her. The officer pulled her back, and Rupert pulled her forward, keeping her in place until one of the paramedics pushed the dog back, and Ang struggled to keep her footing when the tension in the leash eased. They loaded Krista onto a flat stretcher. Everything was moving so quickly.

"Where are they taking her?" Ang asked, finally yanking away, scrambling for Alfur's leash. He was trying to get into the ambulance. She finally caught him, yanking him back, wishing she didn't have to be so rough with him when all they both wanted was Krista.

"Central." The officer moved her toward the sidewalk.

Alfur whined, pulling his leash from her hand as the paramedics finished loading Krista into the ambulance. Ang couldn't stand it. She pulled free again. "Alfur!" The officer grabbed at her, and Ang spun on him. "For fuck's sake, get your hands off me! Let me get her dog, goddamnit. Come here, Alfur."

She got to the back of the ambulance as the paramedics were shutting the doors. The medic closing the door stumbled over Alfur, who was on his back legs.

"God. I'm sorry," Ang said. "He's just worried about his mom."

"You know the victim?" the paramedic asked.

"Yes. Her name is Krista. She's my friend."

The paramedic handed her a phone. She struggled to take it with one hand on Alfur's collar and the other holding Rupert's leash. The tinny sound of music came from the still-attached headphones.

"Can you notify her family? She'll be at Central."

The paramedic rushed around to the driver's side of the ambulance. Seconds later, the vehicle sped away, sirens blaring. When it was gone, the scene fell eerily quiet, and Ang stared at the empty space the ambulance had left. The crowd dispersed. Everything around her receded as she stood near the empty intersection flanked by small houses. When she glanced toward where Krista had been, there was a glistening pool of blood, more blood than…

Her stomach lurched; bile filled her mouth. She turned away and spit it into the gutter.

"Ma'am?" Ang registered the officer's voice but didn't react, concentrating on not vomiting.

The blood was so dark. "There's so much."

"The remediation team will take care of it when we release the scene."

Ang's own blood rushed in her ears. They'd just taken Krista away in an ambulance, and people needed to know. Her family. She needed to tell her family.

A hand rested on her shoulder. "Ma'am? Do you want to sit down?"

"I need to get back to the store. Call her family."

"I can help you, but first, can I ask a few questions?"

Ang turned toward the officer, trying not to gape at the blood again. He was so young. Alfur and Rupert pressed against her legs.

She nodded, staring. "But what happened?"

The officer gestured toward the dented car. "Vehicle versus bicycle. As far as we can tell, and based on the driver's story, the victim was riding her bicycle northbound when a vehicle, also moving north, struck her, causing her to strike another vehicle parked at the curb."

Several officers continued to assess the scene. A young man leaned against a late-model car, running his hands through his hair while he spoke to one of them. Ang wondered if he was the driver.

She took in the scene again, feeling a sense of numbness wash over her, praying she wouldn't vomit again. None of it made sense. Krista's bike was lying a few feet away. A broken side mirror of a dented car with the same color paint rested on the asphalt next to the bike.

"Is she going to be okay?" she asked, terrified of the answer.

"That's a question for the emergency room docs." The officer took out a small notebook. "I'd like to ask you few questions, starting with the victim's name."

"Krista Ólafsdóttir."

"Spell the last name?"

She did.

"Age?"

"Twenty-seven."

"Address?"

Ang couldn't answer that or next of kin, except for Asta's and Uncle Raggy's first names. In fact, she couldn't answer any questions. She invited the officer to come to the shop with the hope of finding the information there.

Swifty looked spooked when the police arrived, but she turned their questions to him. He provided the information and helped them contact Krista's sister and parents. She wanted to go to the hospital, but a steady stream of people began flowing into the shop, some of them customers, but most of them were from the neighborhood. Word had spread quickly about the accident. Every time she considered closing the store, more people came in. All of them knew Krista, and no one knew of their recent...

Their recent what? Would she ever find out what they had together? Would Krista be okay? She couldn't think about the alternatives. Numbly, she took care of the customers along with Magnus and Kayla, answering questions as best she could, even though she knew nothing. Everyone was shocked and dazed.

The hours crawled by.

Swifty stayed in contact with Asta, and he relayed information as it finally came in. Each update came with the same statement: they'd have to wait and see. Ang had never felt so useless, so scared, so alone. She wanted to call Kat and Geri, but she hadn't told them about her and Krista yet. People were all around her, but they knew nothing about her and Krista, and she had no one to turn to. So she did what she did best, she worked as she waited.

CHAPTER TWENTY-FOUR

"A nything new from Krista's family?" Ang asked, leaning heavily on the maintenance counter.

Swifty shook his head. "Nothing since they took her into surgery. Asta said she'd keep us posted. She knows everyone here is anxious about her."

Ang glanced at her watch. In the last update, Krista's sister had informed them that the main concern was managing arterial bleeding from the hip, and they'd taken Krista into emergency surgery. But that had been a couple of hours ago, and she was worried. She wanted to do something, to go somewhere, to be useful. Yet, it was her responsibility to stay at the store and keep it running. It was what she thought Krista would have wanted.

"I was thinking about sending one of those fruit sculpture things or something to the hospital. What do you think?" Swifty asked after a customer dropped off a bike. He picked at one of his fingernails.

"I think she'd love it but probably in a day or two when she can enjoy it?" Ang said, holding back tears because she desperately wanted to see Krista, to make sure she was okay. She hated not being at the hospital with her and being so removed from what was going on that she wanted to fly out of her skin. It was jarring and terrible to have been slowly forming a connection and finally being so close over the weekend just to be left on the periphery during such a traumatic time. It wasn't as if she could just blurt out how things were with them now, though, or that she needed to be included in... what? She didn't have a clue.

Swifty scratched his neck. "Yeah. She's probably out of it, huh? Maybe some flowers then? I'm terrible with this stuff." His response brought Ang back to the moment.

"Yeah. Flowers would probably be good." Truthfully, she thought the idea of sending flowers to a hospital was a weird custom. There was never enough room for them, and they always got in the way. But it was finally something she could do to take her mind from the interminable waiting. While Swifty asked each of the associates if they wanted to chip in, she focused on picking out an arrangement. It was something she would have asked Ann to do at Lithium, but she wanted to do it, and by the time she was done, another half hour had passed, and she was back to waiting, keeping her internal turmoil to herself.

"You look miserable. Why don't you just go home and hang out there?" Swifty said, catching her sitting at the computer with her arms wrapped around herself and gazing into space.

"I think I'd go crazier there, to be honest."

No one at the shop was able to concentrate, but no one wanted to leave because Krista's sister was their link to staying updated. Alfur stayed by her side, as did Rupert. At times, it was hard to have the two dogs crowding her, but mostly, they provided comfort.

Finally, it was time to close the store. Ang was headed toward her bike when she realized there were two dogs to manage, and then it dawned on her, Alfur needed someone to take care of him until Krista got out of the hospital. In a weird way, being able to take care of him made her feel closer to Krista. It gave her a purpose that she found she needed. She left her bike at the store and called a ride to take them home. On the way, she checked the visiting hours at Central and found she could drop the dogs off at home and get there shortly before they ended.

❖

The *whoosh* of the revolving door into Denver Central Hospital blew warm air over Ang when she stepped in. The chill from the short walk from the parking lot made her wish she'd changed from the shorts she'd worn to work, but the inside temperature of the hospital was comfortable. A quick check at the front desk pointed her to the orthopedics floor, and when she arrived at the nursing station, the charge nurse directed her to Krista's room. She wondered if this floor was cooler than the lobby because she was suddenly freezing. Or maybe it was nerves, the closer she got to seeing Krista. She was afraid of what she'd find.

The door was open when she neared the room, the low sounds of a television spilling into the hallway. She poked her head in. The room was dimly lit, the overhead lights off, with only the flickering blue light from the television and the indirect lighting above the headboards. An elderly woman with a corona of wispy white hair was lying in the bed closest to the door and glanced at her before directing her eyes back to a game show. The curtain was drawn between the beds. Ang stood there, uncertain. The pool of blood flashed through her mind.

"You might as well come in. The rest of the Swedish bobsled team just left, including the sasquatch-looking fellow. Thank goodness. He bellows every word he says. She's on the other side." The woman in the other bed motioned to the curtain without breaking her gaze from the television.

Feeling like an intruder, she tentatively entered, finding a woman who bore an uncanny likeness to Krista sitting in a chair next to the bed and scrolling through her phone. She looked younger, so Ang figured it was Asta. She might have left if Krista hadn't lifted her hand, drawing Ang's attention to the bed.

"You finally came." Krista's voice was groggy, but her smile was a good sign. She wiggled her fingers as if indicating she wanted Ang to hold her hand, and Ang moved to the side of the bed to take it. She wouldn't have guessed Krista had been in an accident, except for a scrape on her chin.

"I came as soon as I could," Ang said, finding it hard to make her mouth work because she'd been clenching her jaw.

Krista squinted, appearing to have difficulty focusing, but then she smiled. "I knew you would."

"I hope it's not too late. I just wanted to, um…" An overwhelming urge to cry swept through Ang, and she held up the small stuffed animal she'd picked up in the hospital gift shop on the way up. It was a sheepdog because they didn't have any resembling Alfur. She smiled, but tears slid down her cheeks. All she could think about was Krista's twisted and motionless body lying in the road in a pool of blood.

"I'm Asta. Krista's sister." Her eyes looked bruised, as if she'd been crying, but she stood and offered a box of tissues. "You must be Angelique?"

"Yep," Krista said with her eyes closed. Ang choked back a sob; she was so relieved at the sound of her voice, even as drugged up as Krista must be. "A glorious name. Angelique. Angelique. Angelique. It just rolls from your mouth. It's so nice."

The words were slurred, and Ang laughed as she wiped her nose. She looked at Asta with a shrug. Her throat was tight. She couldn't speak.

"She's still a bit out of it from the second surgery."

"Second surgery?" Ang managed to say.

"She's only been back in the room for an hour. The first surgery was to repair the damage to the femoral artery, but it started to seep again, so they took her back in and found another small tear they'd missed. She'd already lost so much blood. The doctor said if the accident had happened at rush hour, she might not have made it because she was minutes from bleeding out. All these years being a blood donor finally paid off, right, Krissy?"

Krista nodded almost imperceptibly. Her eyes were closed, and she mumbled something incomprehensible.

Ang couldn't help it. She envisioned the pool of blood again. There was so much. The memory haunted her thoughts, and she knew it would replay in her dreams along with the thoughts of how they'd nearly lost what they'd only just begun. How could she go on without finding out what they could have together? "How's…how's everything else?"

"Thankfully, her pelvis and hip are intact. Badly bruised, but there's no fracture. Krista's talked about you before, but she's been asking for you constantly since she got out of surgery. Swifty said you witnessed the accident?"

Ang tried to focus on the good news about the extent of the injuries, and her heart beat a little harder about Krista asking for her, but the pool of blood in her mind wouldn't go away. She cleared her throat. "I arrived there after the ambulance arrived. The paramedics were already—" Her voice cracked, and she cleared her throat again. "They were helping her. Alfur came to the shop alone and, um, he—"

"Alfur. Where's he? I can't move my legs with the squeezy things on them." Krista made a motion to sit up, and Asta put her hand in the middle of her chest to keep her from moving.

"Be still, Krissy. The things on your lower legs are to help with circulation."

"I have to find Alfur."

Ang squeezed Krista's hand. "He's fine. He's at my house. I took him home. He's keeping Rupert company."

Krista settled and returned Ang's hand squeeze. Her glossy eyes locked on Ang's. "You have him? How does a dog mom lose her dog kid? I did. But you fixed it. You found him."

"I'm sure the police would have kept him safe."

"But he would have been so scared." Krista's expression revealed what she must have looked like as a child, and tears welled in Ang's eyes again.

"He misses you, but he's fine," she said.

"You said Alfur came to the shop?" Asta said.

Ang nodded. "I thought maybe Krista let him run ahead, but when she wasn't right behind him and he ran back the way he came, I followed and…and she was only a block away."

"My good boy. He was watching out for me," Krista said. Her eyes were half-closed, and she seemed calmer now. "He held my hand when I was trying to stay awake."

Asta looked at her sister. "I can come get him tonight if you want. He's going to hate staying at my apartment, but I can probably take him to our parents' house tomorrow. You just missed them. Uncle Raggy and they left right before you got here."

Ang wiped her nose. "It's been a long day for you. I can keep Alfur tonight or as long as you need me to. He and Rupert have sort of bonded, I think."

"I knew they would love each other," Krista murmured. Her eyes were completely closed now. Asta watched her with an affectionate expression as Krista's chest rose up and down with a slower cadence.

Ang wanted to cry again watching them. She was a mess.

"I swear. She loves that dog more than life." Asta swung her eyes back to Ang and eyed her up and down before she pointed at her clothes. "You look cute in that, by the way. You and Krista can pull it off. You're both like REI models. I just come off like I'm playing dress-up when I wear those kinds of clothes."

Ang wanted to argue because Asta looked like a hipster, appearing comfortable in what appeared to be hemp or bamboo clothing, dangly beaded bracelets, and a large-brimmed hat. For once, Ang didn't feel like a stuffy corporate type in the formfitting T-shirt and long shorts she was wearing. They were some of the clothes Krista had given her. "I offered to pay her for them. She wouldn't let me. I'd love to pay you."

Asta waved her hand dismissively. "I closed down the online store months ago, and I already wrote it all off. We're good."

"Well, thanks." Still holding Krista's hand, she faced the little sheepdog toward Krista on the tray spanning the bed and then studied her watch. She didn't want to go. She wanted to curl up next to Krista in the bed, but she felt like she was intruding. "I guess I should leave now. Visiting hours are over."

Asta flapped a hand, beads clicking. "They already told us they don't kick family out as long as they're quiet and don't bother the other patients."

Ang was about to argue that she wasn't really family when the gravelly voice of the woman in the next bed piped up over the low sound of the television. "You can stay if you get me another cookie."

Asta covered her smile with a hand and moved around the bed. "Thanks, Mrs. Galveston. I'll get it for you." She turned to Ang. "Sit down. I'll get the cookie and take a quick bio-break."

With that, she was gone, and Ang was alone with Krista, who was now sleeping. Before she sat, she pushed the tray spanning the bed to the side, green Jell-O wiggling in a small container, uneaten and glistening. Krista stirred, squeezing Ang's hand. She hadn't even opened her eyes. After a moment, Krista still hadn't let go, so Ang hooked the chair leg with her foot, pulling it closer to the bed so she could sit.

"I hoped you'd come," Krista mumbled, her eyes still closed.

"I wanted to come earlier." Ang squeezed her hand, watching her. It was almost too intimate, her stare. But she couldn't help it. She was so beautiful, even in the hospital after two surgeries. Ang wanted to memorize her. She'd nearly lost her. Tears spilled down her cheeks again.

Krista smiled in her sleep, and Ang watched the corners of her mouth curl up. She was always so quick to smile. "Do you remember the park?" Krista's lips moved, but her voice was so quiet, Ang wondered if she'd even spoken at first. "You were so pretty," Krista said. Her eyes opened, soft and unfocused. "Even prettier up close. I was so nervous."

Heat rose up Ang's neck. "Those are the drugs talking."

"Really. You're so pretty. But you're all business. It's frustrating."

"I'm sorry." They were the words of so many past girlfriends. None of them had made her feel the way she felt about Krista, but it had still hurt to hear them, especially now from Krista, too. She vowed to change.

Krista weakly squeezed her hand. "Don't be sorry, beautiful. It's okay."

"I'll try not to talk so much business."

"It's okay. It's kinda hot." This was a different Krista, a totally unreserved Krista, whose filters were muted by pain medication.

Ang was amused and a little surprised.

Krista shifted a little, and a grimace replaced the lazy smile.

"Are you okay? Do you need anything?" Ang asked.

"You're all I need."

It was the drugs, but she liked the sound of it even if she didn't know how to reply. Ang felt like she was peeking into a private place inside Krista's mind. It made her heart swell to hear the words, but she wondered if Krista would be embarrassed if she heard herself while sober.

"Know what the last thing I remember is? Hurrying up to get ready for work. I couldn't wait to see you."

"Are you sure it wasn't your new boyfriend Rupert you were missing?" She couldn't help teasing.

"Oh, Rupert. I love him. I'm so glad you got him. He's gonna be good for you." Ang was relieved for the slight change of the topic, but it wasn't for long. "I was excited for him, too, but it was mostly you. I always love going to work, but I like it a lot more since you're there. I'm so tired. I'm just gonna rest my eyes, 'kay? Don't go, though. Promise?"

"I promise." Ang stared at their hands and ran her thumb across Krista's knuckles, feeling better having talked to Krista, even if she was sky-high.

"How long have you two been dating?"

Ang jumped and tried to slip her hand away, but Krista held on, even in her sleep. She hadn't noticed Asta come back. Krista's eyes were closed again, but the little smile remained. "We aren't dating."

"Could have fooled me. She likes you. She may be stoned, but I can tell when she likes someone. It doesn't happen often. In fact, it doesn't happen at all. I tease her about her commitment issues all the time. Looks like she's gotten over them."

Being told Krista didn't get involved made Ang happier than she had any right to be; maybe she was special in that regard. Still, they'd just…what? Had sex? True, but there was more to it than that. They'd danced around it just that morning. There was something more than sex between them, something they wanted to explore, but in the meantime, they were in this limbo state of not knowing what might happen. She wondered how much of this conversation was being absorbed by Krista. "She's my boss."

"Temporarily. She told me about how you're helping her out. I assume you like her, too, based on you being a high-powered executive and all. I mean, why would you agree to work in a bike shop otherwise?"

Ang asked herself the same question—again. This time, she found she agreed with Asta. She wasn't just filling the time until she decided what she wanted to do next. It was because of Krista. She enjoyed hanging out with her. She liked the coziness of the shop. She liked the excited customers. She'd never have guessed she'd be in this place in her life just a few weeks earlier. In fact, she'd thought she knew exactly where she'd be: flying all over the United States visiting the retail stores of Lithium. There would have been no cuddles from Cleo. No Rupert. No bike rides. No Krista.

"Did I get too personal?"

The question brought Ang out of her head, and she sat up straighter. "Not at all. I'm sorry. I was just thinking."

"It's me who's sorry. I have a habit of trying to get into people's heads. Did Krista tell you I was going back to school to become a therapist? I've always been nosey. But I'm good with people, and I love to help them, so I figured, why not?"

"She mentioned you'd gone back to school. She's really proud of you."

"She's proud of *me*? She qualified for the Olympic biking team. Did she tell you?" Asta rubbed Krista's blanket-covered leg, looking so proud of her sister. Ang shook her head. "Well, the crash at the race for the summit happened, so she doesn't bring it up much. She's never been one to brag. I'd tell everyone who would listen. She would have won, too."

"The race for the summit?" Ang asked.

"The summit race, yes, but I was talking about the Olympic gold medal. The times of the winners weren't even close to Krista's on basically the same course. She'd have set records if she'd competed." Asta squinted at her. "You sure you don't want me to pick up Alfur?"

"I'm sure. I can keep him as long as it takes." Ang wasn't just being nice. She liked having an important part of Krista's life close to her.

Asta seemed relieved. "I would have had to take him to my parents' house, anyway. They have these two Pomeranians who just bully him. They're tiny monsters to him, and he's so patient with them, but you can tell he's miserable when they gang up on him. I'd keep him at my place, but I live in a tiny apartment, and I'm never home. He'd hate it there. I love him, though. I'd move if I needed to take him in, you know if…" She shook her hands in front of her as if she couldn't stand to think of the alternative. "But it didn't happen." She blew out a breath. "Anyway, are you sure?"

"Absolutely. I can bring him into work with me every day. Keep his routine as normal as possible. Besides, Rupert loves him."

"Rupert?"

"My dog. Krista helped me pick him out at the shelter."

"Oh. Okay. For a second, I thought you meant a boyfriend, but you and Krista seemed like you were…anyway…well, then." She stood straighter and smiled. "Yes, it would be great if you can keep him. Do you have keys to Krista's place so you can go get his bed and stuff?"

Ang didn't, and Asta said she'd drop it off at the shop the next day. "Oh, speaking of the shop, is there a certain place she keeps her passwords? I have to get into the accounting software to work with inventory. She told me she was going to hand it over to me this week, but, well…" She glanced at Krista sleeping in the bed. "This happened. I suppose I could get it from Swifty."

"I don't have a clue about anything that goes on at the shop, but her passwords are always the same." Asta gave her a phrase that matched the one for the employee schedule. "If it's not that, I can't help."

She'd promised to stay, and if she didn't have both dogs at home, she probably would have. But when the night nurse came to check on Krista and told them she'd probably sleep all night due to the lingering effects of the anesthesia and sedatives the surgeon had prescribed to keep her from moving around, they decided to leave. Drained to nearly zero as she drove home, Ang was relieved Krista was supposed to make a full recovery, although she'd have a long rehabilitation because of her badly bruised pelvis.

Ang hadn't allowed herself to wonder how things would go with Krista after their night together, and now it was impossible to predict. All she knew was that Krista would require time to get better, and it meant Ang would have to run the store, which she would gladly do. Her biggest strength was crisis management. Besides, it was a good excuse not to start searching for a new job. She was surprised at what a relief that was. She seriously didn't know if she wanted to go back to a career where she'd have to continue to work so hard to just exist as herself. It was bad for the soul.

CHAPTER TWENTY-FIVE

The next morning, Ang arrived at the store early again. She was dragging after a series of bad dreams. No mystery there; they were about Krista. Both Cleo and Rupert slept pressed up against her, Rupert against her back and Cleo against her front, as if they sensed her mood. More subdued than any of the others, Alfur took up the foot of the bed. Once they were close to her, she fell into a deep and dreamless sleep. They woke up to the alarm that came too soon in almost the same position they'd fallen asleep in.

Again, because there was the matter of both dogs to transport, she drove to work, which landed her there earlier than usual, so she didn't start setting up the sidewalk display. Instead, they went into the back to start their day by making a pot of coffee, a requirement if she was expected to function. When the two dogs curled up on Alfur's bed, she was just a little bit jealous.

As she waited for the coffee to brew in the shop's ancient and low-tech Mr. Coffee, which made a surprisingly good cup, she noticed a row of boxes standing near the back door, indicating a delivery had come in after-hours. A wave of appreciation flowed over her for Swifty, who made sure business continued even in light of Krista's accident. She was lucky to have him.

Scanning the bill of lading lying atop the boxes, she was pleased the bikes she'd put on order for customers were already in, as well as a few more of the Cannondales and Treks she'd noticed were fast sellers in the few short weeks she'd been working at the store. Things were clicking into place for her, and she was happy she was getting a better understanding for what the customers were into, which reminded her she wanted to pull a report to check out the inventory and sales records to get a better idea of trends.

When she approached the desk, she noticed a zippered sweatshirt draped on the back of Krista's chair. She looked around to make sure no one was around and picked it up, burying her face in it, breathing in the scent of Krista. Warmth filled her chest, and she was transported to her night with her. Only three days ago, it had started to feel like weeks. Instead of putting the sweatshirt back, she slipped it on.

The password Asta had suggested worked, and as she pulled up the sales and inventory software, she felt just a little guilty for snooping in the system before Krista officially gave her access. But no one anticipated Krista getting in an accident, and there was work to get done, and Ang figured she could get focused on some helpful process optimization to surprise Krista when she felt better.

When the software opened, she found it very similar to systems she'd used in the past, so it was fairly easy to navigate, and she was able to send the inventory and sales lists to her email so she could do analysis when she was home. She'd have little free time to do it at the shop when it opened. While she was in there, she noticed a couple of reconciliation error messages, and she decided she'd get to those after she got a cup of coffee.

Stirring sweetener into the cup, she leaned against the counter. A sudden memory of Krista hovering above her in bed made heat rise up her neck, but just as quickly, a memory of Krista lying on the pavement in a puddle of blood replaced it. The contrast was chilling. She wasn't sure what she'd be doing now if she hadn't been able to talk to Krista the night before. But even drugged-up and groggy, Krista had been Krista, and Ang knew she'd be fine once she healed. She took a moment to be grateful the accident hadn't been worse. With a sigh, she pushed away from the counter. It was time to open the store.

Ang was rolling the first bike out when Swifty showed up. He looked like she felt, tired and worried. Both the dogs came from the back to greet him, and with a faint smile, he bent to give them scratches.

"Nothing can lift a spirit like the love of a dog," he said, and she liked him more for it.

"How's Dirk doing today?"

"Cranky but getting stronger. The doctor thinks he can give him his last infusion on Thursday, which means he'll probably get to come home next week."

"Wonderful. I'll bet you'll be relieved to have him home."

"Not as much as he'll be. But it'll be nice."

"Anything from Asta this morning?"

He shook his head and began to help her set up. "I guess no news is good news."

"Krista was really out of it, but I got to talk to her a little when I visited last night," she said. "It sounds like she'll be fine."

He nodded as he stood a bike in its stand. "I think so, too. I swung by after I left Dirk. I snuck up after visiting hours. She was sleeping."

"I know she'll be disappointed she missed you. Do you suppose you could give me Asta's phone number? I'm keeping Alfur."

He sent the number to her via text and was headed toward the back when he paused. "We're going to need access to the inventory system to input the stuff from last night."

"You don't have it?"

He shook his head. "Krista recently migrated to a new one, and she hasn't given it to me yet. I usually handle inventory, but she was ironing out a few bugs before she gave it back to me."

Ang sent him the password, which he seemed surprised at her having, and he went back to get the maintenance counter ready, and she took care of the front desk. It was interesting how they'd fallen into a routine so quickly.

The morning passed slowly for her, and, as much as she wanted to know how Krista was doing—as much as she *obsessed* about it—Ang didn't call Asta. So when Asta showed up just before lunch to ask Ang if she wanted to go with her to Krista's to pick up Alfur's food and a few other things, Ang was relieved.

"She's still drugged up to keep her from moving around too much," Asta volunteered on their way to Krista's house. "There hasn't been any more bleeding, which is good. The doctor came in this morning and said if things stay stable, she can leave the hospital by Friday, give or take a couple days. She's lucky she didn't fracture her pelvis or hip. She'd be facing a three to six-week stay. Right now, it looks like it'll be about six weeks to fully recover, although she could stay sore for up to twelve. Knowing her, she'll heal fast and be back to her normal self in no time."

"You sound pretty confident." Ang decided to trust Asta's certainty. She knew her sister better than anyone, and Ang was a believer in positive thinking. "What's going to happen to the kid who hit her?"

"The police said he doesn't have a record, and he obeyed all the laws. He just didn't see her. He'll probably get a fine and maybe a driver improvement course. He's beside himself. He said he normally rides his bike to school, but his girlfriend spent the night, and he'd just dropped her off. None of us blame him. He knows who she is from the shop. He said he'd pay any medical bills his insurance doesn't cover."

"He looked pretty upset at the scene. I'm glad you're feeling confident in her recovery."

"I watched her walk away from that twenty-five-cycle pileup on a switchback during the race to the summit five years ago. It turned out she'd fractured her right tibia, but she still finished the race. She was in a cast for eight weeks. Two days after getting it off, she did the Leadville 100. Not her best time, but she heals fast. My bet is that we'll have to beg her to stay off her bike."

Ang relaxed a little for the first time since the accident. She'd never been in Krista's house, and every detail was fascinating to her, from the art to the throw pillows. Ang would have pored over every detail given the opportunity. But Asta quickly gathered Alfur's things, and they were out in just a few minutes. Asta even packed one of Krista's T-shirts so Alfur would be more comfortable being away from home, which Ang thought was a nice consideration as she hugged the sweatshirt she still wore to her. After they loaded the stuff into Ang's car, Ang dropped Asta at her car so she could get to her next class.

Swifty was happy to hear the good news about Krista when she relayed it to him. The poor guy was taking it hard, and she didn't blame him. She'd only met Krista a few weeks ago, but he'd known her most of her life.

When she went into the back room, she was ready to get some work done. Remembering the errors, she went into the program to try to fix them. However, when she got there, the errors were gone. She shrugged. Swifty must have taken care of them.

There were a lot of other things she could do, but alone in the back office, she took a few minutes to breathe and think. The image of Krista lying in the street kept trying to make its way into her mind, and she chased it away with the image of her in the hospital bed, which wasn't awesome, but she looked like the Krista Ang knew, and the image was a testament to how lucky Krista had been that the accident hadn't been worse. The next few weeks probably wouldn't be easy, and she didn't even try to envision any specific details. The only thing she knew was that she would help out at Sol Cycle until Krista came back, and she'd help in the meantime any way she could, even if it was just to walk Alfur or drive to doctor's appointments.

There was a reason she had made the unexpected decision to work at Sol Cycle, and maybe this was it.

CHAPTER TWENTY-SIX

After five days in the hospital, Krista was ready to get out. The sunshine when they exited the wide doors stung her eyes, but the outside air and warm breeze was a balm against her skin.

"Thanks for letting me stay at your house," she said again, peering up at Angelique from her wheelchair.

"I'm surprised you chose to stay with me," Angelique said, walking beside her. "From what Asta told me, you had plenty of offers."

Krista studied her. "You didn't offer just to be nice, did you?" A sudden shyness overcame her. She'd accepted her offer eagerly, and now she was worried Angelique might not have really meant it.

"I *am* nice, but being nice isn't why I did it. I kind of like your company. Besides, Alfur has made himself at home, and Rupert seems to think they're best friends now. We're going to have to do a slow transition when Alfur finally leaves."

"And here I was thinking that you just wanted to spend more time with me."

Angelique smiled, causing her pulse to quicken. "It was definitely a major factor."

The comment eased her mind, and she wondered where she'd sleep. Certain hopes crossed her mind, but she wondered if Angelique was on the same wavelength. "I really don't want to be a burden. I'm stiff but can walk, sort of. I don't plan on using this much, if at all." Krista lifted the oversized and ornately carved wooden stick tucked between her knees. It was ridiculous, but if she was going to have to use a cane, she was going to do it in style, and what better style than Gandalf's staff? When she'd bought it while on vacation in New Zealand several years ago, she'd never expected it to do anything but act as a decoration in the corner of her living room.

The orderly parked the wheelchair next to the main entrance and went back for the rest of Krista's belongings. The valet took Angelique's ticket, retrieved her keys, and ran toward the parking garage, leaving them alone for the first time in a while.

"Is there a pipe carved into the staff?" Angelique leaned to inspect it, and Krista inhaled her scent. She knew she was on the mend when stirrings of desire erupted in her from breathing in the lotion or perfume Angelique wore. It took her back to the night they'd spent together. Every time Angelique visited, all Krista could think about was kissing her, but Angelique had kept a respectful distance. Was the longing in her eyes Krista's imagination?

"Are you leering down my shirt?" Angelique whispered.

Heat rushed up Krista's neck and across her face when she realized she'd been caught, but Angelique didn't stand to take her assets out of her line of sight. She glanced around to make sure the orderly was at a safe distance.

"I'll let you ogle mine when you tuck me in tonight," she whispered back. Angelique's crooked smile was the reaction she'd hoped for.

The orderly came back to the chair as Angelique's car was pulled around, and Krista was relieved to be going home with her. They hadn't been able to talk about the night they'd spent together because of the semi-private room.

The drive from the hospital was quick, and a pang of jealousy hit Krista when they drove by the park where people were biking. It would take a lot more than getting hit by a car to make her not want to get out there again.

Angelique must have noticed the riders, too, because she peered over, cocking an eyebrow. "What's this about you being on the Olympic team?"

Krista sighed. "Who was telling you stories?"

"Asta brought up your previous accident when she told me what a badass you are and how fast you heal. There are also photos of you on the winner's platform at various races at the store."

"I was trying to qualify. There's a big difference."

"She said you were close to it."

Krista tried not to think about her competitive racing days. "My competition scores were good enough, but I had the accident. I broke my leg, and my endurance and speed have never been the same. Definitely not Olympic caliber."

"It must have been devastating."

Krista wanted to change the subject. Not many people remembered her racing days, so over time, she'd talked about it less and less. Most people just assumed she'd been crushed about her shattered dreams, and it was easier to let them think that rather than try to explain her real emotions around it. But Ang was going through something similar with the whole change in careers, so she wanted to be honest.

"The thing is, it wasn't devastating. It was a huge change in the direction of my life, but I wasn't as upset as I probably should have been."

"Interesting."

"Well, I grew up hanging out at Raggy's store around cycling. Not to brag, but I was good at it, too. I didn't really get into competition or speed trials until high school, but I competed in local events, and I did well. Being at altitude gave me an advantage. It was natural for Raggy to encourage me to compete since cycling is his life, and once my parents realized how natural I was at it, they encouraged me, too. There was a long time when I really liked it. Most of my friends were into it, so I was immersed. I loved it. I still love it. But when it became the sole focus of my life, the shine went away. Once you get on the train, it's hard to get off. You have schedules, events, training, appearances, the whole shebang, as Swifty likes to put it."

She paused for a moment, remembering some of the good times. It wasn't all bad, but at one point, the bad outweighed the good, and that was when she wanted to get out. "People tell you what to do every minute, where to be, when and what you're allowed to eat. I started to hate it when it became a job. And I hated that I hated it. People were so supportive. I didn't want to let them down. When the accident happened, it changed everything. I started training for the summit race with commitment, and I ended it with a decision to quit. I actively resented how biking had taken over my life. I wanted more. I realized I didn't want cycling to consume my life."

Angelique glanced at her. "But it still does, doesn't it? I mean, you own a cycle shop."

"It's hard to explain. Not *having* to do it brought my passion back. I didn't set out to own a cycle shop. It just sort of happened. Raggy wanted to retire and asked me if I wanted to take it over. I figured it depended on whether I could get the loan or not. The process went through without a hitch, so now I own Sol Cycle. My whole way of living life changed after the accident. I was once a lot like the rest of my family—everyone except Raggy—they're all driven and hyper-focused. It was a like a switch flipped. If things worked out, cool. If not, also cool. I have my business, I have Alfur. I don't need anything else. The rest just happens if it happens. Even my house just happened. I was renting, and my landlord had to sell, and I went from paying rent one day to paying a mortgage. What they see as my lack of ambition bothers my parents, but the business keeps them from worrying about me, and they have my brother the doctor and my sister the psychotherapist demonstrating enough drive for all of us."

Angelique turned down an alley, and Krista wondered what she'd said to cause her pensive expression. "It isn't my place to say, but I met your family at the hospital, and your parents spoke about your drive, as did your sister and brother. You might want to reevaluate their perception of you. They're all very proud." A garage door halfway down the alley rose, and Angelique angled the car in. "We're here. There are two steps up whether we go in through the front or the back, so I'm going to park in the garage. We'll just take it really slow, okay?"

Krista was glad their arrival interrupted the conversation. She hadn't felt like her parents were proud of her in a long time. Hearing it from Angelique made her question the last five years. Krista took her hand before she opened the car door. "Thank you for making me come here."

Angelique's eyes grew wide. "I didn't make you. Did I? I mean, I didn't intend to make you."

Krista chuckled. "I was just kidding, but I wouldn't have been able to manage the stairs at my sister's walk-up apartment with no elevator, and my parents planned their trip to Baltimore to celebrate my brother's new job months ago. My mom was going to cancel her flight and just send my dad until you asked me to stay with you. You're a lifesaver."

Angelique rested her hand on Krista's cheek. "I'm happy to do it. Besides, Alfur is here, and he misses his mom."

"You really are the best." Krista kissed her palm, and they both got out.

Krista thought it would be easy to make it into the house. She'd been practicing walking up and down the halls in the hospital during physical therapy. But the two measly steps up were a killer. And neither of them had factored in the dogs. When Angelique opened the door, they would have knocked Krista back down the stairs if Angelique hadn't warded them off. Krista couldn't blame them. They were as ecstatic as she was, so when she got to the top step, she gave them as much love as she could without bending too much. Appearing to sense her weakness, their demeanor became more careful.

The walk through the house into the living room took far longer and cost way more energy than she expected, and when she eased herself into the recliner, she was worn out. She closed her eyes and took a long breath, relieved to be sitting. When she opened her eyes, both dogs were sitting patiently in front of the chair, watching her.

"You two are ridiculous." She laughed. And then she noticed the room. "You changed everything. And I mean everything. The furniture. The floor. The paint. Even the art." She ran her hands along the dark-green, microfiber chair she was in. "This is so comfortable."

Angelique appeared pleased. "It has an electric reclining function. The button is on the side."

Krista pushed the button, and the chair slowly reclined, bringing her legs up, and a new level of relief flooded through her. She closed her eyes and sighed. "I might not leave this chair. Ever."

"That was the idea."

"Please tell me you didn't get it just for me to recover in."

"I wanted a comfy chair, anyway, but I also wanted to have something you could get in and out of easily. The next thing I knew, I'd redecorated the entire living room."

The white carpet was gone, replaced by dark wood, a few brightly colored rugs, and new paint. The rest of the seating area had more cushy-looking couches covered in the same dark-green microfiber, with bright throw pillows and lap blankets. Dark wood tables and credenzas interspersed the couches and chairs. "It's beautiful. Still very tasteful but so much warmer."

Angelique scoffed. "Leona is going to have a coronary."

"Leona?"

"My mother. Wife to Horace. My parents."

"Your mother has an aversion to comfortable furniture?"

"She has an aversion to anything with personality. She prefers her homes to be showcases. She will call this 'pedestrian' and 'gaudy.' She, who decorates with the perfect and elegant gilt frames, gilded wallpaper, and furniture with carved accents. Too much color is in bad taste. She'd truly flip out if she knew I had Kat smudge the whole house, too. Had to get all the bad energy out. Reset everything."

"You smudged?"

"Don't look at me like that. It works. Geri and Kat came over when I cleared the old furniture out, and we cleansed the house of all the negative. Can you feel it?"

"I think I do." Krista actually could feel it. The house seemed more...flowy. Open. But she'd never felt the bad energy. The one time she'd been there, all she'd felt was raging desire. She believed in intentionalism, karma, the power of attraction, and things like that, though, so it made sense to her. "The important thing is that you feel it."

Angelique raised an eyebrow. "Said the woman who believes in elves." But she laughed and turned in a circle. "I felt like I needed the color. It really ups the vibration."

Krista liked this Angelique, the almost mystical Angelique. "Life should be filled with color."

"And art. I noticed you have a lot of art. Nice art. Interesting art. I've always wanted to collect it, but the things I'm drawn to didn't really go with my sterile furniture."

"How…did you go to my house?" Krista was disappointed she didn't get to witness Angelique's first reaction to her home. She'd really worked to make it her own space.

"Twice with Asta. The first was to get Alfur's stuff and then again yesterday to get a few of your things to make you comfortable here: a blanket, your pillows, pajamas, clothes, that sort of thing. Don't worry. I didn't snoop. Asta collected it all."

"Somehow, I don't picture you as the snooping type, but I don't have anything too crazy to find if you did. I'd love to invite you over when I'm back on my feet. Especially my backyard in midsummer. It's like a magical garden. My favorite thing is to lie out there in my hammock. The injury is going to make it hard for me to plant flowers, but I'll figure it out. The doc said four to five weeks if I'm lucky, so fingers crossed."

"She said four to five weeks for the bruising of the bone to go away. It could be up to three months before the pain is completely gone."

Krista laughed. "I'll be back on my bike in just over three weeks, tops. Mark my word."

Angelique stood, crossed her arms, and gave Krista a look. One she had probably leveled at many a coworker. "Your sister said you heal quickly, but don't push it. The doctor said no work or physical stuff until she gives you the all clear."

"Yes, mistress." Krista said it as a joke, but when Angelique raised one disapproving eyebrow, Krista knew she was serious, *and* it was a complete turn-on. Something she would have never thought she'd like. Angelique wielded a unique power over her, and she liked it. "I'm especially looking forward to getting cleared for the physical stuff." She lifted her own eyebrow. She teased, but she really did look forward to being close to Angelique again. The memory of their night together was the one thing that had helped her get through the boring, and sometimes grueling, days in the hospital. Now here they were, and she was too tired to do anything about it. One thing was for sure, she was going to do everything in her power to get her stamina back so she could do *all* kinds of things about it.

CHAPTER TWENTY-SEVEN

All the air seemed to have left the room, but Ang couldn't tear her eyes from Krista's. She'd probably meant it as a joke, but when she'd said she was looking forward to being cleared for the physical stuff, a particularly vivid memory of some of the physical stuff they'd done hit her hard.

"Me too," she said and turned to go make them both lunch before she said anything more.

It was only a week since the night Krista had stayed over for dinner, but it had been a week of worry, forced patience, confusion, and frustration for her. It wasn't appropriate for her to wish Krista would hurry up and get well just so they could have a repeat. It wasn't right at all; nevertheless, she did. She couldn't help it. Sex with Krista was amazing. Everything with Krista was amazing.

Ang started making tuna sandwiches and thought about the muddle of emotions Krista stirred up in her. The sex was mind-blowing, but it wasn't the only inspiration for the strong sensations marauding through her. She cared about Krista. She'd been on her way to caring about her before the accident, but when the accident happened, she'd realized just how much she already cared. Being faced with the possibility of not having Krista in her life made her the only thing Ang could think about. All she wanted was to be with Krista. She had it bad, and it scared her how quickly it had happened. But Krista wasn't into commitments. She'd said so in the car on the way home.

It was like a gut punch.

Ang didn't factor into her plans. Sol Cycle and Alfur were all she needed.

She had wondered why Krista didn't have a girlfriend, wasn't dating anyone, never talked about a recent ex. Someone like Krista could have her pick of women. But Krista was single by choice. It was how she liked it. No commitment.

Ang's phone rang, and the Lithium prefix came up on her caller ID. She silenced the ringer and watched the silent display as the call rolled to voice mail. Conflicting emotions overcame her, stunning her. The anger and resentment weren't a surprise, but the sense of loss pervading everything was. She'd been so busy working at the shop and worrying about Krista, she hadn't put a whole lot of thought into Lithium or the call from HR last week, and when thoughts had tried to sneak in, she'd distracted herself with work or the dogs. Her last day at Lithium seemed so long ago, but it had only been a few weeks. Even so, things felt undone with them. She hadn't signed anything, and she hadn't received anything in the mail. All voice messages had merely asked her to call them back. Sometimes, she'd wondered if she should check her old Lithium email in case it was still working, but she hadn't wanted to be reminded.

A message flashed, telling her of the voice mail. She left the phone on the counter and got back to work making lunch.

She opened the pouch of tuna, and Cleo, who hadn't bothered to come out when she and Krista came home, came running. She jumped directly onto the counter, never mind the rules. Cleo pretended not to care by sitting and licking her paw, but she never took her eyes off the pouch, playing cool. Ang thought about shooing her off, but instead, she put some fish on a small plate and gave it to her. It was an emotional day. Cleo deserved a treat.

When Ang finished the sandwiches, she brought them out to the living room only to find Krista fast asleep in the recliner. She placed a light blanket over her and put her sandwich in the refrigerator. She ate her own standing at the counter, wondering who'd tried to call her, but instead of listening to the message, she opened her laptop and decided to do some work for the shop.

She took care of the schedule for the next two weeks and made a note about hiring two temporary sales associates when Rajib and Hill went home for the summer once finals were over in May. She then polished up her proposal about creating a deep clean service plan. It was a sore subject, but she'd gently introduced the topic to Swifty, who went through the work orders with her, and despite insisting that no one was taking advantage of the service by getting an inexpensive service just to get the deep clean, she'd been able to show him that more than half of the customers *were* doing it. It meant the customers liked the service. So instead of getting rid of it, they decided that maintenance over a certain dollar amount would still be given the deep clean, but anything under would be an a la carte item performed for a nominal fee.

In addition, customers could buy packages of the cleaning service so they would get a discount for buying more, and instead of doing the deep clean along with things like chain tightening and spoke tuning, they would charge for it and throw in the other. The shop would get paid fairly for the time Swifty put into them. She couldn't wait to tell Krista about it and get her approval. In the meantime, together, she and Swifty had taken it upon themselves to do a trial of the change to get an indication of how the customers would respond. So far, things were going well, and Ang was sure Krista would love the idea.

While she was in the shop's server, she logged into the inventory and accounting system to check inventory. Swifty was keeping track of most of the inventory again, which made him happy. He'd confided in Ang how it had hurt his feelings when Krista had taken it away from him during the change in systems, and he worried she didn't trust him to do a good job. It took so little to make him happy. The positive change in his mood was worth letting him take inventory over. It meant a lot to her to witness firsthand how she was making a difference in the shop. It wasn't like overseeing a multi-billion-dollar division, but in a way, it was just as satisfying getting similar outcomes on a micro-level because she was more closely involved with the actual people involved.

There were a few more things at the shop she'd like to change, such as the number of high-end bikes they routinely sent back for refunds. Swifty said the high-end bikes gave credibility to the store, but it was better to rotate the stock than to let them gather dust. She didn't get the logic, but it appeared to be working, so she took his word for it. She hoped to get more info from Krista when she'd recovered a bit more, but until then, she wanted to avoid shop talk to keep Krista's stress levels down.

While she was logged in, she noticed a new reconciliation error. Swifty's explanation of it being a common error occurring between updates sounded solid, and he knew how to fix it so she wasn't so much worried about it as much as she wanted to understand the process, so she ran a few reports with different interpretations of the data and downloaded them to her home office printer so she could go through them while Krista slept.

She cleaned up the lunch dishes and fixed a cup of coffee, intending to take her work out to the back deck, but when she walked past Krista sleeping so peacefully in the recliner, she decided to work in the living room just to be near her. She curled up on the end of the couch opposite Krista's recliner and started to study the sales reports.

Maybe it was the kind of report she ran, but almost as soon as she started to study the reports, she found a pattern. Someone was intentionally moving certain line items from accounts payable to receivable and back again. It was most likely a process error, but having pinpointed it meant she could fix it. She loved sinking her teeth into things like this. It was why she'd been so proud of having developed the Success Factors methodology at Lithium.

By the time she unraveled everything, she understood why the tax and rebate ledgers were off, and her gut instinct about the high-end cycle orders and returns costing the company money was substantiated. Not a lot of money but enough for them to want to stop it. She just needed a gentle way to bring it up. She'd learned the hard way that Swifty had a tendency to take things personally. Satisfied, she closed her laptop and restacked the reports she'd run and stood to stretch. She'd been at it a long time. The living room had grown darker as the sun started going down. She glanced at Krista and realized she was watching her.

"How long have you been awake?" she asked.

"Not long. I was enjoying watching you work. You get a little furrow right here," she said, rubbing the space between her own eyebrows.

"Oh, yeah?" Ang rubbed her forehead in the same spot and made a mental note to stop the furrowing thing. She didn't want it to become a permanent wrinkle. It wasn't vanity. Or at least, not *total* vanity. Her mother had a permanent wrinkle from frowning so much, and she didn't want to turn her face into a mask of permanent disdain or disapproval. If it meant Botox, she'd do it.

"What were you reading to make you appear so serious?"

Krista didn't need to think about work yet. "Just the schedule for the shop for the next two weeks." It wasn't a lie, just an omission.

"Have I told you how grateful I am that you came along when you did? If I didn't have you picking up my slack, I don't know what I would have done."

"You would have figured things out," Ang said.

"Maybe. But maybe not."

"It helps to have Raggy coming in to help. Your uncle is a good guy. Sometimes a little out there, but in a good way."

"Wait. What? Raggy went to the shop?"

Dang! He'd asked her not to say anything. "After the accident, he wanted to make sure you didn't have to worry."

"He visited me every day in the hospital and never once mentioned that he was helping at the shop. Besides, I have you and Swifty. I don't have any worries."

Ang wasn't prepared for how that simple statement gave her a sense of purpose and belonging. "You have a lot of people who care about you."

Krista smiled. "I know."

"Raggy's girlfriend has been bringing in cookies and muffins. I need to start riding my bike to work again just to burn off the extra calories."

"Hold the phone." Krista carefully pushed herself into a more seated position. "Did you say 'Raggy's girlfriend'?"

Ang nodded, confused. "Hilde." He hadn't told Ang not to mention this.

"This is the first I've heard of a girlfriend."

Ang was surprised. It wasn't like they'd tried to hide being together. "Is this a new girlfriend or something?"

"Raggy hasn't had a girlfriend since Aunt Ing died before I was even born."

"I feel like I outed them or something."

Krista looked preoccupied but waved her hand. "There are many wonders in a cow's head."

Ang shook her head; this conversation was getting weirder and weirder. "What?"

"It's something Raggy says when something unexpected or impossible happens. Him having a girlfriend is one of those things."

"Is it an Icelandic thing?" When Krista nodded, she laughed. "He's always saying funny things. There was something about a raisin and a hotdog the other day."

Krista laughed. "Yeah, 'it's the raisin at the end of the hotdog.' He says it when he's happy with something. He's full of them. My dad says you can take the man out of Iceland, but you can't take Iceland out of the man. That's Raggy."

The more Ang heard about Krista's family, especially Raggy, the more she wanted to get to know them. They were so unlike her family, which was just her mom and dad. It was probably one more thing out of thousands that drew her to Krista, whose life was filled with color and life, a thing she'd realized was missing just before she'd transformed her living room, which was hopefully just a start.

Chapter Twenty-eight

Despite missing lunch, Krista wasn't very hungry when Angelique made dinner. She'd lost her appetite in the hospital and thought she'd get it back as soon as she got out, but even when Angelique offered to make chicken tacos, her favorite food, she just didn't have an appetite. Angelique insisted she eat something, claiming she wouldn't heal if she didn't give her body the nourishment to do it, so she relented to some chicken noodle soup, which she forced herself to eat. After a few spoonfuls, her appetite came back with a vengeance, and she ended up finishing a second bowl. The general fatigue she'd worn since the accident began to fade away.

"Did you get a second wind?" Angelique said, taking her empty bowl. "Your color is a little better."

Krista pushed the recliner back to ease the pressure on her hips. "I think your cooking woke up my appetite."

Angelique snorted. "I can only be credited for wielding the can opener. You can thank Wolfgang Puck. He makes a mean canned soup."

"You can tell old Wolfgang I'm a new fan, then."

Ang grinned and flashed finger guns at her. "I will the next time I bump into him."

Krista sat the recliner up. "And on that note, I think I'll visit the little cyclist's room. I'll be right back." With the help of her Gandalf staff, Krista managed to get up and shuffle toward the hall.

"Do you want help?" Angelique asked.

Krista turned and winked at her. "I'm going to do my best to do this on my own, but I'll give you a shout if I have any trouble." She said it with more confidence than she felt. There were two things she'd needed to do before they'd discharged her from the hospital. One was to walk from one end of the hospital wing to the other, and the other was to go to the bathroom by herself. She'd managed both, but the bathroom had been harder than she'd thought, and there were rails to hold on to there.

"I'm sure you'll be fine," Angelique said, "but can you leave the door unlocked, just in case?"

"Sure thing." Krista took her time. A fall could cause a relapse, which had been drilled into her by the discharge nurse.

When she got there, she was able to lower her soccer shorts and ease herself onto the seat with minimal effort, which was a huge relief. The built-in bidet and dryer was a wonderful bonus, making it so she didn't have to twist to clean herself. She shook her head at the simple things she took for granted every day.

Getting up was much harder. Using both hands to push herself up, one on the counter, the other on the staff, her shorts and underwear slid to her ankles. She cursed under her breath, knowing she couldn't bend far enough to reach them and pull them back up.

Taking a deep breath, she took a moment to think about her options and tried to get a handle on her sudden tears. All because she couldn't pull up her pants? And what was this wild swing of emotions? She had been fine just a few minutes ago. She had to figure this out because there was no way she was going to call for Angelique. The thought alone was too humiliating to even consider. She surveyed the room for anything she could use to hook her shorts and pull them up. But there wasn't even a plunger or toilet brush in sight. As unsavory as the thought was, both of those options were better than having Angelique find her in this predicament.

It occurred to her that the staff was smooth, and she could slide the bottom of it between her feet, under the shorts, and sort of shuffle forward, and maybe her shorts would move up the slant of the staff to a point where she could reach them. She positioned the staff under the crotch of her shorts and began to move forward. It worked. Her shorts rose up the slant.

Too late, she realized the hem of one leg opening had gotten under her heel. She lurched sideways, a hand on the counter kept her from falling, but she dropped the staff, which fell to the floor and clattered loudly on the granite tiles.

She was leaning against the counter with her shorts tangled around her ankles and her frustration mounting when the bathroom door flew open, and Angelique appeared. Krista couldn't even move to cover her bare ass without tripping over her shorts, so she just dropped her head into her hands with agonizing embarrassment.

"Are you okay? What happened?" Angelique wrapped a towel around her waist.

Krista dropped her hands, laughing with embarrassment. "It's stupid. I can't bend to pull my shorts up." She noticed Angelique trying not to smile, which made her laugh, and then Angelique began to laugh. It soon became the kind of laugh where tears rolled down their cheeks.

Without making a big deal of it, Angelique slid Krista's shorts up and stepped back when Krista was able to finish the job. Even through the embarrassment, she found the gesture intimate and sweet, causing something to wrap around her heart in the most incredible way.

"What?" Angelique asked wiping her tears away, and Krista realized she was staring at her with what was probably a goofy smile.

"You."

"What about me?"

"Everything." Krista took her hands and pulled her until their bodies were close, and she kissed her. Really kissed her. Angelique in her arms again was a revelation, and she sank into the kiss in a way she hadn't known she could. Her body responded to memories of the last time they were in each other's arms, and she craved the intimate contact she'd been daydreaming about ever since.

Angelique leaned back without letting their bodies separate. The pressure was distributed across Krista's front, and while it ached a little with the weight against her, it was a good kind of ache. "Should we be doing this?"

"I can't think of anything I'd rather do. I've thought about nothing else since they cut back on those pain pills, and my mind hasn't been in a haze, and even then, I think I dreamed about you, touching you, kissing you, doing this." Krista slid her hands down the back of Angelique's shorts, gliding over the silky-smooth skin of her perfectly round ass.

Angelique made a sound low in her throat, reminding Krista of the first time they'd made love, and she kissed the expanse of throat Angelique exposed when she threw her head back. "I'm afraid I might hurt you."

"I think doing this standing up is actually the best way to do it, if I can manage to keep my hips relatively still. Therein lies the challenge."

Angelique took a small step back, and Krista's hands slid from her shorts. A sound of disappointment rumbled from her throat, and Angelique rested her hands on her hips. For a second, Krista thought Angelique was going to deny her the thing she ached for, but when she saw the hungry glint in her eye, her lower body reacted in a delicious way. Angelique looked like she wanted Krista as much as Krista wanted her.

Angelique held her index finger up. "I will do this only if you tell me exactly what to do. I do all the work, and you tell me immediately if something hurts, are we clear?"

Krista nodded, swallowing hard. She loved when Angelique was like this, taking full control and not having it any other way. Except she was telling Krista to tell *her* what to do. It was a dominating submission, and it wound her up tighter than a spring. She'd never experienced anything like it.

"I'm going to take your clothes off. Is that okay?"

Krista swallowed hard again, nodding. "Take my shirt off first and play with my nipples."

Angelique bit her bottom lip, one of the sexiest things, Krista had ever seen, and lifted the hem of Krista's T-shirt, baring her stomach. She bent to kiss the exposed skin and Krista hissed at the hot trail of kisses Angelique's lips left above the top of her shorts. She braced herself against the counter. As Angelique raised the shirt higher, her kisses went higher until Krista raised her arms to let the shirt slip over her head, but Angelique seemed distracted by her braless breasts, and Krista stood willingly with her arms in the air and her T-shirt partway over her head while Angelique sucked and teased her nipples. Krista moaned and rolled her head back, the threads of sensation making their way from her sensitive breasts to the pulsing wetness between her legs. She struggled to keep her feet flat on the floor and not lift one to wrap around Angelique like she wanted to.

Angelique continued to kiss her way up to Krista's neck and finally pulled the shirt all the way off. She stood back and ran her nails gently down Krista's torso, hooking her fingers into the elastic of Krista's soccer shorts and fanning her fingers around the top of them, slowly pushing them and Krista's underwear lower until the top of her pubic hair was exposed, at which point, Angelique dropped to her knees and peered up at Krista, waiting.

"Tell me," she said, her deep brown eyes appearing almost black with desire.

"T…take my shorts off." Krista's heart felt like it would pound right out of her chest.

"And your underwear?"

"Yes. Both."

Angelique did as she was told, her nails again skimming along the skin of Krista's legs, careful to avoid the area close to Krista's groin where the surgeon had repaired the artery. Her soft lips followed the trail until she reached the insides of Krista's knees, where she licked and gently bit the soft flesh.

When her shorts fell to her feet, Krista carefully stepped out of them, her bare ass against the cold granite. She held the edge of the counter tightly, not because she was afraid she'd fall, but because it was all she could do not to pull Angelique up, to strip off her clothes, and explore every inch of her with her tongue. Just the thought of Angelique's legs wrapped around her neck while she slid her tongue inside made her center spasm.

"Stand up," she said.

"Don't you want me to put my mouth on you first? While I'm on my knees?"

Krista wanted everything. "God, yes," she said.

"Are you able to spread your legs a little more?"

Krista inched her legs apart but wasn't able to spread them as far as she wanted, but Angelique was able to slide her tongue between Krista's swollen labia, tracing the folds, trailing deep within her and finally settling on her clit, which ached for attention. When Angelique placed her lips over it and sucked it, Krista could barely hold still, and the act of holding still only heightened her pleasure. She foresaw herself orgasming in Angelique's mouth, and the thought took her right to the edge.

"Put your fingers inside me. I want you inside when I come."

Angelique slowly teased her hand up Krista's leg, caressing the trembling muscles of her thigh before her fingers teased her wet opening while her lips and tongue worked Krista's clit. Angelique ran the tips of her fingers lightly around the outside, until Krista couldn't stand it anymore.

"Inside. Please. Inside."

Angelique slid her fingers deep inside while she sucked her clit. Krista moaned, wanting to rock her hips, but she didn't. Her orgasm built and rolled inside until it was a ball of electric energy pulsing and constricting, putting out shockwaves, until it finally bellowed outward, rushing from the center of her body, lifting every nerve and shaking her to the edges of her skin. Every muscle in her body contracted and released in rhythmic pulses until she remembered to breathe. The sensation rolled through her like a crashing wave that she rode until her heart, hammering in her chest, resumed a normal pace.

Angelique left her fingers inside as she stood, and she ran her other hand over Krista's hip and up her side, around her back, and she pressed her body against Krista, careful of her injury, holding her close.

"Your body sings when you come. I can hear it, and it vibrates in my chest. It's beautiful." Angelique kissed her slow and hard while the last of Krista's orgasm gripped the fingers deep inside her.

"Take me to your bedroom. I want to lie down, and I want you to let me do to you what you just did to me."

Angelique did exactly that, and Krista forgot all about the issue in the bathroom and the sense of helplessness she'd faced. Instead, she felt the power of desire and fulfillment fill her as she showed Angelique just how much she loved pleasing her, too.

Chapter Twenty-nine

Ang would have liked to stay home all weekend with Krista out of the hospital, but she was now filling in for her at the store. Even with Swifty and Raggy there to help, she was needed because of the warmer weather. How had Krista done it before hiring her? Then she remembered. Krista had worked seven days a week, which needed to change.

Ang laughed at herself. Who was she to talk? If she hadn't left Lithium, she'd still be working seven days a week herself. She dragged herself into the shop, and thankfully, the bike ride helped invigorate her. It was just her and Rupert, though. She'd left Alfur home to keep Krista company.

Swifty had already opened the store by the time she got there. Magnus and Hill showed up shortly after. With the maintenance desk and sales floor covered, she was able to check on work orders and inventory, which was a constant task. Initially, she'd thought the inventory system would have kept everything in order, like the one at Lithium, but it wasn't completely set up, so with Swifty's reluctant help over the last few days, they'd gotten it up and running, and in the first couple of hours at work that morning, she was able to configure the final preferences to fully automate it with the scanners. It even created the vendor orders that simply required a review and submission. Once completed, it was all scan and verify, cutting the work of managing inventory by half.

Krista's setup had been perfect, and Ang and Swifty only needed to complete the initial input, then turn it on and fine-tune the workflows. She hoped to do a similar thing with the work order process on the maintenance side. She couldn't wait to show Krista when she came back to work in a few weeks. The trick would be to keep her mouth shut about it in the meantime.

Swifty stuck his head into the back from the maintenance counter. "Hey, Ang. Can you watch the desk for a few minutes? I'm gonna skip on over to the Bean for coffee. You want anything?"

"Sure," she said getting up. "Hey, thanks for clearing the error from yesterday. I just got the inventory workflow online, which should keep everything in sync so you shouldn't have to do it anymore. All we have to do is scan in and scan out, and we should be fine. I'll start on the work order workflow next."

Swifty flapped his hand. "I'll believe it when I see it. You and Krista keep telling me it will make things easier. I just see more work. You want your usual?"

She gave him her order and some cash and took a seat behind the counter. He was a good guy. Easy to work with and always there to lend a hand. He'd also made the last week so much easier than it might have been. He wasn't the biggest fan of the new software system, but he was starting to warm up to it. He said he liked the old system of writing it all on a ledger and then having Krista key totals into the spreadsheets, but she'd kept promising him the new way would save them a ton of time. Ang was grateful they'd gotten past his initial distrust. The last week had been pleasant between them. Some people just hated change, but she knew how to bring them along.

After Swifty left, Raggy came ambling in and headed to the back desk. As always, his appearance made Ang smile. He filled a room when he entered it, and it wasn't because he was tall or wide. Physically, he probably wasn't much bigger than Swifty. It was his happy-go-lucky personality, fast smile, and sparkling light blue eyes that did it. He reminded her of Krista. Even at eighty, he was a handsome man.

"Hiya, Ang. How did Krista settle in yesterday?"

"Very well," Ang said. She wasn't about to tell him specifics since they'd spent the rest of the evening in bed, but she did fill him in on her progress.

"I'm so glad she has you. I know she didn't want her *modor* to fuss over her, and Asta has the attention span of a puppy." He looked around. "Did Swifty take the day off?"

"You just missed him. He's out getting coffee. Want some?" She lifted her phone. "He's probably ordering now. I gave him enough cash."

"I wouldn't mind a few drops if it's Mr. Beans. I don't care for the maiden's piss they pour at the other one."

Ang laughed. She'd learned the hard way how strong Raggy liked his coffee when she accidentally took a sip from his cup. She texted Swifty before returning her attention to him. "I wasn't expecting you today," she said.

"I took in a few bikes yesterday after visiting with Krista, and I thought I'd work them up. Hilde has plans with a friend to shop and go to lunch, so I came in. I've missed coming to the shop. It's different when it isn't a real job."

She could relate. "Hey, I want to run something by you. Do you have a few minutes?"

He followed her to the back, and she showed him the bike returns causing the errors. She hoped he'd talk to her about why rotating expensive stock through the store was necessary. It wasn't that she didn't trust Swifty; she just didn't understand his logic.

Raggy pursed his lips and scratched his head. "I'm no good with computers. My phone is as high-tech as I get, and I only use it to make calls and take pictures of elk and fish."

"It's okay. It was a long shot. I was just hoping your experience with the sales tax and vendor rebates might trigger something. I'm pretty sure the system isn't recalculating the sales tax when we send a bike back, and it's probably the same with the rebate, but the rebate shouldn't even trigger on the returns."

He pulled on his ear, thoughtful for a few seconds. "You say returns like you have a lot of them."

"We do. Mainly just the high-end stuff we send back for rotation."

He shook his head. "I'm not so sure about this rotation stuff. It must be something Krista has worked out. When I ran the shop, we only did high-end for special orders. I don't think we did a single return on a special order in the forty years I ran the shop. And we never did enough volume on them for the rebates. Maybe one or two a season." He stared at the screen and then tapped his finger on it. "I'm not sure if I'm looking at this right, but is it true there are a half dozen high-end sales in the last two months? Better business than I ever did. I'm proud of my Krista."

Raggy's obvious affection for Krista made her smile, but what he offered didn't clear up her confusion about the returns.

When Swifty returned, she was grateful for the caffeine. She and Krista had stayed up pretty late, and Krista had still been asleep when she'd left, so Ang guessed she was worn out, too. They'd been inspired to continue what had started in the bathroom, and it had gone on until the small hours of the morning. No complaints from her, though. Just the opposite.

Raggy slurped his coffee noisily. "Not as good as mine, but it'll do." With that, he made his way over to the table to work.

After a few drinks, Ang settled into her analysis of the spread-sheets again, and there it was. It finally stood out to her, and it was so obvious. She'd been making it complicated in her head all along. The software was just not recognizing the returns because the lading records weren't being zeroed out. Probably a simple process error.

She mentally patted herself on the back. She couldn't remember the last time she'd done manual bookkeeping, and it had been a while since she'd untwisted something this complex. She still had it, though, and without bothering Krista.

She leaned back in the office chair with a sense of satisfaction. "Hey, Swifty. Can I talk to you for a second?"

"Sure. Let me just..." He laid his bike wrench down. "Okay," he said as he came to where she sat at the computer, wiping his hands on a shop rag. Raggy continued to work on another bike at the other end of the bench. "What's up?"

"I've been going crazy trying to figure out the reconciliation error in the new system."

Swifty grunted. "Yeah, good luck. Krista couldn't figure it out, either. But the override I do takes care of it when it comes up, so I wouldn't worry about it."

So much for not telling Krista. If Krista knew about the error, she'd be curious about what cleared it. "What override are you doing?"

He flapped his hand dismissively and turned back toward the workbench. "I just clear the error message."

"You aren't correcting it?" This meant she would have to go back in the records and correct them all. Not fun. But not awful.

He turned back, his expression showing just how much he hated to be challenged. "The numbers are all correct. They just weren't in the right columns. I can't move them around because the software won't allow it, so I just go in and take out the bit of code throwing the error. It's a bug."

"The software should do it all for us if we input the numbers correctly."

Now he sounded annoyed. "I'm putting them in right. It's a bug."

He was wrong, but it didn't matter. She would correct the input data and show him how she did it. Hopefully, it would bring him around. Frustrating as it was, she reminded herself that it had been less than a month, and she was still earning his trust. It seemed some things were the same no matter what size the business was. "I'll put in a ticket with the software vendor. In the meantime—"

"Krista already did that. They weren't helpful. I just made it not a thing. The numbers eventually add up, plus or minus a few dollars. It's not even worth the time to investigate. I've been telling her as much."

She wished she hadn't brought him over to talk about it now. She should have just fixed it and then showed him how to do it going forward. She kept her voice level and deliberately kept her corporate tone out of it. "That's the thing. The numbers don't add up. They show we owe more sales tax than we do, and we need to return rebates we didn't earn. So—"

He blew out an impatient breath and threw a rag he'd taken out of his back pocket onto the workbench. "Krista will get the money back when she does the taxes. It's a nice bonus during the slow months. And the vendors don't care. It's the cost of doing business." He picked up the rag and stuffed it into his pocket again.

She was glad he wasn't their accountant. "That's not how it works." She tried to hide her growing frustration, but some still slipped into her voice. She was good at her job, and she refused to have to prove it to every entitled…no. This was not Lithium. She softened her tone. "The books have to reconcile correctly."

"No one cares."

That made her angry. It reminded her of all the men in her past who were less qualified than her yet felt the right to be condescending. She could deal with them. But she couldn't use the same tactics here. This wasn't a corporate office where each employee was just a number, and verbal evisceration won arguments. It was a small business, and each employee was unique, necessary, and encouraged to give feedback even if they had no idea what her true capabilities were.

"I do," she said. "Krista does. But most importantly, the IRS does." Hopefully, he could understand the last point.

"Oh, so you speak for Krista now?" Contempt laced his words.

She stood. "Not at all. Look, Swifty, I get it, you—"

"You don't get anything. Things were working just fine around here before you came in. You were hired to make the schedule, hire temps, and do some marketing, not to muck everything up."

Ang took a deep breath and forced herself to be still. The story of her life. Everyone else got to be jerks, and it was up to her to maintain the peace. God, she was tired of it. But she'd learned her lesson the last time. He was quick to temper but cooled down quickly, too. She'd drop it for now and let him calm down a little. "I'm sorry I've introduced more change than you're comfortable with. I'll do better."

His shoulders lowered. "Sounds like a good plan."

"I'll talk to Krista about this and—"

"There's no reason to talk to her. I said it's fine. You need to mind your own business."

And now he'd crossed a line.

"If she tells me to drop it, I will." This time she made sure there was ice in her voice. She no longer had to pretend his behavior was appropriate.

He stepped closer, but she refused to move. "This is just too much." He threw the rag on the floor this time. "You just go ahead and waste more time on this. Whatever it is you think you'll find ain't gonna be there. And I won't continue to work here if the thirty-two years I've put in gets discounted by a corporate honcho who's here for a month. You don't know squat about a small business."

Raggy, who'd stopped working and was watching everything, held his hands up and walked closer. "Hey, now. Swifty, let's chill."

He spun to face Raggy. "I *am* chill. I just don't think I should have to put up with the BS you're both flinging at me right now."

Ang knew better than to retort. When employees exploded like this, out of nowhere, the best thing she could do was let them calm down. It almost always turned out to be personal stress, and he had more than his share of that right now with Dirk. A huge wave of compassion washed over her. She looked to Raggy, hoping he'd jump in. Swifty trusted him.

Thankfully, Raggy did. "You have had a hell of a bad patch lately, Swifty. No doubt. Especially at home. Let's just take a few minutes and figure things out. Dirk is getting better and—"

Swifty pointed his finger at Raggy, his face red with rage. "You leave his name out of this. You just leave it out. This has nothing to do with him. Nothing!" Spittle flew from his mouth.

"Wait. Wait. Wait," Raggy said.

"I'm not waiting for anything. You can all go to hell. You take your witch hunt and have fun with it. It's no longer my problem."

With a glare at both of them, Swifty stomped out. Ang remained where she was, hoping he'd come back, watching him walk away, but he finally marched out the front door without another word.

She turned to Raggy, who wore a bewildered expression, one probably matching her own. Just minutes ago, they'd all been working companionably. It was nice. They were sipping coffee while Swifty talked about Dirk being home before his final round of chemo. Swifty had been ecstatic about almost being finished.

Then he'd exploded, reminding her of all the men she'd worked with who felt justified in expressing all their messy emotions and bad behavior, yet held her to the narrowest of lines lest she get blasted about how emotionally unstable she and all women were. The hypocrisy was overwhelming.

"How did that happen?" she asked, dropping into her desk chair. "*What* happened?"

Raggy looked shell-shocked. "He was not the man I've worked with all these years," he said. "We did nothing wrong."

"But why do I feel like I did?"

"Do you want me to call Krista?" he asked.

Ang told him she wanted to do it in person and started to tie up her work to go home, dreading the conversation but wanting to be in a loving place after what had just happened. "I'll do it. I can fix this, but I want her input. Thirty-two years deserves a second chance. We'll give him some space, and I'll ask Krista what she thinks we should do. She's really good with people, and she'll probably have suggestions." She glanced up, realizing she would leave the store with two less people. "Damn. I can't leave the store with both Krista and Swifty gone."

Raggy shook his head. "I've got things here, Ang. The sooner we fix this, the better."

CHAPTER THIRTY

K rista exited the bathroom with a smile, her staff in one hand and a trash picker-upper thingy in the other, a gift from Angelique so she wouldn't worry about dropping anything while she was home alone. This time, when her shorts fell to her ankles, a simple pull of the trigger to pull them back up was all it took. Genius.

She was halfway down the hall, swinging her new favorite tool, when her phone rang. Swifty's name displayed on the caller ID, making her smile.

"Hey, Swiftman. How're things?"

"To be honest, not so good." The admission was not like him.

Her concern flared. "Is Dirk okay?"

He blew out a loud breath. "He's fine. He's home, actually. The doctor let him come home for a few days before his last round."

Relief poured over her. Briefly. But why was he not so good? "What's up, then?"

"Ang is what's up."

"Okay," she said, dragging out the last half of the word. Angelique had said things had been fine at the store. Had she been keeping things secret?

He paused and then let it out in a gush. "She's out of control. Changing all our stuff. She went ahead with taking away the deep cleans on all work orders. She told me all inventory decisions have to go through her. To top it off, she's accusing me of messing up the books in the new software. I have to tell you, Krista, I'm starting to think it's her or me."

Krista listened with calm until the last sentence, and something like dread settled over her. She wasn't in a place to deal with this, and if they couldn't resolve their differences, no matter which way it went, it would hurt. "Wait. What? What the hell happened? We all agreed to leave the deep cleans alone. She told me herself she wasn't interested in changing anything there. Inventory is all you. It always has been. And what about the books? I'm the only one who has access to the new software."

"I'm just telling you what's going on. She was in the books today, and she saw the error we've been trying to figure out, and she let me have it, saying I was doing something wrong."

Krista was confused. "But *you* don't even have access to the new system."

"She doesn't care. She's always thought she was better than us because she's a bigshot, and we're just a small neighborhood bicycle shop. It's all about the bottom line with her. She doesn't give a care about our customers who come to us because we *aren't* a big corporation. They'd go to REI if it didn't matter to them."

Krista shuffled to the recliner and sat. Angelique had never even hinted at any of what he was describing. But it wasn't like Swifty to get so upset. Not even when it was about Dirk. This was all out of the blue, and she didn't like the feeling of impotence she had being so far out of the loop. "I'm sure there's a misunderstanding. I'll talk to her when she gets home."

"Gets home? Is she coming over to your house? Did she already call you?" He said it like someone had stuffed a cat turd in his mouth. Not that she and Angelique's relationship was a secret, but it was also none of his business. So why did she suddenly feel guilty?

He sounded like he thought she'd already taken Angelique's side. And truthfully, if she was to pick sides, she'd pick Angelique's, even if some of the information Swifty gave her was solid. She raised her chin. There was nothing to hide. "I'm at her house. Staying here until I can get around a little better. Everywhere else is nothing but stairs."

"When did you two get so friendly?" She didn't like his tone and was about to say as much when he continued. "Wait. Are you sleeping with her?"

This was not the Swifty she knew, and her personal life was not up for discussion. "It's none of your business," she said calmly. At least she was outwardly calm. Inside, she was royally pissed off. But someone had to stay levelheaded. "Even if we were, I wouldn't tell you."

"Oh, great. Now you're mad at me, too." He sounded like a petulant teenager. What was happening?

"I'm not mad at you," she lied. "Just confused. You're acting weird. You don't just get pissed at people. You don't sound the way you sound right now. What's going on?"

He let out a long breath. "You want me to tell you what's going on? Remember a couple weeks ago when Ang got all pushy about the deep cleans and started nosing around about the sales trends?"

Krista took a deep breath and let it out slowly. Swifty was the one who'd been out of line back then, not Ang. "Right. I asked her to look into our processes. But you weren't behaving like yourself, then, either. In the meantime, you've accused her of a few things I can't imagine she would do. Especially the part about hacking into our books."

"If you don't believe me, just check the access logs. You'll see she was in there today. She might be in there right now. She's very interested in our taxes and total sales. She's nosing into everything."

Now he sounded paranoid. "She has no reason to be interested in those things."

"Exactly.

"These are some major claims, Swifty. I'll talk to her when she gets home to get her side of the story, and I'll come down to the store tomorrow, and we can have a meeting and go through all of this together."

"She'll just justify everything and make it sound like I'm the bad guy." His voice was getting louder again. He sounded almost panicked. Was he worried about his job? He needed it, she knew, but no one had indicated it was in jeopardy. She wished she was there to deal with this in person. It would be so much easier. He'd never raise his voice in person.

She tried to calm him down. "I'm sure she won't. She didn't do it last time. In fact, she owned up to her part in it."

"She's a different person around you. She shows her true self when you aren't there. She's been a total dictator the whole time you've been out. She comes and goes when she pleases, and she spends all her time on the computer."

Krista didn't want to keep talking about Angelique when she wasn't there to answer for herself. "Let's make sure we talk this out when we all meet tomorrow."

"Well, I'm not welcome at the store anymore."

She didn't understand. "What do you mean?"

"I don't work there anymore."

What? The feeling of dread surfaced again. "Are you saying she fired you?"

"Basically. Let's just say it was a mutual decision. I don't want to work there if she is."

"She isn't authorized to fire anyone." That kind of thing wasn't up to anyone but her.

"I'm not going back to the store. I don't want to be anywhere near her."

"You are not fired, Swifty. I'll talk to her when she gets home, and we'll straighten this up."

"Krista." He sounded relieved but wary. "I can't lose my job. Dirk is on my insurance. She has to go."

She didn't blame him for being scared. His whole life was on the line. But his outbursts were so out of character. She guessed everyone had their limits. "Don't worry. I won't let that happen."

When they hung up, Krista logged into the store's server and noticed someone had logged in using her credentials. There was no way of knowing who it was, though, and it was hard to believe Angelique would go in without telling her. Of course, she'd been out of commission for most of the week, and business needed to go on, but Angelique would have at least talked to her before doing it.

They hadn't known each other long, but she trusted Angelique. Sure, there had been some hiccups, but she chalked those up to taking initiative, not to mention Angelique was still in a steep learning curve. She'd even owned her part in the previous argument. That showed major leadership skills. Everything was going well. Actually, Krista didn't know what she would have done if Angelique hadn't been there. There was no way she had a hidden agenda like Swifty suggested. If she did, Krista was in trouble. Not just at the store but personally. Krista's heart was involved now.

Alfur got up, and a rattle of keys in the kitchen told Krista that Angelique was home. It was barely noon. On one hand, she was glad she was home so they could talk, but it also meant she'd left only two sales associates to run things. Not ideal for this time of day.

Krista shuffled into the kitchen to find Angelique leaning against the counter, brows furrowed, deep in thought. She probably was if she'd just fired Swifty. Even her posture made Krista uneasy. Rigid, arms crossed in front of her, looking ready to let someone have it, like she was about to do battle in a difficult board meeting. It wasn't the person Krista knew, and she sensed a gulf looming between them. Krista hesitated to interrupt her thoughts, which only irritated her, but her business was at stake.

Angelique glanced up. A small smile fluttered to her face, giving Krista a brief sense of normalcy, but then the smile was gone, and the distance was back. "What a day." Angelique came around the counter for a hug, and Krista happily stepped into it, her mood buoyed when their connection reengaged.

"Bad day? You're home early," Krista said when they parted.

Angelique nodded and sighed. "And it's not even half over. I wasn't planning to work the whole day. I wanted to spend some of it with you."

That last part made Krista feel better. "Everything okay?" She wanted to hear Angelique's side before telling her about the call with Swifty. Angelique paused, and Krista's unease resurfaced. Why didn't she want to tell her about the confrontation with Swifty? What other things was she not saying?

"You should be focusing on getting better, not worrying about work."

Krista gave her what she hoped was an encouraging smile. "Why don't you let me make that decision?"

Angelique returned the smile. "Fair enough. I keep reminding myself that I've handled worse days at an executive level. This is nothing."

Krista was certain Angelique didn't mean it, but her words came off as a slam. If it wasn't a slam, what did she mean? A small business like hers wasn't as important as Lithium? "I don't think the scale of a business makes the problems any less important."

Angelique blew out a breath. "Try telling my ex-boss, Robert."

"I think I would, given the opportunity."

"He'd never give you the chance."

Krista wasn't sure why they were talking about this, but she didn't like what Angelique implied. Swifty's call had set her on edge, and she didn't appreciate Angelique's suggestion, like she wasn't capable of holding her own with some corporate asshole. Krista was pretty sure she could hold her own just fine if put in the position. Sure, she didn't have the business degree, and she didn't have hundreds of people working for her, but she was more than capable. And she'd been running her own business for four years. She wouldn't let anyone minimize her abilities. Coming from Angelique, the implication stung more. Especially since Krista had admitted how hard she'd worked to overcome her insecurities.

"You don't mean to imply I'm less of a business person because I only run a small business, do you?"

Angelique looked surprised. "Definitely not. I'm sorry if it sounded like I was."

She sounded sincere, and most of Krista's anger fell away. "I'm sorry. It didn't. You were saying you were having a bad day. Please tell me about it."

Ang placed her hand on her forehead as if she was thinking. "Where do I start? I'm not sure how it happened exactly."

"What happened?"

"Swifty kind of went off on me today." She shook her head. "No. Not *kind* of. He definitely did. One minute he was fine, and the next, he was accusing me of going on a witch hunt."

"A witch hunt?"

"His exact words. There was a specific error coming up in the software, so I asked him to help explain how the records were updated so I could fix it. I tried to be neutral about it, but he became very agitated and accused me of trying to blame him for it."

Embarrassment made it hard for Krista to absorb some of what Angelique said. The books were the center of any business's success, and the possibility of Angelique thinking she was an ineffective business owner tapped into her worst insecurities. "First of all, Swifty has absolutely nothing to do with the online bookkeeping. The new software is all me. Can I ask how you got access?" She'd wanted to remain fair-minded, to figure out how best to respond to Swifty's call, and this defensive response was not the way to do it, but she couldn't help it.

Angelique appeared confused. "It's the same password as the scheduling spreadsheet. I was trying to take care of things while you were out."

"And you thought bookkeeping was your responsibility?" Angelique drew back as if Krista had raised a hand to her. As someone who rarely lost their cool, it shamed Krista that she'd made Angelique wince. She struggled to get her emotions under control and soften her tone. "Of course, you did. I said I'd train you."

Angelique's shoulders lowered, but the furrow between her eyebrows told Krista she wasn't completely appeased. "Maybe I overstepped. I made some assumptions. I knew you were wrestling with the system, and I hoped to smooth it out and maybe even automate a few things before you got back. To surprise you. Now, I see it just made you uncomfortable. By the way, you should think about changing your passwords."

Angelique's tone said she was not appeased at all, and Krista didn't want her to be angry. Angelique's day was obviously already off to a terrible start, and she was just adding to it. So recently out of the hospital, she probably shouldn't be attempting to have this conversation anyway, but what was she supposed to do? She couldn't ignore it. Things were going on without her knowledge or input, and she was not cool with it.

"Well, I feel like shit for ruining your surprise. I just want to know what you're working on. But let's not talk about this now. Since you're already in there, please keep doing what you're doing. I'll figure out the thing with Swifty."

Krista thought her tone was obviously calmer and open but was surprised when Angelique still looked pissed. "I'm getting the feeling you're upset with *me*." She folded her arms. "As if you're trying to manage *my* responses or something. *I* was the one attacked today."

Krista held out her hands, even though her own impatience flared, and she worked hard to tamp it down so she didn't throw more fuel on the fire. She wasn't sure if she was upset with Angelique or mad about not being kept in the loop or just grappling with the conversation with Swifty. "I didn't mean it the way it sounded, but something is off, and I want to figure it out. Especially since I wasn't there when it happened."

Angelique appeared to cool off a little, and she dropped her arms to her sides. "Can I help you figure it out?" She sounded tired but concerned now.

Krista, also tired, leaned against the counter. "I'm not sure where to start. Did anything else happen I should know about?"

"He ended up storming out."

Angelique said it without emotion, so Krista couldn't tell what she thought about it. "What was it about?"

"To be honest, I don't know. But I don't want you to worry. It's my issue to fix."

There it was again. Krista watched her own fingers drumming on the countertop. "I really don't like being left out of the loop."

"You need to concentrate on healing." Angelique's voice was still flat, and Krista felt like she was being brushed off.

"You need to stop telling me what I need to do." It came out harsher than she intended it, but she was getting frustrated, and it didn't help that she'd been standing for longer than she had since the accident, and she was trying not to take the goddamned pain pills that made her fuzzy.

"Oh." Angelique appeared startled again. Krista hated it, but she also hated that her business was on the line, in addition to a lifelong friendship, and Angelique was acting as if it wasn't important enough to let her in on the plan. She had to get things back on track.

"Look. Swifty called me. He told me his version of what happened. I was trying to give you the opportunity to do the same, but you're brushing me off, and what I *am* hearing is different than what he's saying. So, yeah. I'm upset. I don't want to be. I don't want to jump to conclusions. But this is some serious shit, and no one is telling me the things I need to know so I can fix it." As she spoke, her voice got louder. All the frustration was starting to come out, and as it did, it became more pronounced. By the time she paused, she wasn't quite yelling, but from the expression on Angelique's face, it looked like she might as well have been. "I'm sorry I sound angry. I'm not. I'm mostly frustrated."

"You do sound angry, which makes it hard to respond rationally." Angelique stood tall and clasped her hands in front of her. Her stance was formal and practiced, her expression deliberately devoid of emotion, a visible and painful representation of the widening gap between them, and Krista hated it. She didn't want this divide. She wanted to go back to that morning when they were still wrapped in the warm bedsheets they'd made love under the night before with such passion, albeit carefully. Great. In trying to make herself feel better, the reminder that she couldn't even make love to Angelique the way she wanted to filled her with embarrassment.

"Why don't you tell me what happened and try not to hold back like I'm some kind of invalid?"

Ang took a step back. "This has gotten completely out of hand."

Krista dropped her head back. "I agree. But are you going to tell me what happened, or am I to take everything Swifty told me as the complete story? By the way, it doesn't come across as very flattering toward you. I'm trying to remain neutral, to hear both sides out, but it's becoming more difficult the more we talk."

Angelique held her head high, and Krista got a very good idea of how she'd represented herself at her corporate job. It was hard not to feel intimidated, and that made her even angrier.

"I'll tell you *what* happened, but I can't tell you *why* it happened. Swifty will have to tell you why, if he hasn't already. What I do know is that stress makes people behave in ways they normally wouldn't"—she lifted an eyebrow—"and I am trying to apply some understanding to Swifty right now because he's been under a lot of stress."

From the raised eyebrow, Krista knew she was applying understanding to her, as well, which just pissed her off even more. "Okay."

"I told you I went into the accounting software. I noticed an error message. I investigated, and it looked like there was a reconciliation issue going on. I suspected an input issue. I asked Swifty about it. He said it was a known bug that you two discovered. But just by the numbers, it didn't add up. Like, maybe he didn't understand it, but he thought he did. So I tried to dig in, to figure it out. It makes me nervous when the accounting doesn't add up."

Krista bristled at the last remark, as if Angelique was saying no one was taking the books seriously enough, as if her experience was so much better than theirs. "And I take it Swifty didn't react well to the interrogation."

"I wouldn't call it an interrogation, but no, he did not take it well. I tried to stay unconfrontational. But he just snapped. He acted like I was accusing him of something. I never once inferred he was responsible for it because I never suspected him of anything other than an input error."

"Are you sure your tone wasn't accusatory, or maybe the words you chose might have caused him to think it?"

Angelique paused. "I'm not some fresh-from-business-school supervisor, Krista. I know how to work with people."

"Something obviously set him off. He has never acted like this before. This is the second argument between you two."

"An argument would imply two people were involved. He was the only one who yelled. He's the one who stormed off. Not me. I maintained my professionalism."

Krista couldn't help getting angrier. "He's been under a ton of stress. Did you take his home situation into consideration? Who fires someone when their husband is going through chemo?"

Angelique just stared for a couple of seconds. "I did not fire him. He quit, but I don't think that particular nuance will matter to you. He's not the only one under stress, Krista. But in fact, I did take his home situation into consideration. It's the reason I didn't yell back at him when he raised his voice. It's the reason I didn't come home directly to tell you all about how unreasonable he was. It's the reason I decided to give it until tomorrow before I tried to talk to him again." Her voice remained measured but grew tighter. It was obvious that she was holding back. She even took a few steps backward. "You know what? I think I'm going to take a ride. Somehow, you're convinced I'm the bad guy here, and I don't think I like it."

Krista hated the way Angelique was talking to her, as if she was just some kid who didn't have a right to her own reactions. When she turned and left, Krista didn't try to stop her. She needed a little space to figure out what was happening. But as she stared at the empty doorway, sadness threaded through the anger and frustration, and she wondered how they could fix it. *If* they could fix it.

CHAPTER THIRTY-ONE

A ng's thigh muscles burned, but she didn't slow; she just kept flying down the bike path taking her past Cherry Creek Reservoir and down to Parker. She pedaled for miles, hoping the exertion would expend the anger raging inside her. Anger and hurt. The look in Krista's eyes had said she thought the whole thing with Swifty was Ang's fault. Krista hadn't been there to see how hard she'd tried to keep the discussion civil, battling her own anger. She hadn't lashed out. She'd remained cool, hoping to keep things from escalating, yet they had. He'd still stormed from the store. Had still quit.

Ang wished she'd had the chance to wait a little longer before bringing Krista into it, wished for the opportunity to follow up with Swifty before telling Krista what had happened. But Swifty had beat her to it. Krista deserved to be in the loop, but not stirred up when she needed to be resting, and some of what Krista had repeated was blatantly wrong, such as Swifty being fired. With that kind of information, no matter how Ang had handled it, Krista would have focused on finding her responsible. She didn't blame Krista for being protective of a person she'd known all her life, but Krista didn't have all the facts, and now, just like always, Ang was the one who had to do all the work to make everyone okay again. When would it be someone else's job? When would *she* be allowed to get upset?

It wasn't the most mature response, but she resented it. All of it. The way Swifty had behaved, the way Krista had reacted. She never got to act that way. She always had to keep it together. Even when she'd quit Lithium, she'd done it with a modicum of restraint. She hadn't yelled. She hadn't argued. Yes, she'd used some choice language, but she'd maintained her cool. When would she get to lash out at someone, behave badly, get to be the victim?

The answer was always the same.

Never.

She was a Black lesbian woman. The world she lived in didn't give permission for Black lesbian women to respond in any way that made people—specifically people who were not Black lesbian women—feel uncomfortable. They didn't like it.

Ultimately, she didn't *want* to be the person who lashed out. She liked being calm. She liked remaining in control. She liked not having to worry that she might have hurt someone or been unfair by saying something in the heat of the moment. Once something was spoken, it could never be unspoken; once a hurt happened, there would always be a scar.

So she rode. She rode until she thought she'd better turn back before she wouldn't have the energy to make it home. And as she approached her house, physically exhausted, her mind was still going a million miles an hour, trying to figure out how to make it right with Krista. She'd told Krista that stress made people behave in ways they normally wouldn't. It wouldn't be fair if she didn't give Krista the same benefit of the doubt. And maybe Krista would do the same for her.

After putting her bike up on the hook, she went into the house, and her spirits rose when Rupert greeted her with his usual excitement. But when Alfur wasn't right behind him, she knew that something was wrong. There was no sign Krista had ever even been there. Not her clothes. Not her pillows. Not her blanket. Not even her toothbrush.

Everything was gone.

There wasn't even a note, but the trash picker was on the counter.

Its pathetic existence twisted her heart.

Ang had been in this position before. Too many times. All the others had left, and she knew she'd made them do it. None of them had ever felt like this, though. Like she would have gladly changed everything about herself to prevent it. Like she could have said something to stop Krista from leaving. Like she and Krista could have fixed the situation together if she had just asked Krista to help. Instead, she'd decided to do it all herself, driving Krista away.

Thinking about Krista struggling with all of her stuff filled her with sadness. Her own pride wasn't enough to keep her from making sure Krista was okay.

The phone rang a few times. Ang expected to be dropped into voice mail, but Krista answered, surprising her.

"Where'd you go?" Ang asked.

"Asta picked me up."

"You're supposed to avoid stairs."

"She took me back to my house. I only have the front steps to worry about."

Ang wanted to ask her how she was going to manage without the garbage picker, someone to make sure she took her meds on time, and a reminder to eat, but those questions felt too personal now. The distance between them seemed absolute and painful. "You didn't have to leave."

"I think we both should take a little space." Her voice was cold.

"I shouldn't have left." It occurred to her that it was the second time she'd left a difficult situation recently. She'd never been a person who just left, and now she'd done it twice.

"Our conversation wasn't going anywhere. I was acting like a jerk." Ang's hopes rose. Maybe she was reconsidering. "But I'm not sure we're good for each other. I get insecure around you, and I don't act like myself."

Ang's hopes plummeted. "Where do we go from here?"

"I'm not sure."

"Should I even show up for work?"

"It's up to you."

"We're down two people with you and Swifty out," Ang said. Part of her wanted not to care. But she did.

"I don't have the right to expect you to stay, but I can't manage the place right now."

"I'll keep working. We can discuss the next steps when you're ready to come back. It was always just a temp thing anyway." She said it, but even as it came out of her mouth, she wondered if she ever actually thought of it like that.

"True."

Ang was about to end the call, but... "And Krista?"

"Yeah?"

"*You* were never a temp thing for me." Krista didn't answer, but Ang heard her take a shaky breath. "Anyway, I'll send you status reports." Krista didn't say anything, so Ang gave what she asked for: space. "Bye."

Ang hung up and was at a loss about what to do with herself. She wasn't a crier. She hadn't cried after Portia had left or any of the others. Not after leaving Lithium. She wanted to cry now, though. It was a pressure that started in the middle of her chest and rose inside her. It got to the back of her throat and stopped. She was so used to holding in her sadness, she didn't know what to do to let it go. So she sat in Krista's recliner. Cleo and Rupert settled in the chair with her, one on each side of her lap.

And she cried.

She thought it would bring up all the feelings associated with being walked away from by every woman she'd ever dated, but that wasn't it. What she felt was simple. For the first time, she felt like she wasn't in control.

Chapter Thirty-Two

K rista wanted to cry. The day was not turning out the way she'd thought it would, especially in light of how it had started. She'd woken up beside the woman she'd slowly been falling in love with since their second random meeting in the park, feeling like things were exactly how they needed to be. It was amazing and unexpected but perfect.

How did things take a turn to have her lying on her living room couch, wondering what the hell had happened?

She wished Swifty had never called her.

She tried to walk through the discussion that had changed her day from sun-stained bedsheets and kisses good morning to accusations and storming out. She hadn't seen it coming. How did Angelique go from a warm, loving person into a cold corporate robot right before her eyes?

If only Angelique had called her about Swifty. If only she'd asked for help. But she hadn't. She'd let him spin out of control. She'd let him storm out. Why hadn't she said there was a problem with Swifty as soon as she'd walked in the door? They could have worked on it together. Instead, Krista was forced to pry it from her, as if Ang didn't respect her and Swifty's lifelong relationship.

As if she didn't think Krista could handle it.

Krista's business was her life. The people she worked with were her family. It wasn't just a job for her or a way to make money. It was an extension of who she was. Sure, she sometimes struggled with the administrative side, but Sol Cycle was part of a community. It was part of the local schools, it was a cornerstone of the neighborhood, and it was a legacy. The people who worked there, some of whom only worked a summer or a few semesters, were family. Angelique acted like they were simply cogs in a machine.

How had Krista been so wrong about her?

She didn't blame Angelique for Swifty's...what? Meltdown? Tantrum? Either way, whatever was going on with him was unexpected. He'd always been easygoing. One of the warmest people in her life. Someone who took in strangers and advocated for groups he was passionate about. Even though his happy place was working on bikes, he'd always been quick to jump in and do other things. He was a truly caring person, and he got along with everyone.

What made him snap?

And why now?

Maybe she'd introduced too much change with the new system and a new manager when there was already too much on his plate, especially in his personal life.

Krista was doubting herself now. Everything was going smoothly until she'd started having insecurity about her ability to run her store, and those doubts started when she'd met Angelique. It wasn't Angelique's fault, but she highlighted all the things Krista didn't know. It took a long time to get the confidence to ask Raggy to stop giving her "pointers," but she had, and she'd been doing a good job on her own. The switch to the new software was a small setback, but it was in the name of progress, and she had to find ways to reduce administrative tasks. It was a step forward.

As much as it pained her to recognize it, she'd made a mistake bringing Angelique in. She could see it now. What had she been thinking? It was too good to be true. Angelique was so capable, ridiculously smart, and she was an expert on how to manage retail stores. Someone like her was beyond the workings of a local bike shop.

And Krista felt threatened.

Which was stupid.

Back in college, as captain of the cycling team, although she'd been the best cyclist, she wasn't voted captain for her talent; she was voted captain because she'd made the team work as a synchronized unit. A unit working to support each other, to give their best. And they'd won a national championship, which in turn had progressed her on the Olympic path. A path she'd sabotaged when the pressure got to be too much.

Was that what she was doing now? Sabotaging something else just as it was going great?

A good business person wouldn't be threatened by someone with talents greater than theirs. They'd use their leadership capabilities to encourage people to find new and better ways to use their talents, enhancing the business and supporting the others.

She shook her head. It was too much to take in. What was the use of thinking about all of this now?

She'd blown it with Angelique. There was no way to get past the way she'd treated her. All because of her insecurities. She'd known what Angelique was when she'd hired her. She knew someone like that would find things to change in her little bike shop, but she'd only been focused on one thing: getting to see her more often. She should have just asked her out, but she'd been certain Angelique would say no. Someone like her didn't want to go out with a person who'd never had a serious relationship in her life, someone incapable of sticking with anything, even when she loved it.

Hiring her for the shop had been the next best thing. And Krista had sabotaged it. The minute she'd gotten comfortable with Angelique, she'd started to see what it might be like to be with her on a long-term basis, and she'd flipped out. She should never have moved in, even though it was only until she could get around on her own. That was what did it. She could see herself doing it forever. So she'd ruined it.

With the help of her pain medication, she fell into a deep and dreamless sleep.

CHAPTER THIRTY-THREE

Ang parked her car on the quiet street and dropped her chin to her chest, trying to summon the courage to do what she was about to do. Before she could talk herself out of it, she got out, and she and Rupert walked up to the tiny house on the corner, only a couple of blocks from the cycle shop. Huge houses stood all around it, making it appear even smaller next to their modern facades, wrought iron fences, and elaborate landscaping. The house was well taken care of with newly painted cedar siding, neat flowerbeds, and freshly mowed grass. Ang couldn't think of one thing she'd change about it. A little library box even stood in the corner of the front yard, constructed as a miniature version of the house, complete with tiny replicas of the bicycles hanging from hooks on the screened in porch. This was the home of a person who was content in life, someone who enjoyed the simpler things. She wondered if she should be disrupting their life by coming by unannounced.

Swifty was on his knees with his back to her, elbow-deep in a muddy hole in the corner of the lawn. The cords of his earbuds draped over his shoulder and down his back, just as he wore them in the store so they didn't get tangled in bike parts. Pieces of PVC pipe and a sprinkler head were laid on a towel next to him, and Ang debated interrupting him just as he glanced over his shoulder. Surprise defined his face before he turned away again and lowered his head. She didn't expect him to be happy to see her, but she regretted coming now.

She almost walked away, but he sat back on his heels, dropped his tools, and stood, peeling his gloves off. He pulled one of the speakers from his ear as he faced her. "How'd you find out where I live?"

"Google. You can find just about anyone these days."

"That's disconcerting."

She nodded. They stood there for a few seconds while Ang tried to figure out what to say. She regretted not figuring it out on the way over, but when she'd left her house, she had nothing specific on her mind except for trying to fix things. The shop didn't open until noon on Sundays, so she'd gotten into her car before she could talk herself out of it. Now that she was here, she was at a loss for words. Stalling for time, she surveyed the property. "I'll bet your yard is beautiful in the summer."

"It will be if I can get the sprinklers fixed. I didn't blow them out in the fall, and I have leaks in at least three of them." He seemed to be having a hard time meeting her eyes.

"You had a lot going on in the fall."

"Yeah."

"I want to apologize for yesterday," she said. "I never meant to accuse you of anything. I don't have anything to accuse you of. I'm not sure what I did, but I definitely did something. And I'm sorry. You need your job. The shop needs you. I'm there temporarily, and I'll leave you completely alone if you come back."

He rubbed the side of his neck, staring at the ground. "I don't know."

Ang could barely catch what he said, it was so quiet. "Please. Don't let me be the reason you leave a job you so clearly love."

"You aren't the reason."

"I triggered you, whatever the reason was."

He took a few steps toward the house. "Come sit with me on the steps. My back is killing me."

She followed him to the concrete steps leading up to his screened-in porch. He sat on one side of the center step, and she took the other. "It's a little chilly in the shade," she said.

"It's going to be in the seventies today."

"Another beautiful day in paradise."

"Look, Ang, you didn't do anything. I've been doing something terrible, and the pressure got to me yesterday. I'm ashamed and angry at myself, and it's not your fault."

She had no idea what he was talking about, but he was talking, which told her she should be relieved. What he said meant that all the things Krista thought about her, and some of the things she thought about herself, weren't true. But it wasn't like it made a lot of difference. Krista still thought she was capable of being a corporate automaton, and she must think she was, too, at least deep down, if she'd been questioning it.

"I appreciate you telling me, but I wish I hadn't triggered it. Is there anything I can help you with?" she said.

He stared at his hands. "I don't think so, but I guess I should be honest about something."

She watched him in silence for a few seconds while a parade of expressions—indecision, fear, anger, among others—flashed by on his face. Finally, he blew out a big breath and sat a little straighter, staring into the branches of the elm. He kept his gaze there when he spoke.

"I've been kind of running a side business from the shop."

"What kind of business?" She couldn't imagine what it might be.

"Selling bikes."

"I'm not sure I understand."

"I started selling custom bikes to members of the bike clubs and to some of the athletes and their families."

"On your own? Not through the shop?"

"I needed the money. Insurance doesn't pay all the bills, and our deductibles are so high. I had what I thought was a solid plan for selling a few bikes on the side and keeping the retail markup. On the higher-end bikes, it can be a few thousand dollars."

"You were taking the store's profits on sales?"

"They weren't sales the store would have made." He was looking at her now. His eyes searching hers, possibly for understanding. "I would never steal from the store. Never. I thought of it as more of a commission on sales I drummed up myself. I used the store's vendor agreements and wholesale pricing to finance the bikes, but since the invoices are payable forty-five days after delivery, I just paid it directly as soon as I got paid, so the store didn't incur any charges."

"How could you do it without Krista figuring it out?" And why was he telling her all of this?

"I sell to friends or friends of friends in various bike clubs and to some of the competitive teams who want custom bikes. A lot of it's through word-of-mouth. I make the orders over the phone, I have the bikes delivered after-hours so Krista doesn't see them, and I deliver the bikes. Cash on delivery. I pay the vendors and keep the markup."

Ang was shocked at the simplicity of the scheme, but more about his deception with Krista. She knew Krista would have worked with him if he needed anything. "I have a lot of questions, but I need to think about them before I put my foot in my mouth again. But first, why would loyal customers of the shop deal directly with you?"

"I let them believe they're working through the shop, and if they suspect I'm doing something a little off-the-books, well, they're saving a few thousand dollars, so they don't care. But they trust me, which helps."

Things started to fall into place. "This explains why the tax and rebate entries weren't matching."

"At first, everything was manual, so I just kept it off-the-books. But Krista installed the new system. Now, because it's electronic, it hits our books as soon as the bikes get delivered. When she asked, I told her they were mistakes or returns, and then I was able to override the error by making it look like a return in our system without processing it back to the vendor and making a personal payment to the vendor. The taxes became a problem when Krista started up the new system. I was able to zero it out manually in the spreadsheet, but you can't do it in the system. Things just got weird when you two started trying to figure it out, and I panicked. I found a way to suppress the error by just commenting out the code, but I hadn't found a way to zero out the ledger. I figured I'd create a process when Krista turned inventory back over to me, but she kept on trying to figure it out. The thing is, it's not costing the store anything." He sounded like he was still trying to convince himself he wasn't stealing. "I wouldn't be selling the bikes if it did. There are taxes, but the rebates more than make up for it, so the store is actually making a little bit on it."

There was one thing she didn't understand, something that made her feel lost. "If you think it's not costing the store anything, why have you not told Krista about it?"

He ran his hand over his face. "Good question, one I keep asking myself. I've gone through it a lot in my mind. I guess I'm technically diverting sales, and it's sleazy."

At least he wasn't delusional. "I don't want to make you feel worse, but the tax thing is a big deal. The *way* they get paid matters. If the store goes through an audit, they could get in trouble. Some of what you're describing sounds a lot like how money laundering is done."

"Oh jeez." He hung his head. "I didn't think of it like that. I've gotten things twisted into an even worse knot than I thought."

Her mind automatically went into problem-solving mode, and then she stopped it. That was what got her and Krista into the place they were now. "I think the thing to do is to tell Krista."

He stared at his hands clenched in front of him. "God. I don't think I can. She'll never forgive me. *I* can't forgive me."

"I get it. But she adores you, and she'll listen."

"How do you get past something like this?"

"You've had a lot on your plate, Swifty. She understands that part of it. I'm sure she'd rather hear it from you and have a chance to fix things rather than finding out some other way. As far as I can tell, there's time to fix things at this point."

He glanced at her and dropped his head into his hands, and it took her a few seconds to notice he was crying.

She rubbed his back. "Hey. I can be there with you. You don't have to do it alone."

He glanced at her, roughly swiping the tears from his cheeks. "You probably wouldn't offer that if you knew I called her yesterday and basically told her it was you or me."

Krista had said that he'd called and that he'd been angry, but not that. No wonder she'd been wound up so tight. Ang tamped down a flare of anger. It had been a shitty thing to do, but he didn't know he'd probably destroyed their relationship. Wait. No. She'd done that. She had to own up to that. But this wasn't about her. "You were upset. People say things when they're under stress. It was obvious you weren't acting like yourself."

He swung his head from side to side. "You're giving me too much credit. I panicked and tried to save my own butt. She said she wanted to talk to you first."

"Interesting." The conversation with Krista made a little more sense now. Krista had already heard Swifty's side, with much of it intended to make Ang look terrible, yet she still waited to hear Ang's side of it before casting judgment. Krista had every right to be angry. Even if she didn't believe Swifty, it was her shop. Ang should have told her what was going on and shouldn't have tried to keep things from her, even if she was doing it out of concern for her health.

"Swifty, I can't tell you how Krista's going to react, but we have to tell her so she can fix it. I shouldn't be the person to tell her, but I can be there to support you. Do you want me to be there?" He just nodded and wiped his eyes, a gesture that squeezed her heart. "Come on, then. The shop opens in a little over an hour. Let's go to her house and find out if she'll talk to us."

Ang was afraid Krista might be completely done with her, but it was the right thing to do to help fix the situation with the books while it was still contained. She couldn't pretend that she didn't want to beg Krista to give her another chance, but it would be unfair to pressure her about that while her business and a life-long friend were on the line. She had to give it some time, let Krista get the books fixed first. At least maybe she'd get to see her. That would be something.

CHAPTER THIRTY-FOUR

The text from Swifty asking to come over was a surprise, but even more surprising was him bringing Angelique. After all the things Swifty had said about Angelique, Krista never expected they'd share the same space again. But with the prospect of Angelique being there in a few minutes, the thing on her mind was the way Krista had left her house without leaving a note and how cold she'd been when Angelique had called to check on her. Plus, Uncle Raggy had called for his daily check-in with her that morning, and he'd spoken as if he thought Swifty was responsible for the whole ordeal. When she'd asked him what had happened, he'd told her she should talk to Angelique. He seemed to have taken her request for him to back off at the shop to heart, and no matter how much she'd asked, he'd kept saying Angelique needed to tell her. It was all so confusing, and Krista didn't know what to make of it.

Krista was out back, and when the gate squeaked open, Alfur ran to investigate. She closed her eyes and took a few deep breaths. She was in physical pain as well as emotional. After the way they'd left things the day before, she was nervous about seeing Angelique, too.

When they appeared from around the corner of the house, Angelique unclasped Rupert's leash, and the two dogs ran out to explore the yard. With all of her conflicting emotions, along with the mystery of the visit, Krista was on edge. "Sit." She motioned to chairs near the cushioned lounge chair she reclined in. "I'm at a disadvantage with you both towering over me." She tried to summon her composure.

Swifty pulled over a chair for Angelique and then slid one over for himself. How civil. Interesting. "The yard looks great, Krista. You've done a lot of work since the last time I was out here," he said.

"Thanks. I'm a little behind on my planting this year, and it will be even longer before I can get to it. But I'm pretty sure both of you didn't come down just to talk about my landscaping." Her words came out sounding a bit harsher than intended, but it was better than confused and heartbroken and full of regret, which were the other feelings she had swirling inside.

Swifty gave a nervous laugh, and Angelique gave him an encouraging nod. What had changed between yesterday and today? "Well, Ang came to my house to check on me today."

"You did?" Krista asked, glancing at Angelique.

"I wanted to ask him to talk, and he did." She gave him an encouraging smile. "You want to take it from here?"

"Um, yeah, sure." He picked at the corner of his nail. "I told you some of this yesterday, Krista. But I also omitted some things and lied about others. I feel terrible about it, and I don't expect you to just let it go. I deserve…well, I deserve whatever you want to do about it. Anyway, I know why the accounting errors are occurring, and I've been sort of massaging the books for a while because… because I did something stupid, and the software isn't equipped to manage it the way I wanted it to."

"Oh…kay." Krista answered, a sinking sensation filling her stomach. "Explain it to me."

Swifty told her what he'd been doing, and Krista tried to not to get angry, but she *was* angry, and the more he explained, the angrier she got. She loved him like an uncle, and she'd trusted him with her business, and he'd jeopardized it. He'd taken advantage of her trust, which was hard to accept. Not just hard to accept, it was betrayal of the sort she'd never experienced and never ever, *ever* expected from him. It was a gut punch. A kill shot. It was so overwhelming, she was frozen inside, almost unable to grasp the magnitude of what he said.

"Wow," was all she said for a few minutes.

"Can I interject here?" Angelique asked.

Krista couldn't take it if Angelique added to the list of things Swifty had done, the hardest of which to accept was how he'd caused her to doubt herself, which contributed to her taking it out on Angelique. All the drama of the last two days had been unnecessarily caused by Swifty and his damn pride. Not only would she have helped him if he'd asked—hell, she'd been offering it all along—but she and Angelique would have never gotten into the fight, and she wouldn't have pushed her away just as she was falling in love with her.

Who was she fooling?

She'd already fallen in love with her.

And she'd maybe ruined it.

"Go ahead. Lay it all on me," she said woodenly.

"Swifty didn't mention why he was doing this," Angelique said.

"To pay medical bills that the insurance doesn't cover for Dirk's treatment?" She already knew.

"There's more to it. When Dirk got diagnosed last year, he wasn't covered. All of last year was out-of-pocket for them. He has insurance this year, but last year ruined them. When I searched his address this morning, there was a listing about the house being in foreclosure and going up for auction soon. He's in bankruptcy now, and he's saving the money from the bikes to buy an RV so they won't be homeless."

Swifty wouldn't look at her; his eyes were red and watery.

"Is this true?"

He pressed the palms of his hands into his eyes. "Pretty much."

"I don't understand. You could have had coverage through the store."

"Both of us were healthy at the beginning of last year. Insurance coverage for me was costing the store way too much because of my age."

Krista remembered a day over a year and a half ago; she'd been on the phone with the insurance broker, and Swifty was in the back when she'd been working with the insurance broker, trying to get the best cost for coverage that would include Leticia's pregnancy care and not drive up the copays. Their broker had mentioned that Swifty's age skewed the average of the store demographic before she could mute it. Now she wanted to throw up. "I should never have discussed it in front of you. I would have figured it out, even if it meant paying higher premiums."

"You were going to have to take the cheaper plan for the store, but Leticia needed the good plan to cover her pregnancy."

"I would have figured it out," Krista repeated, trying to remember how everything worked in regard to the insurance decisions at the time. Everyone was covered. She wouldn't have allowed it otherwise. How had Swifty ended up without coverage? And then she remembered. "You said your nephew was able to find you a great plan at a fraction of the cost."

Swifty was stooped, his elbows on his knees, staring at the ground. He dropped his head into his hands. "I lied. At first, I thought we could, but between Dirk and me, we made too much to get on a discount plan, and the other plans were too expensive."

Krista couldn't believe she'd fallen for it. She still didn't know how the whole insurance thing went. Every year, she winged it, trying to look like she knew what she was doing, but she had no clue. She always just went with the broker's recommendations. She'd thought it was too good to be true back then, and now she knew it was. She'd failed at keeping her employees—no, her *family*—safe. All of her fears were true. She was a terrible business manager. Things had also escalated in the last days because she didn't know what she was doing.

"Why didn't you tell me?" she asked, staring into space, ashamed.

"After being shut down for almost a year during the pandemic and still paying our salaries, I knew you'd depleted a lot of our cash reserves, and you were struggling to make payroll. Dirk's young, and I only have a few years until I qualify for Medicare. I thought it was worth the gamble to go without insurance for a while. We hardly ever used it anyway." He flung his hand out in apparent aggravation before running it down his face. "I was wrong. The hospital has worked with us as much as they can, but it's still so expensive. I refinanced the house and sold both our cars to get Dirk on the stem cell treatment that finally made him respond to chemo. I don't regret one penny of it. But, yeah, a lot of Dirk's treatment was out-of-pocket last year until we qualified for discount insurance at the start of this year."

She hated that she couldn't get up and move around. Lying there and listening to this was torture. "I'll call the hospital. I'll figure it out."

He waved his hand. "Believe me, I have. The hospital has programs to help, and they wrote off a huge chunk of it. I also got assistance from various nonprofits that help folks in this kind of situation. I haven't figured out exactly how much has been taken care of, but the bills keep rolling in, and I have to go through them with the hospital and doctor's offices to figure out what's covered by what program, and I get tired of it sometimes, so I let the bills pile up, and then I start all over again. It's just a lot."

Krista struggled to sit up, and Angelique helped her. The conversation almost made her forget they were still…whatever they were, but Krista couldn't help but remember what they'd been to one another. Had it just been the morning before? It seemed so much longer. Her heart ached.

She held herself upright. Her pelvis hurt so much it throbbed, but she had to connect with him. She rested a hand on one of his arms. "Swiftman. Why didn't you tell me? Why are you insisting on doing this alone?"

"There was nothing you could do. I was embarrassed. You told me not to take myself off the insurance, and I did. Take your pick. When things got bad with the bills, I was already embarrassed enough for taking help from the hospital. I didn't want to admit to you that I needed the help."

She shook her head, not believing how all this could happen. "And then you came up with the bike thing to bring in money."

He hung his head, and his shoulders shook. He was crying, which made her cry, and all of the feelings of the last...not even twenty-four hours careened through her. "Yeah. I thought it was a perfect plan. No victims. I was ashamed about taking business from you, but I justified it by telling myself I wouldn't have been selling bikes otherwise. I wouldn't have been making sales in the first place. I just never thought about the tax thing. If I had, I swear, I wouldn't have done it. I'm just an old idiot."

She squeezed his forearm, her heart breaking for him. "You are not an idiot. You're pretty smart, actually."

"Please don't give me praise. I may have tried to justify it, but I still didn't tell you. That alone says everything. It was wrong."

Krista didn't know what to say and was glad when Angelique stood up. "This is awkward, but I have to open the store," she said. "Swifty, do you want a ride back?"

He looked at Angelique, his eyes swimming with tears, and Krista saw appreciation and something else that bordered on awe in them, and she didn't blame him. She felt the same thing when she looked at Angelique. How could she not, when Ang was capable of doing what she'd done to get all of this into the open so they could all have a chance to fix it?

"I can walk. It's just a few blocks, and the air would be nice. Thanks for being here. It really helped." He didn't meet either of their eyes as he spoke.

"I'll see you, then. Okay?" Angelique rested a hand on his shoulder, and he reached up to pat it.

"Why are you working today? Isn't Raggy holding down the fort?" he asked.

"He and Hilde had a prior thing, and I told him when I left yesterday that I'd come in. It's Sunday, our short day." She called Rupert and didn't look at Krista.

"You can leave him here if you want," Krista said without thinking, her mind more on the fact that Angelique was working seven days a week and hadn't mentioned it, even at her angriest. Or that Raggy had been at the store when things had flared up yesterday. God, Krista had put her foot in it. "They're having fun. I mean, unless you want him with you at the store."

Angelique hesitated, and Krista wondered if she'd put her in an uncomfortable position. "If it's not too much for you."

Relieved, Krista relaxed. "Not at all. They take care of each other, and it keeps Alfur from getting in my lap. I miss him, but I can't take the pressure yet."

Angelique gave a little wave and turned to go. "Well, then, I'll see you two later."

Krista watched her leave and wondered if she could fix the mess she'd made of things.

"You two *are* a thing, then," Swifty said.

"I'm not sure, actually," she said, looking away from his questioning eyes. She needed to focus on fixing the books instead of pining away for a relationship that had barely begun before it ended...although, it was hard to figure out which was her priority since she felt like her life was empty without Angelique in it.

Chapter Thirty-five

A ng sat in her car outside Sol Cycle after work. If Rupert hadn't been at Krista's, she would have just gone home. Tired and confused, she'd had time to think throughout the day, and her head was a mess. She wanted more time to get some perspective, but at the same time, she couldn't wait to see Krista again. The more she thought, the more she wondered what the hell she was doing. A little over a month since she'd quit her job at Lithium, and she still hadn't figured out what she was going to do with herself. It also occurred to her that taking the job at Sol Cycle really had been an odd thing to do. She hadn't been thinking clearly. She should have learned something from Kat and Geri's reactions. They'd told her she was out of her mind. She'd agreed, but it was fun. Until it wasn't. Really, though, she'd just wanted to spend time with Krista.

God, this thing with Krista.

It had always been about Krista, hadn't it?

In some ways, it was as if she'd put her life on hold and jumped into someone else's life. Like she was bewitched. She didn't think about her future or what happened or any of her old goals or dreams. None of it mattered after Krista.

How did it happen? Was it healthy? Sustainable?

Was it even real?

Or was she just avoiding facing her unknown future?

She rested her head against the steering wheel.

What now? She didn't have a clue, but she needed to pick up Rupert.

She put the car into drive, and before she knew it, she was parked in front of Krista's house. A note was taped to the front door saying to come in. She knocked, cracked the door open, and announced herself. The dogs came running. She thought about taking Rupert and just leaving, but it would be rude. With a stomach full of anxiety, she made her way to the little sitting room off the kitchen, looking for Krista.

She was in there, lying on the couch, a book open and facedown on her chest, watching as Ang entered the little room. The two dogs went right in and lay on the colorful rag rug in the middle of the room.

Krista scooted into more of a sitting position with a slight grimace. "I left the note because I figured you'd get here faster than I could get up."

Ang stood in the doorway, fiddling with her keys, a mix of emotions, mostly regret and loss, sitting like lead in her stomach. "I figured as much, but don't get up. I'll just collect Rupert and get going."

Krista settled back into the pillow. "How was work?"

"Busy for the first few hours and quiet for the last two."

"Sounds about right for a Sunday this time of year."

This was what they were reduced to? Small talk? "Is his leash still out back?"

"On the dining room table." Krista gestured toward the other room. "But can you stay? I mean, just for a little bit? You don't have to rush away, do you?"

Ang smoothed her hand over her head to push her braids back before she realized they were gone. She'd mostly stopped doing it, but it was always a shock when she forgot. "If you're asking if I have something to do, I don't. I should go, though." More small talk sounded painful.

Krista looked disappointed. "I guess I really fucked things up, didn't I?"

Ang sighed. "This isn't only on you. I screwed up, too. It would have probably happened eventually, anyway."

Krista closed the book and tossed it onto the coffee table. "I set you up so you didn't have a way out of the argument. I forced you to leave."

"You didn't make me leave."

"I did. I force people to leave me so I don't have to."

They had more in common than she'd thought. Ang was trapped between going to her and running away. She couldn't move. "That's not what happened."

"You left, and I ran, and here we are, and it sounds like I'm trying to manipulate you into wanting to stay, but I don't want to manipulate you. I just want to fix this." Her voice was so sincere, it made Ang's heart ache.

"I'm not in a very good place to talk." Since she'd quit her job, she'd done everything but think about what was going on in her life, where she wanted it to go, who she even was anymore. Maybe without so much distraction—i.e., Krista—it was time to do some real introspection and find out what she wanted to do, who she wanted to be, and what really mattered to her. Krista was such a wildcard thrown into her life that it was hard for Ang to focus. "My head is all over the place. I don't want to sound like a jerk, but I don't think talking about it now will be productive. I think some time would be good for me."

Krista nodded but looked disappointed. "Take whatever time you need. Just promise you'll let me know when you're ready to talk."

"I promise." She wondered if she could keep that promise, but she would try.

Relief flooded Krista's face, and she squeezed her eyes closed. "Thank you."

Ang couldn't think of anything or anyone more beautiful. "And I'll continue to work at the store." It was a promise she could keep, at least until she figured out what she was going to do with her life. "I assume Swifty will be back?"

"Yes. I told him we'd figure out how to fix the accounting entries to get it all in order and find out where everything stands. Do you think it's urgent?"

"It isn't, but we'll want to do it soon. You wouldn't pass an audit. But let me work with him to figure it out. If it's okay? I don't want to overstep again." Ang knew she should go, but she took a few more steps into the room. Krista was like a magnet.

Krista dropped her head into her hand. "Thank you for talking to him. For the record, you never overstepped. I wallowed in my insecurities, and rather than just admit it, I focused on...you know what?" She shook her head. "I'm not going to get into it. I asked you to help us, and I haven't been letting you do it. From this moment, until you decide to leave, you have my full permission to change anything you think should be changed. You have full autonomy, and I trust your judgment. I'd be a fool to not take advantage of your experience."

Ang wanted to argue but didn't have the strength. Also, she'd already stayed longer than she planned, and Krista on the couch was a temptation. If she stayed much longer, she wouldn't want to leave, which wouldn't be good for either of them. She gestured toward the door. "I think I'm gonna go. Are you okay? Can I do anything before I leave? Help you to bed?" Why had she said that? She had to leave.

"I'm fine here. My bed is a little too high to get in and out of comfortably. As long as I don't try to move too quickly, I'm fine." Krista looked like she had more to say but didn't.

"Well, then. I guess we'll head out." Ang turned to leave.

"There's one thing you could do. I mean, if it's not too much. Could you...I mean, could you...give me a pillow?" Krista pointed to a stack of pillows on a nearby chair.

Ang thought she was going to ask for a hug good-bye and was both relieved and disappointed when she didn't. She picked up the pillow and noticed a small red house on the table next to it. "What's this?"

Krista tilted her head with a half-smile. "I ordered it the same day we got your barbeque grill, when we tried to find one at the garden store, and they didn't have any. You should take it home and put it in your yard."

The sweet gesture tugged at Ang's heart. "Thank you."

"You're welcome."

Ang brought the pillow to her. "Would you like me to…"

Krista sat up, and Ang placed the pillow behind her. When she went to step back, Krista took her hand and pulled her. Ang wanted to resist it, but she couldn't. She sat on the edge of the couch and gave in to all of her feelings for Krista, taking her in her arms. When Krista's arms wrapped around her, she wanted to cry. Krista did. It destroyed Ang's heart to think she'd caused it, but she couldn't find a way to fix it. So she just held on tight, wishing she could change everything. It took everything in her to not kiss her, but that would have led to other things and make everything even more complicated than it was.

When they finally let go of one another, Krista held a hand over her face. "You should go now, before I make a bigger fool of myself."

Everything in Ang wanted to stay, to make Krista feel better. It killed her to know she was doing this to her. This was why she never did the leaving. But she had to be the strong one for once. She had to give them both space to think. She felt like she was leaving her heart as she stood. With Rupert on her heels, grateful Krista couldn't see the tears running down her face, she left.

CHAPTER THIRTY-SIX

K rista sat in her backyard on the lounge chair she'd been
spending most of her days in, soaking up the late afternoon
sunlight. A week from the hospital and she was more comfortable,
but she still needed to stay off her feet. In the span of the week she'd
been home, her backyard had turned from the trimmed back winter
version to the early spring version, with new leaves on trees and
bushes, purple buds on the lilacs, and the long leaves of the tulips,
hyacinths, and bearded irises rising taller every day. This was the
time of year she always looked forward to.

She took all of this in as if from behind a glass wall, though.
Her tender heart keeping her from really enjoying it.

Raggy sat at the patio table, sipping a beer after telling his
version of the blowup Swifty had the weekend before. Now she
felt even worse for having doubted Angelique's handling of the
situation. She needed to find a way to apologize and make it right.
Not wanting to get her uncle even more involved, she turned the
discussion to his and Hilde's relationship.

Alfur groaned as his big head rested in Raggy's big lap. Expert
fingers rubbed his ears. Raggy's bushy eyebrows squeezed together
as he pondered a question she'd just asked about why he hadn't told
her about his girlfriend, even as he'd visited her every day in the
hospital.

He finally turned his gaze back to her. "I wasn't *hiding* anything,
mitt krútt. I was just waiting for the right time. Just trying to learn

how to be me alongside another person after so long on my own. I had to know where to put the love for two great women in my heart."

"How long have you known Hilde?"

"As long as I've owned the cabin." He scratched the stubble on his neck. "Going on thirty years, I guess. She runs the co-op."

A parade of all the faces at the co-op she'd seen and talked to throughout the years filed through her mind. She couldn't pick out who might be the one to have stolen her uncle's heart. "I've probably bought groceries from her."

Raggy smiled. "It would be a feat if you did not."

"Have you been pining for her all this time?"

"Oh, a little crush, I guess, but she only had eyes for her husband, a great man. He passed four years ago this last January. She and I were friends for a long time before I asked her to accompany me to the Caribou Room to watch music, still as friends. She liked me as a friend, so it was on with the butter for me. Then one day, the lodge had a snowshoeing outing, and we took a rest on a fallen tree, and she said she was ready. And that's that."

"So *that's* how snowshoeing factored in. I can't wait to meet her. I mean, aside from all the times I've supposedly talked to her at the co-op." She felt so much better having talked to him about Hilde. It had been hard seeing him every day, wondering why he was keeping this big secret from her. She never suspected he carried such conflicted feelings about sharing his heart again, worried he might be pushing the love and memories of his first wife out of the place of honor.

Raggy flattened his huge hands on the glass top of the table, spreading his fingers and raising his shoulders before letting them fall. "She's been anxious to meet you, too. I didn't bring her to the hospital with the whole family there. She didn't want the first meeting with the family to be when you were not feeling your best."

"I should have you both over soon. Maybe when I'm a little stronger."

"It would be nice." He took another long sip of his beer. "Mitt krútt, there is one thing I have learned these past months, and it is this: I wish I hadn't waited so long to find love after your aunt passed. I'm telling you this because I watched you playing the field, so to speak. It's healthy as a young person, but you were never content. And then you stopped even playing the field. The solitude shows in your eyes. Me? I was content, more or less. But you're young. You have so much to offer. It would be too bad if you waited as long as me to share your heart, to join your road with someone. I thought maybe you had figured it out, but the small flame I saw for a while is gone."

She watched him for a moment. What else had he seen? Had he noticed how scared she was that she wasn't enough for Angelique? "Why are you telling me this?"

"Because I can see you. You're sad and maybe a little lonely?" He put his hand out and rocked it. "You walk your road like the road is just for one. And I see someone else who is probably the same. This person has great affection for you, and yes, I think love, too. And you for her. I don't want you to miss it when it is so special, you know?"

She wondered if Angelique had told him about them. The sting of tears never seemed very far off for her lately, and she rubbed her eyes. She realized that she'd kept her feelings for Angelique from her family much like Raggy had kept Hilde from them. Had she been trying to figure out where it belonged like he had? Now, she had to wait for Angelique to tell her if they had a chance. "It's not my call to make, Uncle Raggy."

"I don't think she'd be upset to hear from you. The road isn't so hard when you're on it with someone."

"She said she needed some space."

"Well, it's your store. She can't be upset if you came in to visit."

"My doctor won't clear me for work until next week at the earliest." Plus, Angelique might still get upset, and she didn't want to upset her any more than she had.

He sighed. "I said visit. Anyway, since when has any person in our family ever followed the rules?"

"Oh, let's see," she said, gazing toward the ceiling as if considering it. All of them," she said with a smile. Maybe the first real smile she'd given in over a week.

"All of them except you and me, mitt krútt."

She and Raggy were the odd ones in the family, the ones who did their own thing and made their own paths. There had been so many times when she'd felt alone and not understood, so many times she'd found that all she had to do was turn to Raggy to know she wasn't really alone. She raised her beer. He did the same. "Skal."

❖

Late April sunsets in Colorado were always magical, with golden light, deep blue skies, and light air. Krista opened herself to the magic as she walked the three blocks from her house to the shop. She'd thought about driving, but getting in and out of the car entailed more effort and pain than she wanted to endure. Besides, she needed to exercise.

The walk invigorated her. She'd stopped shuffling but still moved slower than normal, very careful to avoid tripping or overbalancing, imagining how it might be for her later in life. There could be no stepping up the curb like a healthy, uninjured person might do without thinking about it. She realized how much she'd taken her mobility for granted. Even the broken leg after the accident on Mt. Evans hadn't been as constrictive. The cast had been a pain, but she could roll in and out of bed and swing from place to place on crutches before they'd replaced it with the walking cast. Not so much with a bruised pelvis. She'd never thought about how much she relied on her hips and core muscles until she had to mind how she used them for the simplest of movements.

She smiled when she arrived at the shop. The outdoor planters were already filled with geraniums and petunias, which gave the place a splash of color. She shook her head at Swifty's annual display of optimism in planting flowers before Mother's Day, which everyone from Denver believed was the date for safe planting. But Swifty always said, if the frost or snow got them, the nursery had more. This year, it felt like coming home. She watched a dragonfly land on a strand of decorative grass. Vibrant blue, the small insect promised summer nights when the sky at sunset would be full of them, consuming mosquitoes and other pests, making it pleasant for lounging on porches and decks.

She'd come long after closing on a Friday evening because she could be fairly certain no one would be there, and she could see through the glass doors that the safety lights were the only thing illuminating the shop, telling her it had been closed for the night. She loved nights like this, alone in the back, music cranked up with the loading dock open to let in the breeze. Sometimes, she and Swifty worked on bikes together if he stayed late, too. He loved classic music from the seventies, and they would sing along to bands like Van Morrison and The Doors. But Swifty had already swung by her place on his way home from work to the hospital. She'd sent him to Dirk with a container of homemade *kjötsúpa*, made by her mother with chicken instead of lamb. The soup would be gentle on Dirk's chemo-ravaged stomach.

Being out of the house lifted her mood, which really needed lifting. Six days of no contact with Angelique had made her miss her more than she'd ever expected she would, and as more days went by, she started losing hope that there might be a chance for them in the future. She worried Angelique didn't miss her and wouldn't want to try again. Maybe she'd misread the hug last time.

Uncle Raggy's talk about love was still on her mind. She'd once asked him about Aunt Ing, and he'd said she'd been his forever love, his perfect happiness, and he had no desire to replace it, if that was even possible. The conversation had made an impact on her little self, and since then, she'd wanted the same thing. She wanted a forever love, and she would recognize it when she found it.

Something told her she'd found it with Angelique. She'd felt it in the park, a zing she'd never experienced before, a desire to be around her all the time.

The possibility of having lost her felt terrible.

Sadness threaded through her as she unlocked the door and disarmed the alarm. Alfur wagged his tail, probably happy to be back. The radio tuned to Swifty's station played in the back. It wouldn't be the first time he'd forgotten to turn it off.

The store looked good, even in the dim light. A few of the shelves had been moved around, and a new cycling jersey display was near the front, but the biggest change was near the front door, where all the bikes they moved out front every day were usually stored. Four carts holding at least ten bikes each were lined up against the wall. Genius. It would take a fraction of the time to move the bikes out and back in each day. They took up less space on the floor, too, making more room for inventory. She wished she'd thought of it.

The music grew louder when she and Alfur went into the back, and she was surprised to find Angelique and Rupert. Angelique sat with her back to them, but Rupert jumped right up and wiggled and wagged right over to her.

"Holy hell! You scared the crap out of me," Angelique said, leaping out of the chair. "I sensed someone behind me, but I thought it was just Rupert. How long have you been there?"

"I just walked in." Krista took the leash off Alfur and leaned against the workbench. She would have normally jumped up to sit on it, but her hips were already tight and sore from the walk to the store. "What are you doing here at this hour?"

"It's only"—Angelique glanced at the time on the computer screen—"eight. Yikes. Cleo is going to kill me."

Krista traced a scratch in the workbench with her thumbnail. "Lost track of time, huh?"

Angelique grimaced, running her hand over her hair. "I've fallen back into old habits I vowed to change."

"Nothing here is that important." Except everything was, especially Angelique. God, it was good to see her.

Angelique tilted her head. "You mean to me."

Krista felt like she'd missed something. "What?"

"It's important to *you*. What you mean is, it isn't important to *me*." She said it matter-of-factly.

Krista wondered what she meant. That Angelique didn't care about the shop like she did? Of course she didn't. It didn't represent her entire life. Yet Angelique had stepped up to do more than she'd been hired to do anyway. Because Krista needed her.

A thought hit her hard. She didn't have to be here; she *wanted* to be here. Krista cleared her tight throat. "I misspoke. Something here is important to you. It's obvious by the time and effort you've put into running the place while I've been unable to. Even before that, actually."

Something shone in Angelique's eyes. "Thank you."

"I should be thanking *you*," Krista said.

"I'm thanking you because I think you understand now."

"All I understand is I was terrible to you when you were trying to help me. You didn't need to get involved, but you perceived something threatening the store. Yet, instead of helping you figure it out, I let my insecurities get in the way."

Krista paused. Not just her insecurities about her abilities but also because she worried that Angelique deserved something she couldn't provide. She knew that now. She thought things were different simply because she'd felt that thing she'd been missing, that something different with her, the thing that told her they could maybe last. But that wasn't all of it. Raggy's words about finding her forever person echoed in her mind.

"I know I told you that I had a problem with not being kept in the loop about things, and there's something I haven't told you about, and it's that I've been struggling with some major insecurities about being able to run this place. But I've had time to think. All of that played a small part in it. It's really about how I felt about you... *still* feel about you." Krista stared at the floor, afraid Angelique wouldn't understand or didn't feel the same way about her.

Angelique took a few steps toward her. "You said you thought something here was important to me. It's actually someone."

Krista sensed her debating whether to approach. Under normal circumstances, Krista would have traveled the distance, but her hips were stiff, and she was afraid that if she tried to, she'd fall down. So they stood and gazed at each other, the half dozen feet separating them a gulf of indecision.

Uncertainty clouded Angelique's beautiful face, which tore at Krista's heart. She hated being the cause of yet more of her pain. Ignoring her fear of falling, Krista pushed away from the workbench, but as she feared, her legs didn't move as quickly. Thankfully, Angelique caught her.

"I shouldn't have let you stand there." Angelique pulled the chair over and helped her sit. "How did you get here, anyway? Tell me you didn't walk."

"I walked." Krista tried to mask the pain radiating across her hips.

"I told you not to tell me."

Krista tried to smile, but she couldn't get comfortable in the chair. Standing was actually easier. "I think I should go home and lie down."

"Do you want a ride?"

She hated to say it but nodded. "I overestimated the limits of my abilities because I felt better today."

Angelique picked up her keys. "You've been cooped up for a long time. Let me pull my car around. Don't go anywhere."

Krista couldn't if she'd wanted to. "Yes, my lady."

Angelique gave her a worried smile and hurried out. Krista peered around the back room. She'd missed it here. The bicycles hanging in neat rows from the hooks in the ceiling, the gear neatly stored on shelves.

She glanced at the computer screen Angelique had open to the books. Pleased, she noticed the errors from before were gone, and the totals in each column appeared to be in order. There were also a few reports added to the trends, inventory management, and services modules. The customer relationship module even seemed to be live when Krista thought it would be months before she got to it. Angelique had been busy.

"The car is out front." Angelique stopped behind Krista's chair. The chair tilted a little when Angelique leaned on the back of it. "I wanted to have all of it up and running before I showed you. It's mostly done, but there's still the chron jobs to set."

Krista peered at it. "Chron jobs?"

Angelique waved a hand. "It's just a fancy name for the timers running the analytics at certain intervals and then sending out reports. You picked out a great service management tool."

"I thought it was an accounting and inventory system."

"It is, but it does a lot more. I took the liberty of transferring the schedule into it and finished the work you started on bringing the inventory system into it. I did a few other things, but nothing you have to migrate to, if you prefer doing anything the old way."

"You did all of this in two weeks?"

"You made it easy having all the spreadsheets so well-managed. It just took uploading them into the system and mapping everything."

"This is amazing. And I couldn't get past the reconciliation error." For once, she felt no shame about that. Angelique's abilities didn't make hers any less impressive.

"Swifty disabled some of the error reporting. He's a pretty sharp guy. If he hadn't told me how he'd done it, I'm not sure I would have been able to unwind it either. By the way, we took care of it. The system is running error-free."

It sounded like Swifty and Angelique had gotten past their issues, a huge relief, but a minor dread settled over Krista. She'd been avoiding this for a week, telling herself not to think about it until she got back to work. She braced herself for the bad news.

"What kind of tax bills are we looking at? I really don't want Swifty to deal with any penalties or restitution or paying anything back. I'm going to take care of all of it, even if I have to get a loan."

"There's nothing to take care of."

"Please don't tell me he paid it all back."

"He doesn't have to. The rebates he collected from the vendors more than covered the taxes, and we're all straight on the quarterlies. With the books reflecting the proper accounting now, the reconciliation is working, and there are no taxes or vendor payments outstanding. He really did set it up to be a victimless crime. His words, not mine. We just needed the books to reflect it."

The news settled in like a warm balm, and even with the pain, Krista felt herself relax for the first time since all this had come to light. "So essentially, he just used the store as a wholesaler?"

"Pretty much. I mean, he took sales from you, but like he said, he wouldn't have been motivated to seek out the sales if he hadn't been desperate for the cash."

"I'm tempted to ask him if he wants to keep doing it. We could work out a commission that could help with the medical bills." The idea excited Krista. She hated to think her friend was still under a crippling financial burden, even if the shop's books were clear, and this was a solution.

"I talked to him about that, but he blew me off. Coming from you, he might reconsider."

"I just wish he'd talked to me about it. We all could have avoided so much stress. Has he told you what he's going to do about his house? He's lived there for so long. It makes me sick to my stomach about him losing it."

Angelique studied her hands. "Yeah, me too."

Krista could tell Angelique had more to say but didn't. All she wanted was for everything between them to be out in the open, the good, the bad, and the ugly. Saving people from hard things and making assumptions just screwed things up. "What? It's worse than he told us, isn't it? Don't try to minimize it for me. Let me in."

"The house already went up for auction."

Krista's stomach fell, and she dropped her face into her hands. Her heart ached for Swifty. "Oh no."

"I bought the house."

Surprise, elation, relief, and gratitude filled Krista's chest. "You did?"

Ang nodded. "A good friend of mine is a director at a bank, and she walked me through the foreclosure and auction process. I set up a trust, and when the house went up for auction on Tuesday, I won the bid for less than half it's worth. I wanted to tell you before I told Swifty because I plan to give it back to him."

Words almost failed Krista. Angelique was more generous than she'd even thought. "Just give it to him? Are you that wealthy?"

Angelique shook her head. "Most of my assets are tied up in Lithium stock right now. It's not worth anything until I actually sell it. Buying the house took a good chunk of my savings because they required cash. But I wanted to do this. I couldn't bear for him to lose his house. I wanted to ask you how I should tell him."

Overwhelmed, Krista didn't know what to say. For Angelique to do something like this for someone who had been spiteful toward her was probably the kindest thing she'd ever witnessed. "You…

are…amazing. I've never met a more generous person." Angelique looked embarrassed by the comment, but Krista didn't care. One thing occurred to her, though. "As kind as it is, I don't think he'll accept it. He's a prideful man."

"I know. Do you think he would if I sold it to him? The price I got it for with a fifteen-year mortgage would make his payment much less than the payment he was making on it before. He'd still have his house, I'd get my money back, and with a smaller payment, he could make more headway on the medical bills."

"I don't know. It won't hurt to offer." Krista took her hands, afraid Angelique would pull away. She didn't. "I've been thinking about this—you, me, us—almost obsessively over the last week. I discovered a few things about myself. I don't want you to think you were to blame for any of this. It's my fault. All of it."

Angelique's eyes shimmered with tears. "I'm not without blame here. I let my pride get in the way of Swifty's life collapsing and your rehabilitation."

Krista shook her head. "You had a reaction, and you deserved to have one." A pain spiked through her hips, and she couldn't hide the grimace. "I'd love to talk more about this. But can we do it at my place? My hips are screaming at me."

Krista watched concern fill Angelique's eyes, and her expression made her feel cared for and loved. It was something she thought she might have never seen had she not stopped thinking in terms of them being on separate roads, and hope filled her heart. All this time, she thought she'd been looking for something that promised forever, but she hadn't been. She'd been looking for something that showed her the way to real love. And it was there between them. It had been there since the beginning. There was a way to real love with Angelique. She just had to believe they were doing it together. Maybe this was the start.

CHAPTER THIRTY-SEVEN

A ng pulled up to Krista's house and, although Krista didn't say anything, the expression on her face showed she was in agony. "I'll let the dogs out and then help you up the walk." Sympathy flared within Ang at seeing the normally vibrant woman resting her head against the headrest, her eyes squeezed shut in pain.

The dogs wrestled on the front lawn, illuminated by the porch light as Ang helped Krista from the car. Krista moved slowly and deliberately. "I'm sorry. Sitting made me a little stiff."

"Don't be sorry. You were literally hit by a car. Take as much time as you need. You can lean more on me if it helps." Ang closed the door and brought Krista's hand over her shoulder, wrapping an arm around Krista's waist, enjoying the closeness she'd missed in the last week. Something had changed between them. She wasn't sure what it was, but it felt like a wall had lowered. She'd never sensed one going up, so she wondered if it had always been there, and somewhere in the last week, it had started to lower. Part of her still clung to the idea that she still needed to figure out what she needed to do with her life before she could consider jumping back into anything with Krista, but now she wasn't as sure as she'd been before about it. It might be easier to do if she had someone to help her figure it out. With these hopeful thoughts, she helped Krista up the walk.

Krista groaned as she mounted the three porch steps. "I made a mistake by not taking my medication today."

Ang held back a comment about not being a compliant patient but noticed her looking at Ang as if she expected one. "What?"

"I expected you to scold me about taking care of myself better."

"Would it change anything?" At the front door, she kept her arm around Krista, unwilling to let go.

"Not really." Krista handed Ang her keys. "I guess I overestimated my ability to heal. My hips are screaming."

"The doctor said it would take up to twelve weeks for you to move around *mostly* normally. It's only been *two*." Ang opened the door, waiting to let the dogs rush into the house before them.

"Still, three blocks? You're basically carrying me."

Ang imagined how hard it was for a former athlete to not be able to rely on their body. "I'm happy to do it." Ang helped her to the couch in the living room.

The relief washing over Krista's face when she lay on the couch seemed to radiate from her. She allowed Ang to give her some of her anti-inflammatory and pain medication.

"I've never wanted to lie down so badly in my life," Krista said, propping herself up on her elbow to put the pill in her mouth and swallowing it with a sip of water from the glass Ang handed her. "This pill is gonna conk me out. I'm such a lightweight when it comes to this stuff. I hate it."

"We shouldn't have waited so long to get you home." Ang sat on the low wooden coffee table next to the couch and pushed back a strand of hair hanging loose from one of Krista's braids. The hair felt like silk beneath her fingertips, just like she remembered. Her eyes found and held Krista's, and she longed to find a way back to where they'd been before.

"I miss you." Krista turned her head, kissing Ang's palm, and a light exploded within Ang's chest.

"I miss you, too." Ang took the water glass and put it on the table beside her, feeling more connected to Krista than she had in a long time.

"Do you want to hear my revelation?" Krista said.

Expectation swirled within Ang in anticipation of what she might say. The kiss on her palm told her she didn't need to worry, but more than that, it was the sense that a barrier between them had been removed. Still, anxiety remained.

"I told you it was my insecurity making me behave badly toward you."

Regret poured through Ang. All her life, she'd been told how intimidating people found her, and she'd tried so hard not to be, but an image of her mother flashed through her mind. She knew where the impression originated. She ran a hand over her head and stared at the floor. "I hope I haven't been triggering it. I've been told that, among other things, I can be cold, and I really hope I haven't been cold toward you."

Krista rolled onto her side with a grimace, and Ang took a pillow from a nearby chair to slide between her knees. Relief smoothed her forehead, and Ang ran her hand across the smooth skin.

"Thank you." Krista brushed a hand over Ang's forearm, and it sent a tingle up her arm. "You've never been cold. My insecurities stem from worries of people not taking me seriously. I love owning Sol Cycle. I grew up there. I can't imagine doing anything else, but I'm not sure I have what it takes to keep it competitive with the chains. Most other shops have been squeezed out. The only reason we haven't been yet is the friendly neighborhood thing. But it's changing. All the original homes around here are being torn down and replaced with big houses from people moving in from other states. The college has become a major university, with most of the students coming from out of state. Pretty soon—" She flapped a hand. "I have no interest in selling out to one of the chains, although I get approached about it all the time. I'm not sure I can keep us relevant."

This astonished Ang. Krista always exuded confidence, especially about her business. "Why haven't you told me any of this? I can help you. My career has been dedicated to maintaining relevance."

"I have no doubt you can. You naturally figure things out. Things I struggle with. Like the deep cleans. You were right about them. They take time, and we lose money. But our customers appreciate those little details. And you knew it, too. But I chose to keep them as they were, and you figured out a better way to do them without losing money. I could learn so much from you, but I choose to do things my way, learn for myself. Every time you do something effortlessly when I struggle reminds me of all the things I still don't know. I won't lie. I resented it. I can't just magically learn it all on my own, and I beat myself up for not being able to."

The resentment part stung, but she couldn't focus on it. "Don't beat yourself up. You're more of an expert in your field than I was at the same point in my career."

The comment appeared to brighten Krista's mood, and then her face fell, squeezing Ang's heart. "I hurt you."

"I think I hurt you, too." It felt good to admit it. Looking back, she'd fallen back to her competency for getting things done, and while it wasn't her work hours that had come between her and Krista, she'd still made so much of their relationship about work. She'd thought she was helping, but in a way, she was holding Krista at bay.

Krista looked puzzled. "How so? You've been nothing but supportive."

"My support has not always come from an altruistic place. I think I caused some of the insecurity you mentioned." She thought she'd feel better voicing it, but it actually called up regret and memories of past girlfriends who'd told her she was married to her job.

Krista's brow furrowed. "I don't understand."

"I thought I was helping, but I was also putting up a safety wall between you and me—if we didn't work out it was the job, not me. I guess I was showing off a little, too, pushing you into directions you weren't ready for."

"That wall thing sucks, but the directions you suggested make sense."

Krista was always so quick trying to make her feel better. She appreciated it, but she had to own her own shit. "Maybe. But I could have been more patient, understanding there are benefits to acknowledging the attachments to familiar processes." Ang breathed out heavily, wishing she could just throw away her superhero businesswoman suit and her hang-up about being an old fuddy-duddy compared to Krista's effortless coolness. "And I was stuck on our age difference."

Krista scoffed. "It's ten years. It's nothing."

That reaction gave Ang a relief she didn't expect. "It occurred to me that our life experiences made me uncomfortable, not our age differences. However, I've learned our pasts may be different, but the results aren't dissimilar."

"I don't understand."

"My entire adult life has been about meeting career goals. Similarly, you had your Olympic dreams. You, however, figured out the goals weren't worth what you were giving up. It took me, what? Fifteen years longer to figure that out. I've never owned my own business, either. So I might have some knowledge you don't, but you have quite a bit I don't. Even me being out of touch doesn't matter. The difference is, I don't like being a stuffy old suit. I watched you living your life, being the kind of person you want to be, and I want to be more like you."

"I hear what you're saying, but I have a hard time thinking you don't like the way you are. You're amazing." Krista rested a hand on Ang's knee.

Ang wanted to believe her. She placed a hand over Krista's. "I'm far from amazing."

"Don't fight me on this." Krista eyed her intently. "Raggy and I had a conversation yesterday." And Krista told her about the revelation she'd had of sharing her road. "I was maybe eight. I asked him why he never remarried. He said Aunt Ing was his true love. She died before I was born. He told me he knew the instant he met her that she'd be his one love. He'd never meet another like her. It stuck with me, this expectation that there's a perfect someone out there for me, who would share my road, and until then, I shouldn't waste my time."

Ang's stomach tightened in disappointment. It was the second time Krista had said she didn't want to waste her time. "Am I a waste of time?" Everything seemed to freeze as she waited for the answer.

Krista's face morphed into an unbelieving expression. "I wasted all of my time *before* I met you. I felt a link to you when we first met, as if some external power brought us together. I wanted to know you. Everything." She nearly shouted it, squeezing Ang's hand. "I want to share my road with you." Krista said, breathing hard as if reliving the memory, then she looked away, laughing self-consciously. "Sorry. I got a little carried away there."

Ang watched the feelings coursing through her. "Don't be sorry. I love that I can see your emotions."

"It's just that you're so serene all the time."

Ang snorted, remembering all the times she'd wanted to throat punch someone but had merely straightened the cuff of her suit jacket instead. "Maybe on the outside."

Krista gave her a disbelieving look. "What do you mean?"

"I learned a long time ago that people got really uncomfortable when I showed strong emotions. So I keep them contained."

Krista leaned forward with a mischievous grin. "I've seen you when you come. You were not keeping it contained then."

Heat moved throughout Ang's body, settling in specific places. "That's different."

Krista ran a hand along Ang's thigh. "I think I'd like to see fired up Angelique, then."

"I'm not so sure about that." The resentment she'd built up about being the gatekeeper of other people's comfort shifted within her.

"Try me. If you think you can scare me away with real emotion, you need to know you can't." Krista said it with such conviction, Ang believed her. A feeling Ang could only think to call trust enveloped her. It felt so good, she felt tears sting her eyes.

"Okay, but just remember you asked for it," she said, hoping Krista was right.

Krista laughed. "I knew what I was in for when I offered you the job you were way overqualified for," Krista said, slurring her words. Her pain meds must have kicked in.

Ang traced the top of Krista's hand with her fingertip. "And then things happened, and..." She couldn't say it.

"And what?"

"I lost..." Nope. She couldn't say it.

"You never lost me. I thought I'd lost you." Krista took Ang's hand. She missed the first time but got it the second time. Ang smiled. The drugs had definitely kicked in.

With her heart hammering in her chest, she watched their hands. She'd felt untethered away from her. She couldn't recall ever feeling that way before. She'd loved before, or at least, she'd thought she had, but she'd never experienced this kind of connection to another person. She wanted to call it desire, but it was more. It overwhelmed her. It yearned in the absence of Krista. This was something else. Something major. It had been there for some time, too.

Krista squeezed her hand. "I love you, you know."

The words fell against Ang like a physical weight. She lifted her gaze to Krista's gorgeous eyes, eyes normally clear and bright but which were now bloodshot, with dark circles beneath them. She was still utterly beautiful, but she appeared tired and in pain, but more than that, she looked intense and open. And scared. As if she'd just revealed something sacred, and she waited for Ang to hurt her.

"I love you, too." Ang said, her heart beating like a hummingbird.

Krista gave her a slow smile. "I know that person."

"What person?"

"The one who comes out after we make love and who lives in your eyes when you first wake up. The one who doesn't measure her words. The one who would probably do spur-of-the-moment things without pausing to consider if she should." She giggled. "The person who adopted a hairless cat and pretends to not like her most of the time but who cooks a chicken breast so the cat won't get sick of the same old food every day."

Ang glanced away. "I will not confirm nor deny your ridiculous claims." But she felt seen for the first time in maybe forever. That and telling Krista she loved her was the truest thing she'd ever felt.

Krista lifted and dropped their joined hands. "You have to confirm. Truth is truth."

Ang laughed. "I think you're on drugs, and you're dreaming."

"If it's a dream, I'll take it." Krista's head relaxed into the pillow, and she gazed at Ang with a smile, and then her eyes closed. The smile remained even after her chest rose and fell with the breathing of a person solidly asleep.

Ang continued to watch her, holding her hand as she thought about what they'd talked about but especially about Krista saying she loved her.

She'd said it back, too.

Ang hadn't told many women she'd loved them, and when she had, she'd deliberated for months before saying it, and there'd always been a little doubt. With Krista, it simply tumbled out after a month and a half, with little thought yet absolutely no uncertainty. She was in love with her and had been for a while. Maybe from the start.

Ang placed Krista's hands on the couch and repositioned her on her back, slipping a couple of pillows beneath her knees to take the pressure from her bruised pelvis. Krista didn't wake, but when Ang rearranged the pillow under her head, adjusting her long braids to the side so she wasn't lying on them, Krista ran her hands up Ang's arms and pulled her close.

"Don't forget I love you." She didn't open her eyes, but she took Ang's hand and held it tight.

"I won't," Ang whispered and kissed her lightly on her lips.

Krista smiled in her sleep, and Ang pulled the nearby chair closer to the couch, kicked off her shoes, and got comfortable. There was nowhere in the world she'd rather be.

Chapter Thirty-eight

K rista woke to the sound of a lawnmower somewhere in the neighborhood and Alfur curled up on the couch at her feet. She absently scratched the fur under his chin with her toe. The amount of sunlight streaming through the window told her she'd slept well past her normal 5:00 a.m., and Alfur, used to being fed at the crack of dawn, uncharacteristically remained asleep.

She moved her legs carefully. They were a little tight but not in much pain, a major relief. "Sorry, buddy. I'll get you breakfast as soon as I can get up."

He jumped down and lay on the rag rug, resting his head on his front paws.

She stretched gingerly, the internal bruising sending painful reminders that springing out of bed these days was a longed-for luxury. If not for the pillows beneath her knees while she'd slept, it would have taken five times longer to warm up her lower body enough to sit up. She didn't remember putting them there. She didn't remember falling asleep at all. Her last memory was of talking to Angelique.

Dueling reactions flowed through her. First, the joy of having Angelique near, talking to her, looking at her. Then, the pain of remembering how they weren't what they used to be. She wanted to cry and not because of the pain-med hangover. She missed Angelique so much, it hurt more than her injuries.

Gently rolling to her side, she pushed herself up just as slowly as she'd gone through her exercises. She wasn't as sore as she thought she'd be after her walk to the store. The pain that had blasted through her before she had gotten home and taken the pain pills was the worst she'd ever been in. Even the physical therapy only caused a low throb because of the medication. But she'd tried to go without the prescriptions yesterday, taking only over-the-counter meds. But by the time she'd arrived at the store, the ache had come back with a vengeance.

She rose carefully and shuffled toward the kitchen. As she passed the sliding glass door, someone walked across her lawn. Alarm flared until she recognized Swifty pushing her lawnmower. She opened the door to the aroma of fresh-cut grass, watching him make the last couple of trips across the small lawn. He killed the engine and waved when he noticed her.

She held a hand to her brow to block the sun. "What're you doing?"

"Your lawn needed a trim." He walked toward her, pointing to the far corner of the yard. "And I fixed the door to the fairy house. A screw came out."

Tears threatened again. "Elf house."

Swifty looked confused. "Huh?"

"It's an elf house. Fairies aren't real." She laughed at his even more confused expression. "Anyway, I can pay the high school kid next door to mow the lawn. Thank you, though."

"I like doing it. It's Zen, as Dirk likes to say."

"How is he?"

"Getting better. We'll find out more on Monday after the scan, but the doctor thinks the tumor will be gone or dead. The chemo about killed him, but he's a fighter."

She nodded. "He is."

He pointed at her. "Like you."

She laughed. "Me? No way."

"I heard you took a walk to the shop last night."

Angelique must have called him because it was his day off. Knowing they'd survived Swifty's guilt-ridden blowup made her happy. "Did Angelique tell you I couldn't make it back on my own?"

He shrugged. "You're getting better. It won't bother you so much when you do it again."

She'd missed him. They hadn't spent any time together since he and Ang had come over that day, although he'd called to check in several times. "You wanna come in for a cup of coffee?"

He appeared to think about it but ended up shaking his head. "Don't like to leave Dirk alone for too long." He took a step back.

She was bummed but understood. "Thanks again."

"I figured I owe you." He turned to leave.

"Swifty." She waited for him to turn, which he did, but he didn't raise his eyes. She wondered if they would ever be back to the carefree, almost familial way they'd always been. "You don't owe me anything."

He shoved his hands in his pockets. "I don't know about that."

"I do. You don't owe me anything." She gestured between them. "We are good. At least on my side. Are you good?"

He grinned and finally looked her in the eye. "Mostly. But I think I'm going to mow your lawn for a while if you're okay with it. I want to, so let me, okay?"

"It's a deal."

He smiled and left through the side gate after stowing the mower, and she went back in to feed Alfur and make some coffee. She wondered if Angelique had brought up the idea of selling the house to him. He had to be stressing pretty hard about it. On the counter near the coffee press, she spotted a note lying next to her keys and prescriptions:

Alfur woke me up at 6:00 to feed him. When I left, Swifty was pulling the lawnmower from the garage. We talked about the house. He said no, like you said he would, but I think I finally convinced him when I told him I couldn't afford both houses. Oh, BTW, I told him to come back at noon so you could sleep. Call you later.

Ang

P.S. Don't forget your meds.

P.P.S. There's quiche from the Bean in the fridge, Swifty's treat.

No wonder Alfur wasn't clamoring for his kibble. She checked the clock on the microwave, which displayed eleven, not as late as she thought but still later than she'd slept in years.

She reread the note. Between Swifty coming by to mow and Angelique staying to watch over her, she felt…loved. Fuzzy memories of their talk came back to her and an awareness of being connected to Angelique inundated her, a dream of telling Angelique she loved her. Was it a dream? It seemed so real. And Angelique had said it back. Her heart skipped a beat. Whether it happened or not, the reality existed, and she realized she was all in with Angelique now. Absolutely, completely, overwhelmingly all in.

CHAPTER THIRTY-NINE

A ng rocked the hammock she sat across by pushing away from the deck rail with her foot. It was night, but the shining white lights crisscrossing her backyard gave the area a festive air. She was alone, but she didn't feel alone, which was a major upgrade from the last couple of weeks. Hell, the last few years. Something in her had opened up, and although she didn't know exactly what she was going to do with her life, she didn't really care. She knew it would be all right, and the person on the other end of the phone now was a big part of it.

She switched the phone from her right ear to her left. She'd been on for almost two hours already, draining her AirPods but not her urge to keep on talking, and it didn't sound like Krista wanted to hang up either.

"She pretends to ignore me, but I catch her watching when she thinks I'm not paying attention," Ang said, eyeing Cleo, who sat in the window grooming herself.

"How could she not love you? You make her special chicken."

Ang sucked in her breath at the mention of the chicken, remembering when Krista had said she loved her. She wanted to bring it up. She *ached* to bring it up. But she couldn't. Did Krista even remember? Or maybe she did and regretted it. Ang had thought about it all day, though. She remembered how Krista had looked at her as if she was looking right into her soul, and she remembered how it had made her entire body tingly and how she'd had no power not to say it back. Drugged or not, Krista had said it, and it was everything. Ever since, the knowledge and awareness of loving Krista had lifted her like a balloon, expanding within her, filling her with elation, stretching her skin. Anticipation kept her on the edge of insanity. Not just a surface love but a deep and blazing love, consuming her. She couldn't think about anything else. Even the fear of Krista not remembering didn't matter. She did, and that was enough. It coursed through her, carving permanent reminders anywhere it touched, which was everywhere.

I love her. I love her. I love her.

It was silly, really, how she'd become this person. The one acting like a teenager discovering her first crush, wanting to declare it to everyone, write it on paper, etch it into the bench at work among all the scratches and gouges in the wooden surface, record it in the notes on her phone, write it in the steam on the mirror after her shower. The sensation of it being the best and if it didn't work out, the worst thing that had ever happened to her ping-ponged through her, filling her with elation and dread at once.

"What's she doing now?"

Krista's question brought Ang back to herself. Cleo was no longer sitting in the window. "She moved to her cabinet, still pretending not to stare at me."

"She's such a cool cat."

"I guess she is," Ang said. "She misses you, though." It tumbled from her mouth before she could stop it. "I mean, you let her sit on you for hours at a time."

"I kind of like the weight on my chest. I don't think I could sit in one place for so long anymore, though. She'd be disappointed. But I can get one of those cat carrier things, like those baby carriers you wear on your chest, only for cats and small dogs."

"She would marry you if you wore her around."

"I'm searching for one on Amazon right now." The tapping of keys over the phone corroborated her statement.

"You're crazy."

"Crazy for Cleo."

For a second, Ang thought Krista might say her name instead and disappointment rushed through her when she didn't. This was insane. She was talking to a woman she'd been intimate with. A woman she'd already said she loved. And she didn't know if Krista even remembered. "Have you taken your meds yet tonight?"

"I took the anti-inflammatory, but I'll wait until we get off the phone to take the pain pill. I don't want to fall asleep on you again. I don't want to disappoint you."

This wasn't the first time she'd mentioned disappointing her, and something tickled at the back of Ang's brain. "Do you really think you've ever disappointed me?" The sound of Krista blowing out a breath told Ang she'd touched on something.

"You got the brunt of it when the whole Swifty thing exploded." The deflated way she sounded after the light-hearted conversation made her wish she could go back a minute or two for a do-over.

"I won't pretend that we both couldn't have done better, but how was that about you disappointing anyone?" Ang was confused, and she hated to admit it, but a flare of frustration accompanied the confusion. How long would it take before they trusted themselves with each other?

Krista was quiet for a moment. "Well, there's the whole thing about not being able to fix the accounting issue. I'd been looking at it for weeks, and you pinpointed the issue almost immediately. But it wasn't just that. It's hard to explain. I felt left out, like I'd fallen backward somehow. I'm afraid I don't know why all those emotions came up, and I'm terrified that we might trip across it again. It reminds me of how I felt when I had to quit the cycling team after my accident."

The tickle in the back of Ang's brain became more pronounced. "I've been meaning to ask you if this accident has brought up bad memories of your previous injury."

"I've been thinking about it more than usual, but I think that's normal."

There was something there. Ang wondered if she should press for more. She didn't want to ruin whatever might be happening between them again but then decided it was needed if they wanted to have a chance. "This might be difficult, but do you want to talk about the disappointment over quitting? Because it doesn't sound like something anyone should blame themselves for. There were twenty-five cycles involved in the crash, and you rode into it. You didn't cause it."

Krista was quiet for a moment before speaking. "My injuries were not enough to cause me to quit. I quit because I didn't want to compete anymore."

"It's natural for athletes to lose their nerve after a bad crash like that."

"I didn't quit because I lost my nerve. I quit because I lost my competitive spirit."

Ang was confused. "Couldn't that be one and the same?"

"Maybe, but not for me. I'd been feeling it before that race. I was riding for everyone else but me."

"But you love to ride."

"I do. But I didn't love it when it was supposed to be my one passion. There's so much in life to be passionate about. But I was forced to put all of it into one thing. It sounds stupid saying it out loud. I've never told anyone this before."

She remembered Krista telling her that commitment eluded her. "Do you think that factored into your previous relationships?"

"You mean my commitment issues? How do you know about those?"

"You mentioned it once when we were on the phone. The morning of the accident. And Asta mentioned it, too. She picked up on something between us when I visited the hospital and said she was glad you'd gotten over your fear of commitment."

To Ang's surprise, Krista laughed, and it lightened the mood. There was probably more to say, but at least they'd started the discussion. "She's always been perceptive. She'll make a good therapist."

"Just to be clear, I am one-hundred-percent not disappointed in you. You've apologized, and I've apologized, so I think we're in a good place. Don't you?"

"I think so." No hesitation.

"I'd like to..." Ang began but stopped, afraid to stir up the things that had seemed to settle. God, she was a coward.

"You'd like to what?"

"I don't know." Ang couldn't bear for Krista to tell her they couldn't get back what they once had.

"There's something I'd like."

"Tell me." Ang thought she sounded normal, but they were on the edge of something, and anything coming after this could be irreversible. She felt like she'd driven off a cliff.

"I'd like to pretend the Swifty thing never happened. I'd like to be right back to the morning when we woke up together, and we made love, and you went to work, and I puttered around the house waiting for you to come home so I could ask you how your day went, and you would tell me you had a good day, but you couldn't wait to get home to be with me. That's what I would like. I would like it so much." Krista said it so fast, leaving no doubt that she'd been thinking about it as much as Ang had.

"I'd like it, too," Ang said. Her voice cracked on the last word, but she told herself not to cry even as tears slid down her cheeks. She wanted it so badly, she was choking on it.

"How do we do it? How do we get back to before?"

As much as Ang wanted to ask Krista to come back to stay with her, it didn't seem like the right path forward. "You were staying here. You don't need my help anymore."

"I loved the help you gave me. Have I told you how much I appreciated it? All of it."

Ang gave a small laugh. "You've been very good at telling me." And she had, until all this...crap got in the way.

"Good." Krista paused, and Ang wanted the conversation to return to how they got back to before. "But you're right. I have to focus on getting better, and I think that if I let you take care of me, I'd be pretty distracted."

Ang's stomach dropped. It turned out that, even with the doubt, she'd been hoping for the best. She felt like she was falling into a million little pieces. "Do you mean we shouldn't see each other until you're stronger?"

"I think it might be best. I'd have motivation to recover. Besides, I don't think it would be very fun for you to watch me fall in and out of naps. Because it's all I do right now. I read and nap and occasionally go out to the backyard. Even Alfur is fed up with my pet rock impersonation. I don't want you on the receiving end of how grumpy I get."

She liked that Krista didn't want to be grumpy *at* her. "But we can talk on the phone like this, right?"

"I'd be very sad if we didn't," Krista said.

Ang wasn't ecstatic about it, but at least they could talk. "Okay. It's a plan. We'll talk on the phone until you're stronger."

"I'm doing my exercises as we speak."

Ang laughed. "Don't overdo it. Bad things happen when you overdo things."

"Believe me. I'm following doctor's orders from now on." Krista sighed. "What we talked about before, about the quitting on purpose and problems with commitment? Asta tells me I haven't processed it, and I should get a therapist. I tell myself, she's a therapist, so she thinks everyone should have one. But she's probably right."

"It's not a bad idea," Ang said, grateful Krista trusted her enough to confide in her. All she wanted to do was to hold her and comfort her, but for now, she settled for phone calls.

She kicked the deck to keep the hammock swinging. Cleo stared at her through the glass door, and when Ang waved at her, she put her paw on the glass. It made her hopeful for their relationship growing stronger, and that was what she'd continue to hope for with Krista. For love to work, she had to have hope.

CHAPTER FORTY

A week later, Krista navigated the Sol Cycle website while Angelique walked her through it over the phone. She was pleased with what she saw. "I really like the updates Swifty did. They give me other ideas, too. Did you give him detailed instructions, or did he come up with all of this himself?"

"I gave him a few requirements, but he had ideas. The events page is all his, and he came up with the sale carousel."

Krista still couldn't believe how quickly Angelique and Swifty had become such a dynamic duo after everything that had happened. She clicked on the page to make the carousel spin. "It's my favorite thing so far. It's very sleek."

Angelique sounded pleased. "I thought so, too. What about the job posting?"

"It's good. You took most of what I wrote and rearranged it, making it appear more…" She tried to find the word.

"Dynamic?" Was Angelique reading her mind?

"Yes. That's it. Dynamic."

"We have a few applicants already."

She knew it was coming, but Krista wasn't prepared for the wave of dejection washing over her. "Great. Sad, too, though."

"Why sad?"

Angelique sounded authentically surprised, and Krista wondered if she was anxious to get on with her "real" job search.

She couldn't help but feel a little resentful. "Because it means you'll be leaving." Her dejection increased when saying it out loud.

"I'll still be around. Besides, it's not like we see each other a lot as it is," Angelique said.

She probably didn't mean it the way Krista heard it, but the statement still hurt. "I'm stronger and better every day. Pretty soon, I'll be ready to spend time at the shop. I'm thinking I might start with half days next week."

"Are you sure? You'd be on your feet or sitting upright."

Angelique didn't sound convinced, which irritated her. She wanted to hear excitement. "I'm sitting upright on a stool at the kitchen counter as I speak."

"I guess you're making better progress than I thought you were," Angelique said, and this time, she sounded pleased.

The happiness in her voice made Krista smile. It made her not want to admit that sitting upright caused pain, and she couldn't stand in one place for any amount of time. But maybe by next week, it would be different. She did her exercises religiously, and the physical therapist *did* say she might be strong enough to go to work part-time by next week. Specifically, a ten-percent chance, but Krista kept hoping.

"I'll try not to get in your way when I come back, if you're worried about that. From what Swifty says, things are running flawlessly. I don't want to mess that up."

"I'm far from flawless. In fact, I'm kind of an annoying stickler for most rules."

Krista chuckled. "I'll let you in on a secret. I may not be a stickler, per se, but I'm a bit of a rule follower, myself."

"While we're confessing our flaws, you've been there when my tendency to take over projects happens."

"A forgivable tendency," Krista said. "I know how to stand my ground."

Ang blew a breath that Krista heard over the line. "I lose track of time when I'm working. It's been a problem in past relationships. I've been meaning to tell you." Angelique was on a roll now.

Krista didn't intend to let anything deter her. She planned on becoming and staying Angelique's present relationship. "I'll become an expert at finding ways to make you want to come home at a reasonable hour." Ang's low laughter made her shiver, and she didn't correct herself for accidentally saying come home rather than go home. The way she'd been missing Angelique, the mistake was a wish and not a slip of the tongue.

"I'm not as socially conscious as I should be. I've never volunteered for a cause or marched for justice. I send money, and I've done a few bike rides, but I'm greedy with my time."

This was something Krista was surprised by, but it just made Angelique more human. "Something I have to get better at, too. Maybe we can help each other. I've always wanted to do the Furry Scurry. Alfur and Rupert would enjoy it."

"That run once a year in Wash Park? Sounds like fun," Angelique said.

"What about this age thing you talked about the other day?" Krista waited with mounting anxiety.

"I'm over it. Age is a state of mind. I mean, between the two of us, who's the one who needs a cane to get around these days?" Angelique giggled. "So I guess it's up to you. I mean, if you're into older women."

Krista liked Angelique in a silly mood. "If you ask me, which you did, it isn't a thing at all. I think we get each other, enjoy each other, and have a lot of the same interests, which is what matters to me. And, for the record, I get around just fine…on my back." She wished she could see the expression on Angelique's face. Her own was probably just as funny as she thought Angelique's would be. Had she really said that?

"Are there carnal thoughts going on in that pretty head of yours?"

"I can't deny it. I've had impure thoughts about you since we met."

"The first time or the second?" Angelique asked. "I'm not sure either answer will be good, considering the morose mess you met the first time and the sweaty, hungover mess the second time."

"With legs for days both times."

"Exactly what I thought about you!" Angelique said.

"Yet another thing we have in common." Krista smiled. "I can't wait until I get cleared to work. I can't wait to see you every day."

Krista hadn't felt so good, so *alive*, in weeks. It didn't feel like they were on track to where they'd been before things had gone badly, before the accident, before the thing with Swifty. It felt like they were on their way to a better place. A place where they were on more even paths, where their roads might come together with more substance.

Chapter Forty-One

A ng tossed Rupert a dental chew, which he caught. She watched him circle three times before he settled in Alfur's bed with it. It would be gone in minutes. She'd gotten used to his many unique quirks over the last weeks and wondered how she'd lived without him. She definitely would have worked less if she'd had a dog before, and maybe it would have saved some of the heartache she'd caused because of it. But then, she probably wouldn't have risen so quickly in her career, and there was a good chance she wouldn't have quit her job. Or met Krista. She wouldn't be thinking about leaving Sol Cycle, either. So maybe things did happen when they were supposed to.

"I can't imagine this place without a dog sleeping under the desk," Swifty said as he passed behind her and picked up the wrench he'd left on the desk after their weekly huddle.

She barely noticed. She missed her old job and most of what went with it. She missed most of the people she'd worked with, too and wished she'd kept in touch with them after she'd left. She hadn't returned most of the voice messages checking in on her and telling her they missed her over the last several weeks. None of them deserved it, but she needed a little time to get her head clear. Now, less than two months later, she thought she might start reaching out to a select few. People like Anne and Neil.

She still liked it at the shop. It had never been a major challenge, if she didn't count the episode with Swifty, which was solidly behind them now. But in the time she'd worked there, it had already become familiar to her, a comfortable place. Not as if she'd always worked there, but more in the way of being part of the team and not always on guard. She could be proud of her work there. If she'd learned one thing during her time at the shop, it was the art to maintaining the balance between a neighborhood business and getting too focused on the bottom line.

She wondered what Geri would say if she told her she was thinking of staying. Her hand was on her phone dialing before she even realized what she was doing.

"You caught me during my planning period. This better be good, yo." Geri's voice was playful, belying her words.

"How's your day going?"

"You did not call me to ask about my day. Are you okay?" Geri always could cut right through the facade. Ang loved that about her.

"What would you say if I told you I was thinking about staying at the bike shop?" she asked, her stomach filled with anxiety about the response.

"I'd say, tell me something I didn't know."

Angelique was legitimately flabbergasted.

"But, before you try to argue with me about how mysterious you think you are, let me tell you this: a month ago I would have invoked our blood oath to one another that if one of us did anything that truly scared the other, like finally, completely lost it, we would do the tough love thing and drag them to a hospital for an evaluation."

"That was a joke."

"Not to me, it wasn't. Dealing with adolescents will drive a person to drink if not to darker places. I need you to tell me you will be that friend for me."

"I promise, I am that friend."

"We'll redo the blood part at the next Rockies game. So you want to run a bicycle shop now? Permanently?"

"I think I might. Am I being stupid?"

"Honestly?"

"Like you ever sugarcoat anything?"

"Okay. The honest truth. You love her. You want to spend time with her. You're understandably gun-shy about jumping back into corporate America. You have the savings to hold you over for a while, and maybe after that, you can downsize. Those are the facts. I say, do it. But I give it six months to a year before you're looking for another corporate job. You need the challenge."

Angelique appreciated the cut-to-the-chase honesty. "I love you, you know."

"I know. I know. That's what best friends do. I gotta go. One of the demons needs to discuss his zits or something. See you Tuesday. Rockies against the Cubs. It's gonna be a good one."

Ang said good-bye to Geri and refocused on her project list, pleased that many of the ideas were already in progress or had been completed. Geri was right. It gave her a huge sense of satisfaction to help make Krista's life easier when she finally came back, but after a while, the challenge would be gone, and she'd probably get bored. Until then, she'd have fun continuing to improve workflows for Sol Cycle.

In the meantime, she missed Krista. There had been many a day she'd wanted to drive by her house, dying to see her. But Krista had asked for time, and Ang would respect it. Talking on the phone every day, sometimes more than once, helped.

"How are the website updates working out?"

Swifty's question startled her. She pulled up the tracking report she'd created. Site traffic had increased considerably. She swiveled to face him. "The special we ran over the weekend gave us a spike in visits as well as sales. We also have a couple dozen applications for the new position. I think the update to the website did the trick. Some of the applicants talk about growing up with Sol Cycle."

He tossed his metric wrench on the bench and picked up another tool. "I'll go through the stack of candidates you narrowed after work tonight. Have you set up any interviews?"

"Not until I talk to Krista. I figure it's really up to her and you. I'll give my input based on the resumes, but you two should make the decisions."

"I'm pretty sure she'll take whatever guidance you give. Although, I think you should stick around."

His last remark hit her right in the feels. "Well, my guidance would be to make you the manager. But you won't take it. So I guess I can stick around until the right candidate comes around."

He shook his head. "I'm not a manager type, but I like the sound of you sticking around for a while. It's going to take some time to find someone to fill your shoes."

It was like he was *trying* to make her cry. Krista was her main reason for wanting to stick around, but she would really miss Swifty. They had come a long way in just a month.

Ang's phone rang, and without checking the caller ID, she swiveled back around and answered it.

"Hi, Ang. It's Janelle. From Lithium."

Ang's heart jumped in her chest. Just the sound of her old company's name made her anxious. Two months since she'd quit and it was only within the last week that she'd been able to go through an entire day without thinking about it.

"Have I called at a bad time?"

Janelle's voice pulled her from her thoughts. "No. I'm just stepping outside." Ang went out through the open loading dock to stand near the entrance to the alley. "How are you, Janelle?"

"I'm well. How are you?" Janelle's voice sounded friendly as usual, and Ang thought about all the good people still working at Lithium. It only took a few assholes to ruin it.

"I'm doing well," Ang answered. She leaned against the brick wall. "I suppose you want me to come down to finally fill out the paperwork?" She thought about offering to pay back the salary she'd continued to receive, but a part of her wanted the company to have to ask her for it. They were lucky she hadn't decided to sue their asses. Geri brought it up all the time for promising her the EVP job and then giving it to Carl fucking Davies. Just thinking about it made her blood run hot.

"Yes, but not to sign resignation paperwork. Barbara Daniels would like to talk to you about remaining at the company."

"Barbara Daniels? The owner?" Shock rocked through her. She'd spoken with Barb at a few corporate events, and she'd always been pleasant to talk to, but Barb ran her own companies and foundations. As far as Ang knew, Barb didn't have anything to do with Lithium. Her husband Bharat was the CEO.

"Barb runs Lithium now. Bharat stepped down as CEO due to health concerns."

"I hope he's okay." Ang's concern was genuine. Bharat had always been a good leader. She couldn't blame him for Robert's terrible leadership; well, at least not too much. Responsibility rose to the top, after all.

"He's expected to make a full recovery. But in the meantime, Barb caught wind of what happened and would like to discuss it with you. She wants to offer you a new position. She'll go into more detail, but I have to tell you, the offer is much-deserved and between you and me, should have been yours already."

Intrigued but with reservations, Ang had questions. "Why's Barb handling this? Is Robert involved?"

"Robert is no longer with the company, nor is Carl Davies, as well as a few others. Barb will fill you in. I hate being vague, but if what happened to you had happened to me, I'd never set foot in this building again."

The anger in Janelle's voice gave her a sense of vindication. "Thanks for saying that, Janelle. It helps."

"You know what? Screw it. You didn't deserve what happened. There's been a major restructure as a result," Janelle said. "Your resignation sent a shockwave through the organization. It brought to light a few things going on, and suffice it to say, Lithium has no tolerance for cronyism, quid pro quo, and several of the exclusionary activities we found when we had a consulting company examine every department from top to bottom. We're pretty sure we've weeded most of it out. Barb wants you to be a part of returning Lithium to the respectable company it used to be. You have a history of great leadership, innovative ideas, and a reputation for fairness. She wants you to model it to the rest of the company. She's going to offer you Chief Marketing Officer. I just told you far more than I should have, but I want you to walk into the meeting with all the confidence in the world. I want you in the position so badly, I can't express it."

Ang got over her initial shock, discussed the meeting with Janelle for a few more minutes, and set a date and time. When the call ended, she sagged against the alley wall, overwhelmed by the complete turn of events. She'd woken in the morning thinking about website updates, and now, a few hours later, she sat mulling over the prospect of going back to Lithium. It didn't feel real. She had a lot of thinking to do.

Back at the loading dock, she popped her head in through the door, grateful to see Swifty still working at the bench. He hardly looked up, but his wave told her things were under control when she told him she was taking an early lunch.

A half hour later, she found herself in Wash Park, not remembering the walk over as she took a seat on a bench by the big lake. Her sense of being overwhelmed hadn't eased. One surprising thing kept nagging at her. The remembered smell of the Lithium lobby. Silly, but a shot of excitement had always hit her when she'd walked through the turning doors. Something on her walk must have inspired olfactory memories of the combined odors of the freshly showered crowd arriving at work, the chlorinated water from the fountains in the open atrium, and the floral scent of the huge flower arrangements in each corner. A sensory reminder of how much she'd loved her job made her miss working downtown.

She took it all in and realized that if she went back to Lithium, she wouldn't have days like this, where she could sit on a bench in the park at midday, watching the runners and the walkers, the birds on the water, and the kids learning how to ride their bikes. Loss swept through her as she squinted against the light reflecting from the lake, and she realized she had already decided to go back to Lithium.

Chapter Forty-Two

K rista dusted off the handles of the electric scooter parked next to her Jeep. She'd ridden it only a few times since she'd gotten it, preferring to ride bikes, but it had grown harder and harder to deal with not going anywhere except to doctors' appointments. Stir crazy didn't come close to describing how she felt. She desperately wanted to ride her bike, to get some cardio in and to feel the wind on her skin, but she wouldn't be cleared for at least a few more weeks, no matter how much she begged her physical therapist. But then she'd remembered the e-scooter and instead of asking for approval from the doctor, she decided she'd ask forgiveness if something happened.

A couple of test runs in front of her house gave her the confidence to take it for a spin. Of course, there would always be the risk of crashing, but just being outside carried risk, and she couldn't stop living her life because of what-ifs. She could do this.

She ducked into the house to get her helmet, and Alfur followed closely, performing his little spin dance when she picked up her helmet.

"Sorry, bud. Maybe we can go for a short walk tonight after dinner if this goes well." To appease her guilt, she gave him a couple of chews, which he ignored, but she knew he'd go back to them when she left.

She closed the garage, and a circle around the block gave her the confidence she needed to go for a longer ride. Exhilarated, she took off in the general direction of the park. Just one loop before heading back home would do it. She didn't want to overdo it again, and she had good reasons to not want a setback. A specific beautiful face took form in her mind, making her smile.

The wind flowing over her skin felt better than she remembered. Even going slowly, it only took a few minutes to arrive at the park with its vibrant green, all the leaves filling out the trees, the tulips beginning to bloom, and the early goslings and ducklings trailing their mothers on the lakes. She wished Angelique was with her as she completed a loop around the park. Not wanting to go directly home, it occurred to her she could drop by the shop on the way. The urge to see Angelique overpowered her. They'd been talking every night but hadn't made any specific plans to meet yet, but she yearned to see her.

Just as she turned to exit the bike path to leave, a deep, distinctive bark made her turn. Rupert raced toward her, not twenty feet away, dragging his leash. Angelique followed another twenty feet behind him.

A warm rush of pleasure erupted in her chest as her eyes remained on Angelique, and she scratched Rupert behind the ears, picking up his leash. "I've never heard you bark before, buddy."

"I haven't either," Angelique said, a few steps away, watching Krista as intently as Krista watched her. She reached for the leash but caught Krista's hand instead. She stepped closer. "Somehow, I expected it to be high-pitched. The deep rumble surprised me."

Krista couldn't stop smiling.

Angelique's smile was just as bright as she tilted her head at the scooter. "Are you cleared to ride scooters?"

"I haven't asked. All I have to do is stand on it."

"Something tells me she would frown upon this activity." Angelique wore an example of the very frown, which tickled Krista.

"She frowned upon sex for the first two weeks, and we didn't pay attention to her advice *then*." She liked the sparkle now in Angelique's eyes. "Hey, that's nice to see."

"What?"

"The look in your eyes." Krista's stomach did a little flip as she continued to hold Angelique's gaze.

"You have a thing for eyes, don't you?" Angelique asked.

"Definitely for yours." Another flip.

"You said something similar when I took you home the other night." A soft smile played on her lips. "You were staring into my eyes when you said 'I know that person.'"

A fuzzy memory of Angelique sitting near her as she lay on the couch came to her. The memory had been on her mind a lot the last few days. Until now, though, she hadn't been sure it was real or just wishful thinking. "Right after you told me you loved me," she said. "After I told you I loved you."

Angelique's smile softened. "So you do remember."

"It seemed like a dream until now," Krista said. A wonderful dream.

"Do you remember another day, another memory, one that happened on the other side of the bike path just a little farther up?"

"The day we met." The memory was never far from Krista's mind. She'd had no idea what that chance meeting would mean to her future and her heart.

Angelique gazed into the canopy of the tree shading them. "A lot has happened in the last couple of months."

"Yes. It has." Krista squeezed Angelique's hands.

"Did you mean it?" Angelique asked, lowering her gaze back to Krista's.

Krista didn't have to think. "Probably more than I've ever meant anything in my life."

Angelique's eyes glistened. She rested a hand on Krista's cheek. "I have no choice but to kiss you now, you know."

Krista's heart threatened to explode with happiness and love. "If you have no choice, I suppose I should comply."

"It would be a first." The corner of Angelique's mouth quivered.

"Everything is a first with you. Now kiss me before I have to beg you." Krista never wanted anything more.

Angelique kissed her in a way that told Krista there was no question about their future together. She didn't have the details, but she did have a certainty she'd never had before coursing through her, one telling her they would make things work. The kiss was a single promise, and she answered it back with her own promise, one saying she would be there until the end.

Out of breath, Krista broke the kiss, putting only a fraction of an inch between their lips.

Angelique smiled, breathing heavily. "I definitely have a thing for your eyes. Something you've probably been told a lot."

"Not from anyone who looked at me the way you do," Krista said.

"And how's that?" Angelique asked with a sexy half-smile, like she already knew but wanted to hear it.

"Like you love me back." An eternity of love passed between them with those words.

Angelique nodded. "I really do. I love you so much."

Epilogue

One Year Later

Ang stood in front of the walk-in closet and slipped into a pair of capris. They went very nicely with the flowing blouse she wore. Krista watched while lying on her side in bed, the sheet barely covering her nude body, her head propped on her hand.

"First, you wore suits, then it was a nice pair of slacks and a button-up shirt. Now you've graduated to shorts and a hippie shirt. What's next? Short-shorts and a tank? What are all the cell phone buyers in the world gonna think when they walk into the stores and get accosted by a nearly naked sales rep asking them what carrier and plan they have?"

Ang threatened to throw a sandal at her. Krista put her hands in front of her face, pretending to be scared, which made the sheet slip down to expose her breasts. Ang dropped the shoe and pounced on her.

"I'm pretty sure we'd make more sales if nearly naked sales reps ran our stores. But we don't. We have neat, yet comfortably dressed team members who are relaxed in their appearance, which elevates their mood. Team members in a good mood make more sales than I suspect nearly naked sales reps would make because the air-conditioning can be a little chilly. Dress codes are an archaic form of imprisonment, and it only took me a year back at the company to abolish them once and for all."

The dogs, used to frequent bouts of wrestling, remained curled up on Alfur's bed while Rupert's bed remained unused. Cleo slept on Ang's pillow, snuggled inside Ang's discarded sleep shirt.

"Aren't you glad you got rid of them?" Krista asked, trailing a chain of nibbles along Ang's neck.

Ang fought distraction when she replied. "One of the best decisions I made when I went back to Lithium."

"A distant second only to you talking Barbara Daniels into establishing a charitable foundation that helps working-class people not lose their homes due to medical debt," Krista said.

"Too bad it came too late to help Swifty and Dirk with their house."

"But you snatched it back at the auction and deeded it right back to them."

"I only wish I had time to hide my identity. Now, I have two men and a gardener jockeying for chances to mow my lawn." Ang never thought she'd see three men fighting over her flora and fauna.

"You have the best-looking landscape in the neighborhood."

"*We* have the best-looking landscape," Ang said.

"Which reminds me, I have to take all the moving boxes to the recycler." Krista rolled atop Ang, who enjoyed the weight along the length of her body and the lips making their way down to her breasts. "Have you decided if you're going to New York next week?"

Ang shook her head. "I'm sending Neil. There's no way I'm going to miss Raggy's birthday."

Krista's face lit up with a delighted grin. "Hilde will be so happy. She was trying to figure out an alternate date. She said it wouldn't be right without you there."

"She's sweet."

"Not as sweet as you," Krista said, nibbling on Ang's nipple, causing shivers to run down her spine.

She wrapped her legs around Krista's body and rubbed against her. "You're going to make me late for work again."

"I'm sorry," Krista said, reaching around and cupping Ang's ass.

"You are such a liar." Ang tried to push Krista away but without real intent.

"You've discovered my devious plan."

"It's only devious if you aren't so obvious about it."

"What do you know about devious? You don't have a devious bone in your body."

Ang pulled Krista up and kissed her since the question was rhetorical. Besides, she wasn't about to tell Krista she'd been setting the alarm an hour earlier so she could still have time to make love *and* get to work on time every morning. Krista hadn't caught on yet, and she didn't need to reveal *all* her secrets.

About the Author

Kimberly Cooper Griffin is a software engineer by day and a romance novelist by night. Born in San Diego, California, Kimberly joined the Air Force, traveled the world, and eventually settled down in Denver, Colorado, where she lives with her wife, the youngest of her three daughters, and a menagerie of dogs and cats. When Kimberly isn't working or writing, she enjoys a variety of interests, but at the core of it all she has an insatiable desire to connect with people and experience life to its fullest. Every moment is collected and archived into memory, a candidate for being woven into the fabric of the tales she tells. Her novels explore the complexities of building relationships and finding balance when life has a tendency of getting in the way.

Books Available from Bold Strokes Books

A Fox in Shadow by Jane Fletcher. Cassie's mission is to add new territory to the Kavillian empire—murder, betrayal, war, and the clash of cultures ensue. (978-1-63679-142-5)

Embracing the Moon by Jeannie Levig. Just as Gwen and Taylor are exploring the new love they've found, the present and past collide, threatening the future they long to share. (978-1-63555-462-5)

Forever Comes in Threes by D. Jackson Leigh. Efficiency expert Perry Chandler's ordered life is upended when she inherits three busy terriers, and the woman she's referred to for help turns out to be her bitter podcast rival, the very sexy Dr. Ming Lee. (978-1-63679-169-2)

Heckin' Lewd: Trans and Nonbinary Erotica by Mx. Nillin Lore. If you want smutty, fearless, gender diverse erotica written by affirming own-voices folks who get it, then this is the book you've been looking for! (978-1-63679-240-8)

Missed Conception by Joy Argento. Maggie Walsh wants a relationship with Cassidy, the daughter she's only just discovered she has due to an in vitro mix-up. Heat kindles between Maggie and Cassidy's mother in a way neither expects. (978-1-63679-146-3)

Private Equity by Elle Spencer. Cassidy Bennett spends an unexpected evening at a lesbian nightclub with her notoriously reserved and demanding boss, Julia. After seeing a different side of Julia, Cassidy can't seem to shake her desire to know more. (978-1-63679-180-7)

Racing the Dawn by Sandra Barrett. After narrowly escaping a house fire, vampire Jade Murphy is unexpectedly intrigued by gorgeous firefighter Beth Jenssen, and her undead existence might just be perking up a bit. (978-1-63679-271-2)

Reclaiming Love by Amanda Radley. Sarah's tiny white lie means somehow convincing Pippa to pretend to be her girlfriend. Only the more time they spend faking it, the more real it feels. (978-1-63679-144-9)

Sol Cycle by Kimberly Cooper Griffin. An encounter in a park brings Ang and Krista together, but when Ang's attempts to help Krista go spectacularly wrong, their passion for each other might not be enough. (978-1-63679-137-1)

Trial and Error by Carsen Taite. Attorney Franco Rossi and Judge Nina Aguilar's reunion is fraught with courtroom conflict, undeniable chemistry, and danger. (978-1-63555-863-0)

A Long Way to Fall by Elle Spencer. A ski lodge, two strong-willed women, and a family feud that brings them together, but will it also tear them apart? (978-1-63679-005-3)

Barnabas Bopwright Saves the City by J. Marshall Freeman. When he uncovers a terror plot to destroy the city he loves, 15-year-old Barnabas Bopwright realizes it's up to him to save his home and bring deadly secrets into the light before it's too late. (978-1-63679-152-4)

Forever by Kris Bryant. When Savannah Edwards is invited to be the next bachelorette on the dating show When Sparks Fly, she'll show the world that finding true love on television can happen. (978-1-63679-029-9)

Ice on Wheels by Aurora Rey. All's fair in love and roller derby. That's Riley Fauchet's motto, until a new job lands her at the same company—and on the same team—as her rival Brooke Landry, the frosty jammer for the Big Easy Bruisers. (978-1-63679-179-1)

Inherit the Lightning by Bud Gundy. Darcy O'Brien and his sisters learn they are about to inherit an immense fortune, but a family mystery about to unravel after seventy years threatens to destroy everything. (978-1-63679-199-9)

Perfect Rivalry by Radclyffe. Two women set out to win the same career-making goal, but it's love that may turn out to be the final prize. (978-1-63679-216-3)

Something to Talk About by Ronica Black. Can quiet ranch owner Corey Durand give up her peaceful life and allow her feisty new neighbor into her heart? Or will past loss, present suitors, and town gossip ruin a long-awaited chance at love? (978-1-63679-114-2)

With a Minor in Murder by Karis Walsh. In the world of academia, police officer Clare Sawyer and professor Libby Hart team up to solve a murder. (978-1-63679-186-9)

Writer's Block by Ali Vali. Wyatt and Hayley might be made for each other if only they can get through nosy neighbors, the historic society, at-odds future plans, and all the secrets hidden in Wyatt's walls. (978-1-63679-021-3)

Cold Blood by Genevieve McCluer. Maybe together, Kalila and Dorenia have a chance of taking down the vampires who have eluded them all these years. And maybe, in each other, they can find a love worth living for. (978-1-63679-195-1)

Greener Pastures by Aurora Rey. When city girl and CPA Audrey Adams finds herself tending her aunt's farm, will Rowan Marshall—the charming cider maker next door—turn out to be her saving grace or the bane of her existence? (978-1-63679-116-6)

Grounded by Amanda Radley. For a second chance, Olivia and Emily will need to accept their mistakes, learn to communicate properly, and with a little help from five-year-old Henry, fall madly in love all over again. Sequel to Flight SQA016. (978-1-63679-241-5)

Journey's End by Amanda Radley. In this heartwarming conclusion to the Flight series, Olivia and Emily must finally decide what they want, what they need, and how to follow the dreams of their hearts. (978-1-63679-233-0)

Pursued: Lillian's Story by Felice Picano. Fleeing a disastrous marriage to the Lord Exchequer of England, Lillian of Ravenglass reveals an incident-filled, often bizarre, tale of great wealth and power, perfidy, and betrayal. (978-1-63679-197-5)

Secret Agent by Michelle Larkin. CIA agent Peyton North embarks on a global chase to apprehend rogue agent Zoey Blackwood, but her commitment to the mission is tested as the sparks between them ignite and their sizzling attraction approaches a point of no return. (978-1-63555-753-4)

Something Between Us by Krystina Rivers. A decade after her heart was broken under Don't Ask, Don't Tell, Kirby runs into her first love and has to decide if what's still between them is enough to heal her broken heart. (978-1-63679-135-7)

Sugar Girl by Emma L McGeown. Having traded in traditional romance for the perks of Sugar Dating, Ciara Reilly not only enjoys the no-strings-attached arrangement, she's also a hit with her clients. That is until she meets the beautiful entrepreneur Charlie Keller who makes her want to go sugar-free. (978-1-63679-156-2)

The Business of Pleasure by Ronica Black. Editor in chief Valerie Raffield is quickly becoming smitten by Lennox, the graphic artist she's hired to work remotely. But when Lennox doesn't show for their first face-to-face meeting, Valerie's heart and her business may be in jeopardy. (978-1-63679-134-0)

The Hummingbird Sanctuary by Erin Zak. The Hummingbird Sanctuary, Colorado's hottest resort destination: Come for the mountains, stay for the charm, and enjoy the drama as Olive, Eleanor, and Harriet figure out the meaning of true friendship. (978-1-63679-163-0)

The Witch Queen's Mate by Jennifer Karter. Barra and Silvi must overcome their ingrained hatred and prejudice to use Barra's magic and save both their peoples, not just from slavery, but destruction. (978-1-63679-202-6)

With a Twist by Georgia Beers. Starting over isn't easy for Amelia Martini. When the irritatingly cheerful Kirby Dupress comes into her life will Amelia be brave enough to go after the love she really wants? (978-1-63555-987-3)

Business of the Heart by Claire Forsythe. When a hopeless romantic meets a tough-as-nails cynic, they'll need to overcome the wounds of the past to discover that their hearts are the most important business of all. (978-1-63679-167-8)

Dying for You by Jenny Frame. Can Victorija Dred keep an age-old vow and fight the need to take blood from Daisy Macdougall? (978-1-63679-073-2)

Exclusive by Melissa Brayden. Skylar Ruiz lands the TV reporting job of a lifetime, but is she willing to sacrifice it all for the love of her longtime crush, anchorwoman Carolyn McNamara? (978-1-63679-112-8)

Her Duchess to Desire by Jane Walsh. An up-and-coming interior designer seeks to create a happily ever after with an intriguing duchess, proving that love never goes out of fashion. (978-1-63679-065-7)

Murder on Monte Vista by David S. Pederson. Private Detective Mason Adler's angst at turning fifty is forgotten when his "birthday present," the handsome, young Henry Bowtrickle, turns up dead, and it's up to Mason to figure out who did it, and why. (978-1-63679-124-1)

Take Her Down by Lauren Emily Whalen. Stakes are cutthroat, scheming is creative, and loyalty is ever-changing in this queer, female-driven YA retelling of Shakespeare's Julius Caesar. (978-1-63679-089-3)

The Game by Jan Gayle. Ryan Gibbs is a talented golfer, but her guilt means she may never leave her small town, even if Katherine Reese tempts her with competition and passion. (978-1-63679-126-5)

Whereabouts Unknown by Meredith Doench. While homicide detective Theodora Madsen recovers from a potentially career-ending injury, she scrambles to solve the cases of two missing sixteen-year-old girls from Ohio. (978-1-63555-647-6)

Boy at the Window by Lauren Melissa Ellzey. Daniel Kim struggles to hold onto reality while haunted by both his very-present past and his never-present parents. Jiwon Yoon may be the only one who can break Daniel free. (978-1-63679-092-3)

Deadly Secrets by VK Powell. Corporate criminals want whistleblower Jana Elliott permanently silenced, but Rafe Silva will risk everything to keep the woman she loves safe. (978-1-63679-087-9)

Enchanted Autumn by Ursula Klein. When Elizabeth comes to Salem, Massachusetts, to study the witch trials, she never expects to find love—or an actual witch…and Hazel might just turn out to be both. (978-1-63679-104-3)

Escorted by Renee Roman. When fantasy meets reality, will escort Ryan Lewis be able to walk away from a chance at forever with her new client Dani? (978-1-63679-039-8)

Her Heart's Desire by Anne Shade. Two women. One choice. Will Eve and Lynette be able to overcome their doubts and fears to embrace their deepest desire? (978-1-63679-102-9)

My Secret Valentine by Julie Cannon, Erin Dutton, & Anne Shade. Winning the heart of your secret Valentine? These award-winning authors agree, there is no better way to fall in love. (978-1-63679-071-8)

Perilous Obsession by Carsen Taite. When reporter Macy Moran becomes consumed with solving a cold case, will her quest for the truth bring her closer to Detective Beck Ramsey or will her obsession with finding a murderer rob her of a chance at true love? (978-1-63679-009-1)

Reading Her by Amanda Radley. Lauren and Allegra learn love and happiness are right where they least expect it. There's just one problem: Lauren has a secret she cannot tell anyone, and Allegra knows she's hiding something. (978-1-63679-075-6)

The Willing by Lyn Hemphill. Kitty Wilson doesn't know how, but she can bring people back from the dead as long as someone is willing to take their place and keep the universe in balance. (978-1-63679-083-1)

Three Left Turns to Nowhere by Nathan Burgoine, J. Marshall Freeman, & Jeffrey Ricker. Three strangers heading to a convention in Toronto are stranded in rural Ontario, where a small town with a subtle kind of magic leads each to discover what he's been searching for. (978-1-63679-050-3)

Watching Over Her by Ronica Black. As they face the snowstorm of the century, and the looming threat of a stalker, Riley and Zocy just might find love in the most unexpected of places. (978-1-63679-100-5)